Tales of Hardooth 10

THEY ARE BACK!

Dara J. Carr

Tales of Hardooth 10

THEY ARE BACK!

Dara J. Carr

Foundation PUBLISHER

Tales of Hardooth 10: The Lies We Tell To Survive
All Rights Reserved
Copyright © 2022 Dara J. Carr
Edited by Betty Powell and Linda S. Carr
Artwork by Eric A. Carr

Foundation Publisher
foundationpublisher.com
info@foundationpublisher.com
ISBN: 978-0-9974935-4-2
Library of Congress Control Number: 2016962993
Foundation Publisher and its graphic representation are trademarks belonging to Foundation Publisher.

PRINTED IN THE UNITED STATES OF AMERICA

OTHER BOOKS BY

DARA J. CARR

The Semi-Dragon Tale

Diamond, the Black Dragon

Revenge Cometh Forth

Here Are My Shorts (a collection of short stories)

Volunteer...Spy?

The Original Owlam

What New Things We Can Learn?

The Lies We Tell to Survive

Countless Enemies and Discoveries

Enemies From Beyond

More Troubles, More Enemies

Reflections and Beginnings

What New Occurrences Do We Face?

She is Back!

THEY ARE BACK!

1

Bikaropin waited on the pier. He saw the first ship come slowly sailing into the harbor. When the citizens of Malantroi were taken to Oosam, the elite were on the last ship out. Coming back they were the first. Going to Oosam they were prisoners. Coming back they were now free – after learning a powerful and costly lesson. The elite were able to look back and see their entire city in flames. They came back totally confounded over the fact the city was completely intact. None of the structures had been kept up in seven years. Other than that they were still there (still with a lot of broken doors).

Soolchakan, Bonarain, Kiyalee and Chyning were in Spy watching all of the activities that were going on.

Chyning grunted. "Are we going to have to restore any testicles to any of these men?"

Soolchakan snickered. "No, they didn't castrate any of these Malantroi men in Oosam. They wanted to make sure they could make them procreate so that they had plenty of children to take care of when they arrived back here."

Chyning scoffed. "Good! After restoring one testicle, each, to over eleven thousand men in fifty-nine days…I don't know if I ever want to see another man's groin."

Kiyalee shook her head. "Why so many children? Each family is coming back with at least six children."

Bonarain looked at Kiyalee. "The point that they decided to make to the people of Agrosha was - if you're going to enslave anyone, use and abuse your own children. Leave our children alone." She shook her head. "They supplied them with a *lot* of children in order to keep them busy with that very idea. Most of the women spent the entire seven years pregnant."

Soolchakan took a deep breath and let it out with satisfaction. "Just think…three years and no one has heard anything about any professional slavers operating anywhere in the world."

Chyning snickered. "Yeah, there was that one bunch that tried it four years ago in Jebeltau. They took their catch to Peegruch and…WHAM…the slaves freed and the slavers all sent to the Turgon Wall for life."

Bonarain smiled. "We may have finally arrived at the point where no one will ever try to become a slaver again."

Kiyalee grinned. "That sounds wonderful."

Chyning scoffed. "Now that everyone knows that we exist and…we've scared the *h'oolyach* out of all of them…and the fact that we're anti-slavery, no, one'll dare try it."

"I know that there are a lot of wizards who can't experiment on slaves any more," said Bonarain. "If they want to find out if their spells work on Heyyah, they have to find someone who is willing to be a lab rodent or…battle amongst themselves."

The sails of the ship were taken up in order to make the big craft move even slower for their final maneuvering in the harbor. Bikaropin was waiting on the pier to give the Malantroi citizens an even bigger surprise. As soon as crewmen on the ship started throwing the lines toward the dock, Bikaropin started doing some silly gyrations with his fingers. The passengers on the ship were now staring wide-eyed as the ropes tied themselves to the dock and the gangplank lifted itself into place for disembarking. In actuality, Bikaropin was doing nothing – but wiggling his fingers and waving his arms. Zormun, Ashak, Mobor, Bymin, Ozar, Bak and Porim were in Spy dimension. They were performing the handling of the lines and gangplank. The passengers were all highly impressed and hoping that this was going to be a peaceful and friendly greeting. None of them could possibly win any kind of argument, verbal or physical, with these Owlamites.

Between the City Governor and the Military Commander, they decided the Governor should go down the gangplank first. This would be a sign that they did not wish any military encounter, but a civilized peaceful meeting. It was all that Bikaropin could do to keep from laughing out loud. The consternation of the Council members was getting him tickled in a manner that he had not expected. He wanted them to be awed, however, they were totally overwhelmed with intimidation.

"Welcome home, citizens of Malantroi. My name is Bikaropin of the Fourth. I, and several of my relatives, have been watching over the city, making sure that it was still here, when you got back."

The Governor, Xuzo smiled back at him with a face full of trepidation. He was still baffled, regarding the city being intact. His voice was nervous and shaky. "Thank you, for…watching the city. Has there been any…uh…mischief?"

Bikaropin shrugged slightly. "Unfortunately, quite a lot. There were some who tried to take advantage of the situation. We've detained them. If you wish to incarcerate them or reap some other kind of punishment for their attempts at looting, we'll supply you with all the evidence we have on each one."

Xuzo looked back at the Military Commander, Krezdon, then back to Bikaropin. "Again, thank you. We will have to have a discussion, among ourselves, to determine what to do about those…thugs."

"Yes, of course. It is my understanding, that you have several women, who are in the different stages of pregnancy. We have some large coaches, waiting for you, them and families, in order to make it easier for all."

Xuzo smiled. "I'm sure that the ladies will appreciate that. One thing I am wondering, though…are you here, just to greet us, or are you, now, some kind of keepers, or watchers? Are we free or not?"

Bikaropin snickered. "No. We have no plans of staying. Once all of your city guards and constables have arrived, we'll be on our way. The only reason any of us will stay, is to give evidence, for any trials on the looters that we captured."

Xuzo laughed. "Yes, I suppose that we will need witnesses to the crimes."

Bikaropin gave a slight bow. "Now, if everyone will depart the ship, your transportation awaits you, at the end of the pier."

The people all came down the gangplank, looking at the city. Some had a look of relief, some were crying and some - like the wife of Krezdon - Temela - just wanted to get home and relax.

Three Owlamites, helped the Military Governor Krezdon and Temela, keep their herd of children together. They were Dawuni of the Fifth, Chenny of the Seventh, and Metmiti of the Thirteenth.

Initially the children wanted to run to the end of the pier and start exploring this new city they had heard about, but never had been near before this time.

Dawuni called out to the children. "I think that you younglings should stay with your parents. You don't know the city yet and it is a big place. You might get lost and never find your parents again."

The children all looked back at her with fear on their faces. They immediately ran back to their parents and held onto the hands, pants and dresses until they got to the awaiting coaches.

After getting all of the children into the coach, Krezdon could not help his curiosity. He looked at the three and asked: "Fifth, Seventh and Thirteenth...what?"

Dawuni giggled. "I'm of the fifth generation after Soolchakan, Bonarain, Kiyalee and Chyning. Chenny is seventh generation and Metmiti is thirteen generation from the four originals."

He was not sure whether he wanted to know more or not. He just looked around and saw that there were other Elf women assisting the other families.

Temela whispered to Metmiti: "That woman over there… why is she glaring at us like that? Everyone else seems so kind, but her, she is…"

Metmiti whispered back: "That's Nadiwi of the Second. She's the reason why, Soolchakan and Bonarain are so anti-slavery. I don't know when, and they won't tell us, but when Soolchakan and Bonarain were young, Nadiwi was stolen by slavers and held in bondage, for quite some time. When Soolchakan and Bonarain found her, they did horrible things to the people who held her as a slave and their families. If it were up to Nadiwi, all of you would still be enslaved, imprisoned…or dead."

Temela swallowed hard and just looked down, with a rather worried look on her face. She had been the owner and abuser of several slaves, so she had no argument against this Nadiwi. She headed for the awaiting coach praying that there would be not confrontations.

On the way to their old home, Krezdon pointed out different things to the older children. They looked around wide-eyed with wonder at this new city and home. One thing that he noticed was that he had not informed any Owlamite which house was his, however, they went unerringly to his house without any directions given. This told him, even more, that he should not mess with these people. It was not the fact that they knew too much – they knew literally everything. Militarily he was still helpless against them.

When they arrived at the house. Temela sat there in tears as she looked around. One of the slaves had been successful in demolishing her entire garden. None of the neatly manicured bushes or plants were anywhere to be seen. The entire area was overgrown with weeds. Any flowers that were able to survive through the years were randomly growing in different parts of the garden.

After getting everyone out of the coach, Krezdon led them all inside. There were sufficient rooms, for all of the children, but there were not enough beds for them. Now, he was making mental notes, on what he needed for his family.

Chenny walked over to the fireplace, threw several pieces of wood in, made a strange gesture and a rather large fire flared up. "We'll have something for all of you to eat, very shortly," she said in a very charming manner.

Krezdon almost felt like he had a headache coming on. He wondered if the entire Owlam population were powerful wizards. If they were, then it was no wonder they were able to create such a massive illusion of destruction. He was the ranking member of the military in this city and he felt totally helpless against the Owlamites with every new stunt he saw them perform.

Metmiti came up to Krezdon. "What do you want done… with this?" She held up a whip, that Krezdon had used to beat several slaves to death.

He took the whip and looked at it with disgust. He heard some of his children crying. He looked over where they were. The four oldest were looking at him with terror in their eyes.

"I didn't do anything wrong," wailed one.

"I be a good girl," cried another.

One boy and a girl tried to hide in a corner, hugging each other and crying.

"That's right," said Krezdon calmly as tears welled up in his eyes. "None of you have done anything wrong." He held the whip out to oldest girl. "Here, why don't you be a good girl and throw this nasty thing in the fire?"

All four children now looked at him confused. The girl slowly walked up to him, looking at the whip. She looked up at him fearfully. She held out a shaking hand, swallowed hard and took the whip. She slowly walked over to the fire, looking back several times for assurance from her father. Each time, he smiled and motioned for her to continue. She stared at the flames for a few moments and then tossed the whip in. She was joined by the other three as they watched the whip being engulfed by the flames.

Krezdon came up behind them, knelt down, put his arms out and pulled all four of them together in one big hug. "We will never have one of those vile things, in this house again," he said with tears flowing down his cheeks.

All four children looked back at him, through tears of joy.

Metmiti sent a mental message to Soolchakan that the Military Commander was definitely on the right course.

Soolchakan stood there satisfied as other messages came from the ones assisting the other families, each with their large brood of children.

When they had taken the citizens of Malantroi to Oosam, they needed seventy-five ships. Now, the population was much larger, over 50% being under the age of eight. The ships were now taking them as passengers instead of prisoners so comfort was the primary thing. The return voyages took 115 shiploads of passengers to get all of the Malantroi citizens back home.

At first, King Fonzen and King Zebyuro were rather upset with how much it was going to cost in order to get all of them back to Malantroi. Another load of raw gold ore from the planet Bri halted all of the bellyaching.

It was almost 5489 when all of the trials and punishment phases were over for all of the looters that the Owlamites had captured. They were finally able to wash their hands of Malantroi and go home.

2

Once all of the excitement was over, the First Quartet was sitting in their main room of their apartment in the gorge having a meal.

Bonarain gave Soolchakan a rather inquisitive frown. "I seem to remember…on that day that you finally got off of your butt and came to Fortress Island to rescue me…I remember that there was a Kalash Elf with you."

Soolchakan had a big mouthful of food so he communicated telepathically. **"If you're wondering what his name was…I don't recall. Why are you bringing this up now**?"

Bonarain shrugged. "I was a little out of practice at the time, so I couldn't get full thoughts from him…then we dumped him back in…where was it?"

Soolchakan shrugged while chewing. **"North Paselter, I believe**."

Chyning was confused. "When did we get…North Paselter? All I remember was Paselter. Are there two of them now? And if there are, when did that happen?"

Soolchakan finally finished chewing and swallowed.

"Several years ago, the reigning Queen of Paselter gave birth to twin baby boys – Dolomon and Dolomot. The midwives forgot to tie a red thread around the ankle of the firstborn. Since no one knew which one was the eldest, the King put in his will that upon his death, the kingdom was to be divided equally between the two boys. Since it is the largest and richest kingdom in the world, he hoped that the brothers would remain friends. He made it easier for each one to rule over a smaller area."

Kiyalee looked troubled. "Again, when exactly did this happen?"

Soolchakan shook his head. "I don't remember. It was either 5474 or 5475. What does it matter? That kingdom is on North Chilamte. We haven't lived there in ages."

Bonarain stirred her kwatha. "No, but I remember there was something bothering them. They were on their way to the Turgon Wall to investigate something. I didn't get all of it – like I said I was out of practice. The point is that…they were on their way to the Turgon Wall to investigate something. Some mystery about the Turgons."

Soolchakan nodded. "Yes. As I remember they were thinking something about how the Turgons were using some kind of…weapon."

Kiyalee nearly spit a mouthful of food out. **"Turgons? Using weapons? They're too stupid to use any weapon**."

Bonarain nodded. "Yes, I know. That's why this is bothering me. Why would those people be so concerned about a rumor about the Turgons using weapons…unless there's some truth to it?"

Soolchakan looked around. "Where are the children?"

"Don't change the subject," scolded Bonarain. "We're talking about the Turgons using weapons?"

Soolchakan gave her a stern look. "Where are the children?!"

"They're with Mahanee right now," said Chyning. "You know how she loves to be around children...any children...all the time...even in herds."

He sighed. "Are you really that concerned about the Turgons?"

"Yes," said Bonarain in an uneasy manner. "If they figured out how to use weapons...that could be something disastrous, for all of us."

He hung his head. "If you're so troubled about it, why don't you go ahead and go there and see for yourself?"

Bonarain snarled. "I'M NOT GOING THERE BY MYSELF! We need to go there together and investigate it - together."

Soolchakan was confused. "We're not on the same continent! We left there a long time ago. Why can't we let someone else solve a few problems...without dragging us into the swirling abyss of someone else's catastrophic lives?"

Bonarain folded her arms across her chest. "I wanna know exactly what is going on. If those beasts are getting smarter, then just how smart are they getting? How ambitious will they get? Could they possibly start sailing ships and start conquering? You know that they can climb just about anything with those nasty claws of theirs. If they figure out a way to sail ships and come to the northern cliffs of High Country, we could be in danger EVEN HERE IN THE GORGE!"

He rolled his eyes. "Why can't we just sit down and relax for a while? If you're so interested, we've still got our satellites. Aim one of them at the wall and see what you can find." He smiled. "I'll tell you what – if they have anything more complicated than a club – I'll go investigate with you." He looked back down at his mug of kwatha. "Until then – LEAVE ME ALONE!"

Kiyalee and Chyning were snickering over the exchange.

Bonarain huffed. She hopped to Ghost and then Jumped to the observation room where all of the monitors were located. Elsash was currently on duty with his three wives, Iyona, Balitha and Teedee. The four of them looked up as Bonarain hopped to Home.

Elsash stood up smiling. "How can I help you?"

Bonarain looked at several monitors. Most of them were looking out into space. "I want one of the satellites aimed at the Turgon Wall."

Elsash now looked rather distraught. He glanced at the monitors and then back at Bonarain. "Uh…which part of the wall?"

The three women were also looking rather distressed.

Bonarain huffed. "What do you mean…which part?"

Elsash chuckled nervously. "You should know that… in order to see most of the wall, you have to have at least five satellites aimed in that direction." He sniffed. "Even then, you'll only be able to see about seventy percent of the wall."

Bonarain hung her head. "According to what I've been hearing, the Turgons have some kind of weaponry." She looked up. "I need to see them in action with this weaponry. I need to find out if this rumor is true."

Elsash now looked dismayed. "The Turgons? Turgons using weapons? That is…impossible." He cleared his throat. "Isn't it?" He looked rather helpless.

"I need to confirm that," said Bonarain with a smile.

Elsash turned to his wives. "Are any of the satellites… able to look at the wall?"

Iyona checked the trajectory of the satellites. "Number 22. It'll take a few adjustments. We should have it done by midday." She looked up. "But it'll only be able to see some of the central portion of the wall. By then, Zoo-Idig, Soolchana, Yumitzi and Nemla will be here on duty."

Teedee pointed to one of the monitors. "Number 40 is aimed just south of the wall. If we aim the camera in the right direction, we'll get a shot at the southern end of the wall."

Bonarain shook her head. "Thank you any way." She Jumped back to her bedroom. "**Kiyalee, this is Bonarain, is my personal fighter ready to go?**"

Kiyalee looked up a little surprised. **"Of course it is. I always have our fighters ready. What'd you want it for?"**

"I can't get any of the satellites repositioned anywhere near the wall until midday. I can't get a full look at the Turgon Wall unless I have at least five satellites moved out of their present position. I need to look at the whole thing. The only way I can do that is from my fighter."

Kiyalee shrugged. **"Your fighter is right where you left it on the Chokchakchok ship. Get Majim and Tatab to help you get launched. They're the ones with the duty right now."**

Bonarain Jumped to the Chokchakchok ship in dimension #45. She found Araba on the ship playing with her young daughter Omatena. "Majim and Tatab…where are they?"

Araba was momentarily startled and hugged her daughter. Omatena saw Bonarain and waved with a grin on her face. "Majim is in the other bay servicing one of the fighters."

"What about Tatab?"

"She's watching her little girl, Milyee."

"What about Lamola?"

"She's with her son."

"Are all three of your very young children here?"

Araba had a bit of a guilty smile on her face. "What else would we do with them?"

Bonarain huffed. "Somebody has to take care of all three children while somebody else assists me in getting my fighter ready."

Very quickly, Lamola was assigned to take care of the three children while Araba and Tatab assisted Bonarain. Once she was in her fighter she hopped to Spy and took off. She hopped to outer space in Home dimension, called Elsash and told him that she was going to be flying around, so he should not be surprised if they saw her over the Turgon Wall area, even though she was going to be in Spy.

She flew her fighter to the northern peninsula where the Turgons had been trapped. She started a low level pass over the wall from south to north. She was just over one third of the way when she was shocked at what she saw. She flew back around and landed her fighter. She sat there staring in disbelief.

"Soolchakan, this is Bonarain! I'm here at the Turgon Wall. The Turgons have several...catapults. They don't seem to have any of them aimed at anything. They're just...here."

Soolchakan looked up from the report he was reading. **"Catapults? You said catapults? What...how...WHAT?"** He had to do some thinking in order to get a lot of confusion out of his head.

Kiyalee and Chyning looked up from what they were doing and just stared rather dumb struck.

"Yes, I said catapults. They don't seem to be able to aim or arm the things they're just milling about

looking at them but…they do have some catapults here at the wall."

Soolchakan turned to the two women. He could get nothing from them other than open-mouthed, dumbfounded stares. "**Get back to the Chok ship and get a shuttlecraft. I'll meet you there with Kiyalee and Chyning. We all need to see this**." He shook his head. "After all these years I just don't understand. Catapults? We didn't hear anything about them… back then." He looked off to the side perplexed. "I think." He shook his head. "All these years later and…no one seems upset about this mystery. I wonder why." He grunted in exasperation

Kiyalee and Chyning did not ask any questions. They both Jumped to the Chokchakchok ship, ready to board any shuttlecraft that was ready to go. Bonarain showed up in her fighter. Araba and Tatab had been given instructions to prepare a shuttlecraft. They were doing the preflight as the first quartet boarded.

"It should be ready to go shortly," said Tatab.

Araba hit three switches. "Ready to go now." She looked up expectantly. "Can I go with you and see this…phenomenon?"

"Later," said Soolchakan. "After we do some assessment of the situation. I can understand your curiosity but, I'd like to see the what and where before we start turning it into an event for… tourism."

Both Araba and Tatab looked rather downhearted. They departed the ship as Bonarain took the helm.

Bonarain looked back. "You ready?"

All three nodded as Chyning hit the button to close the doors.

Bonarain hit the main drive. "Hopping to Spy, and, Jump to outside the spacecraft." She looked back. "Now I'm going to Jump to the wall."

Soolchakan nodded. "Go ahead."

In an instant they were directly over the area where the catapults were located.

Soolchakan was looking out the front port. "That's ridiculous! Where'd they get those things from?" He raised his eyebrows. "What is that nonsense? Who paints their catapults in showy colors? And...who paints *flowers* on the sides of their catapults?"

"The Bertheelan warrior women do," said Kiyalee. "They paint that big white, fuzzy-petal flower that grows only on the Island of Bertheel."

Soolchakan shook his head. "Flowers painted on a weapon of war." He huffed. "How ridiculous! There's absolutely nothing *pretty* about war."

"The main reason they do it is so that you'll know that it's a Bertheel catapult," said Bonarain. "They're not trying to make it pretty."

"Still ridiculous," scoffed Soolchakan. "Who cares who made the catapult?"

"They're all over the place," said Chyning. "How many

do they have?"

Kiyalee rolled her eyes. "Does the count mean anything? The Turgons have them! So far I don't see that they know how to use them. But...*here* they are."

Soolchakan looked over the field. "They are...aimed in totally random directions. There's no formation of any kind of a line. Are we sure that the Turgons pushed these things to the wall?"

Bonarain grimaced. "I didn't check on that yet." She looked off to the side with a red face. "I guess we'll have to go to the top of the wall and...read a few minds. We'll get the impression of those who watched the things being pushed to the wall."

Soolchakan continued looking over the field. "Just for experimentation, why don't we land down there among the catapults? Read the minds of the Turgons. See if any of them have an intelligent thought rattling around inside their hollow skulls."

Kiyalee squawked. "What makes you think that we'll get something different? They have animal mentality! How are we supposed to get anything from that?"

"Look at them," said Soolchakan! "Normally when the Turgons get this close to the wall, all they do is start clawing their way to the top. Are any of them going anywhere near the wall? No! They're all mingling around and among the catapults. That tells me that there is something unusual about *these* Turgons already."

The three women all looked down at the Turgons in confusion. Yes, he was correct. Not one of the Turgons was making any attempt at the wall. This was totally foreign to the normal actions of any of the Turgons. Some of them were touching the catapults in different areas or appeared to be inspecting them. They seemed to be trying to figure out how to use the weapons, or at least curious about them. None were attacking the wall.

Bonarain landed the shuttlecraft. The door was opened and they all walked out. That familiar and constant yipping of the Turgons was a little unsettling, however, they all knew that they were completely safe in Spy dimension.

Soolchakan looked somewhat distressed. "Bonarain and Kiyalee, you head north. Chyning and I will head south. Just pick some of them at random and see if you can get anything from their minds. After all this time, I wouldn't be surprised if some of the sentient intellect has somehow...come back...maybe." He shook his head and grunted.

Bonarain and Kiyalee headed north. They each would stop near one of the Turgons and try to read the mind and then move on.

Soolchakan headed south. He was closer to the wall than Chyning.

Chyning noticed one of the catapults had been prepared to launch. The big armature had been pulled back and was ready to hurl a load. There was one Turgon who was taking laps around the weapon as if it were trying...to do...something. There was a well-worn path in the grass surrounding the catapult.

She did what she could to pry into the mind of the big Turgon. She got an impression of hunger. She also saw images in the mind that showed that currently he was looking at the catapult and was trying to figure out how to load and fire the thing. She pulled back in shock. Load and fire? *That* is an intelligent thought. He just could not remember how to load and fire.

She noticed that this particular catapult was aimed, for the most part, at the wall itself. Normally, one would aim the thing at a ninety degree angle to the wall. This one was around eighty to eighty-five degrees.

Then, as only Chyning could think, she decided to try a devious little plan. She reached in one of the pouches she had on her side and pulled some jerky out. She walked over to that "big bowl" on the catapult. While the Turgon was on the other end she hopped the jerky into Home and tossed it into the bowl. She grinned as she moved over to the trigger mechanism.

The Turgon continued his current lap around the catapult. He got to a certain point and started sniffing the air. He crawled up on the catapult. He straddled the armature and looked down in the bowl. He went down, head first and open mouthed, in the bowl to get the piece of jerky. That was when Chyning hit the trigger.

"FIRE ONE," shouted Chyning as the surprised beast was sent flying up toward the top of the wall!

The snarling Turgon did an involuntary half somersault in the air. When it got to the wall, it did not completely clear the top. The shoulders arms and head hit the top of the wall with a sickening splat (that left a big patch of blood on the wall). The lower portion of the body flipped over the wall and the somewhat "shattered" upper part followed the rest of the body and disappeared over the top.

One of the men on the wall swung down hard with a big mace, crushing what was left of the head of the unfortunate Turgon. The man then reached down and cut the tail off. He held his trophy up high and shouted in victory. He then tossed the rest of the cadaver over the wall. Several Turgons ran to their freshly killed comrade and started their macabre feeding. They were not attacking the wall, however they were still hungry.

Chyning was standing next to the catapult feeling a little irritated. "That's my trophy you *doovoft*." She huffed. Her shoulders sagged as she saw Soolchakan heading for her with a rather angry look on his face.

"What do you think you were doing?" He was rather upset. Soolchakan snarled at her again. "Was that really necessary?"

Chyning snickered. "No, but it was fun." She shrugged. "They armed it – I triggered it." She looked over at the feeding frenzy at the foot of the wall. "I can't help it if he got in the way." She tried to look innocent. She could tell from his reaction that it was not working. Her shoulders sagged and she looked off to the side rather miffed.

Soolchakan walked closer with a sinister look on his face. "Did you get any thoughts from him…before you…launched the silly thing?"

"It seems that he was trying to figure out how to load and fire the thing."

Bonarain and Kiyalee were running up to where Soolchakan and Chyning were having their confrontation.

"That sounds like something close to an intelligent thought," said Bonarain.

"It most definitely does," said Soolchakan. He turned his glare from Chyning to Bonarain. "Did you pick up any form of sentience from any of the others?"

"Yes," panted Kiyalee. "Some of them are...thinking. Most of what's in their minds is like pictures or images of what they've observed, but, they're thinking."

Bonarain held up a finger. "I'll be right back." She vanished.

Kiyalee looked around helplessly. "Where'd she go?"

"I don't know," said Soolchakan. "I'm sure she's got a good reason for going to...wherever. Just wait and see what happens."

Bonarain reappeared with Bikaropin.

Bikaropin looked around in shock. "WHAT...WE...HEY, THOSE ARE TURGONS!"

"Very good observation," said Soolchakan. He placed his fists on his hips. "Why is he here?"

Bonarain smiled. "I got an image from one of the beasts." She pointed north. "One of them over there. He had some Elf in his mind. That Elf was showing him how to arm the catapult." She flushed. "I don't remember all of the Elf races. I brought

Bikaropin because, maybe he can get a clearer picture of which race of Elf we're dealing with."

Kiyalee stood there scratching her head. "An Elf race... is conspiring with the Turgons to...do...*what*?" She looked off to the side. "And...why?"

Bonarain smiled. "I don't know. We need to figure out which race of Elf before we can get an answer to that question."

Soolchakan sighed. "I didn't get any picture of any Elf from the minds that I read." He turned to Chyning. "Before your fatal stunt...did you?"

Chyning simply shook her head – still trying to look innocent.

Soolchakan sighed loudly. "All right. We all head for the ones that you got those thoughts from. See if we can get any clear picture from any of them."

They walked shoulder to shoulder heading north. They turned their attention to different Turgons as they walked along. They got to the catapult that was the farthest one north of the group and none had received any image of any Elf.

Kiyalee looked back where they had come from with clenched teeth. "I know that some of them were thinking of an Elf. I *know* it! I *saw* it! It was a little fuzzy as to which Elf race he was thinking about but...I know it was an Elf he was thinking about. Why aren't they thinking about them any more?"

Bikaropin clenched his eyes shut. "Oh no!"

Soolchakan looked at him suspiciously. "What?"

Bikaropin was standing there with his head tilted back and his eyes still shut. "Do you remember what that Teltermak told us?"

Soolchakan narrowed his eyes. "He said a lot of things about a lot of things. Specifically what are you talking about?"

Bikaropin lowered his head. He had an unsettled look on his face. "One of those potions, they made from our...guts! It was made from our brains. He said that if someone drank that potion they became a lot smarter...for a short time."

Bonarain's jaw dropped. "You don't mean...someone has some of those...brain potions and...they're feeding them to the Turgons?"

Bikaropin clasped his hands behind his head. "A little while ago, some of them had semi-sentient thoughts. Now, none of them do, because it wore off." He dropped his arms and sighed. "What else could it be?"

Kiyalee closed her eyes in disbelief. She shook her head. "If that's true, then those potions are able to stay...viable...for a *long, long, long,* time."

Bonarain sank to the ground. "Will we ever get rid of that scourge or memories of the Teltermak?"

Soolchakan held his hands up. "Wait, wait, wait! All of the Elf races were produced from the firestorm weapons. The Teltermak figured out that they could get some super capabilities by...consuming...some of our...anatomy." He dropped his arms.

"It is just possible that…someone else has discovered this same thing about some other Elf race. Consume their guts and you get…some crazy, enhanced capabilities, albeit it temporary."

Bikaropin nodded. "That is entirely feasible. What we have to do is all get in that shuttlecraft, take off and backtrack the trail that the Turgons used to get the catapults to this area."

Chyning scoffed. "What makes you think we can follow any kind of trail like that?"

Bikaropin pointed to the southwest. "Because here comes another group of Turgons pushing another catapult in this direction."

The first quartet followed where he was pointing. There was indeed another catapult being pushed in their direction by several snarling and yipping Turgons. The heavy catapult was leaving a trail in the dirt and grass that would be very easy to follow.

They all Jumped back to the shuttlecraft. Bonarain fired it up and they took off. Following the very clear trail left by the wheels of the heavy catapult was easier than expected. It was rather well used. It took them to a cove on the southern coast of the peninsula two teckfar from the wall. There they found very little as they hovered in place. There were a few trails from the catapult wheels. There were a lot of Turgon footprints. None of them could see anything of use – from their view in the shuttlecraft.

Then Bikaropin gasped. He Jumped from the shuttlecraft to the beach. The quartet could see him picking something up out of the sand. He Jumped back to his seat on the shuttlecraft. He held up an empty yellow bottle.

"Does this look familiar to anyone?"

Soolchakan groaned, leaned over and covered his face with his hands. "That looks like the bottles the Teltermak were using to…bottle our brains when they made the intelligence elixir."

Bikaropin nodded. "Either there are still some Teltermak on Hardooth or…they sold some of the elixir to…someone…who is feeding it to the Turgons."

Chyning looked horrified. "But, who would do that…and why?"

Bonarain sighed. "As soon as, *whoever*, makes their next delivery to this beach…we'll find out then."

"It has to be a diversion of some kind," said Bikaropin.

Bonarain frowned. "Why?"

"The Turgons can't possibly utilize those catapults. They don't know how to arm and fire them. They absolutely don't know how to build them. Someone is giving the Turgons a quick lift in their intelligence long enough to get the catapults from here to the wall. Once the catapults are there, all of the attention is on the catapults in the hands of Turgons. Someone is planning a very dirty trick…somewhere else. As long as all attention is here, this makes a wonderful diversion…and it has been going on for quite a while."

Kiyalee sat there thinking out loud. "The catapults are from Bertheel. In order to get them here, you either take them from Bertheel and go all the way around North Chilamte to the north. That's ridiculous, because the best place to unload the catapults would be on the north coast. The other way is to go all the way around south of North Chilamte."

"Either way, that makes a very long voyage," said Bonarain.

"But somebody is doing it," said Soolchakan. "Why"

Bonarain frowned. "Or...someone is manufacturing phony Bertheelan catapults in order to form another secondary diversion."

Soolchakan hung his head. "*H'oolyach*! I hate plotters. I hate all of this wretched political intrigue." He grunted. "Gives me a headache."

Bonarain sighed. "Yeah. We now have to figure out who is doing it. Why are they doing it? What are they hiding? What do they hope to accomplish with this mess?"

Kiyalee shrugged. "Just keep an eye on this beach and... maybe we'll get lucky."

3

Bikaropin snarled. "We're wasting time!"

"With what?" Bonarain scoffed.

"That last team of Turgons that was pushing a catapult! They have to still have some of the smarts to get that thing going in the right direction." Bikaropin looked around at all of the others. "If we get back to them before their intelligence wears off, maybe we'll find out who is behind this…and how they became intelligent enough to have a purpose."

"Or an intelligent thought," said Bonarain.

"So turn us around," said Soolchakan.

Bonarain swung the shuttlecraft around. They followed the trail to a team of Turgons they had seen pushing a catapult from the beach area to the wall. She landed the craft near the Turgons.

Soolchakan pushed Bonarain back into her seat. "We didn't see any ship close by. Maybe they aren't that far away. They dropped the catapult, gave the Turgons a snort of intelligence elixir and then shoved off. Go back and see if you can see anything from up high."

Bonarain looked confused. "Like…what?"

Kiyalee giggled. "How many ships would be anywhere near the shoreline on the west side of the Turgon wall? Whoever it is, they have to be the ones who dropped the catapult and the elixir off."

Bonarain shrugged. "That's reasonable."

"We'll do some mindreading here on those beasts. You go searching," said Soolchakan.

After Soolchakan, Kiyalee, Chyning and Bikaropin left the shuttle, Bonarain fired it back up and headed back to the cove.

Twelve Turgons were pushing the catapult. They were still making those same annoying yipping sounds they always made.

Bikaropin snickered. "If they were to quit wasting energy with all of that barking and snarling, they might be able to get that catapult to the wall faster." He shrugged. "Oh well, that's their problem."

Soolchakan looked at the set up. "Bikaropin, you go to the left front and read the three in that area. Kiyalee, you go to the right front. Chyning, right rear."

The thoughts of the Turgons were not very manageable. They did not think in sentences, they thought in images and feelings. Some were thinking about the yellow rocks that had the funny tasting liquid. Some were thinking about how they had to keep pushing this thing because the strange food things had promised they could use it against the food things on top of that high thing. Some were thinking about the strange food things.

"Concentrate on those 'strange food things', that has to be the people bringing the catapults and elixir," said Soolchakan.

"I'm trying," said Chyning. "They think about them as strange things but...I can't get any image of them from the thoughts. Nothing that is clear...that is."

"Whatever the strange things are, they seem to have some nasty claws," said Bikaropin. "This little one over here seems to have been scratched by one of the strange things. The bleeding has stopped, but...the claw marks are there."

Kiyalee looked back. "Could that be the Galsino?"

"No," said Bikaropin. "The Galsino don't have a claw pattern like that. This is four claws, all scratching one way. The Galsino grab with all claws and tear flesh. Their claws are talons... two forward and two back. This is a long scratch of four claws."

Bonarain called back mentally. **"I've got a ship. It seems to be more of a river boat than any ship. They're rowing with some very long oars. It only has one mast. It looks like it has a platform, in the middle, where you could place one of the catapults**."

Soolchakan stopped following the Turgons. **"Who is on board**?"

"I can't tell from here."

Soolchakan snarled. **"Come back and get us**."

"I might lose them!"

Soolchakan closed his eyes and hung his head in frustration.

"Are there really that many ships in the area?"

There was no response for several moments. **"I'll be right there**," sent Bonarain flatly.

They watched for the shuttle to appear overhead. As soon as it landed, they boarded as quickly as possible and she took off again. She gained a lot of altitude in order to find the ship again. Once she spotted it she headed back down to get a closer look.

The ship was long and did not sit very low in the water. It appeared a little too thin for a ship used on the high seas. The sides were somewhat low and if it were to end up in choppy waters, the crew would spend most of their time bailing water out of the ship. There was one mast near the middle with a large square sail – that was hanging rather limp at this time. Directly in front of the mast was a large platform area that went all the way from port to starboard. You could park a catapult on that platform. On each side there were thirty long oars. Fifteen in front of the platform and fifteen behind. There was only one crewman per oar. They were rowing in unison so someone had to be calling a cadence.

Bikaropin looked out the front of the shuttle.

Soolchakan saw him scratching his head. "Okay, what do you see?"

Bikaropin shook his head. "I need to get down there to get a closer look."

Kiyalee shrugged. "Jump down to that cargo platform. It looks clear enough for you to landmark. We'll leave your seat open for your return."

"Okay," said Bikaropin. He vanished and immediately reappeared on the platform. The ship was moving and rocking a little so he had to steady himself in order to keep from falling off. Once he got the rhythm he was able to start exploring.

"**I'm seeing Heyyah, Perek, Fastern and Tekaylath-Sar**," sent Bikaropin. "**All of these are normal on North or South Chilamte. I've never heard of them working together though**."

"**Conspiracies can always cross racial boundaries**," sent Bonarain.

"**But which one is in charge**?" Soolchakan sighed. "**We're going to have to follow them to find out**."

Bonarain hung her head. "As slow as they're moving, I don't think this thing has enough fuel to just sit here, hovering in the air above them."

"Land it on that cargo platform," said Chyning with a grin. "It might make it harder for those *bimyocks* to row, but it'll save us some fuel."

"I agree," said Soolchakan.

The craft was easily landed on the platform. There was very little room to spare, however, they were not planning on any vacation time aboard the ship.

Soolchakan saw Bikaropin walking along a central area in the middle of the oarsmen in the front. "**Bikaropin, have you been doing any mind reading down here?**"

Bikaropin looked back at the shuttlecraft. "**Not much good here. All these men are concentrating on the cadence from that guy with the big drum in the aft of the ship**."

Kiyalee stepped out the rear entrance to the shuttle. "**We've got sixty oarsmen, one cadence caller and one *bimyock* on the rudder. Which one of these *doovofts* is in charge**?"

Bonarain looked out the back. "**My guess would be either the drummer or the guy handling the rudder**."

Chyning scoffed. "**Why don't we hop to Observation? That silly drum is giving me such a headache**."

Soolchakan nodded. "**Good idea. Everyone hop to Observation. Then we'll be able to concentrate on some serious mind reading**."

Kiyalee stood there shaking her head. "**The drummer isn't thinking of anything but the cadence**."

"**The *bimyock* on the rudder is just looking for something off to his left**," sent Chyning. "**He isn't thinking about any landfall or any kind of star gazing navigation... unless he doesn't see a ship, in which case, he's thinking of some small island**."

Bonarain had a thought. "**If that navigator is looking for a bigger ship somewhere out here, maybe if I take the shuttle up high, I can see it**."

"**I agree**," sent Soolchakan. "**We're not getting**

anything here. Let's go find a mother ship and find out if anyone there has any positives for us."

They all got back in the shuttlecraft.

Chyning scoffed. "Too bad you didn't get one of the shuttles that was loaded with weapons. We could've given that long ship a bit of a nightmare trying to stay afloat."

Bikaropin shook his head. "Why don't you go back to where your fighter is, get in it, come back and have some fun with it?"

"Not yet," said Soolchakan. "I like the idea of doing that, but…not yet."

Bonarain hit the thrusters and they lifted off from the ship. "Which way do I go?"

"Follow the gaze of that Heyyah on the rudder," said Bikaropin.

Bonarain shrugged. She looked back down at the man controlling the rudder. She followed his gaze, went higher and headed in that direction.

All five of them were scanning the ocean looking for anything that stood out. All they saw, in the direction they were going were three very small islands that were mostly flat and had very little vegetation. Bonarain could not see anything else so she headed towards them. As they got closer they could see that there was some kind of activity, between the scattered trees, on the largest of the three islands.

Soolchakan turned on a monitor, aimed the camera at the island and magnified. "I see some more Perek and Fastern. I also see some Galsino and Heyyah near the huts."

"Look next to the huts," said Bikaropin. "Cages with Turgons in them."

"Yeah," said Chyning. "There's one real big Turgon standing outside the cages. Looks like he's feeding the ones in the cage…some kind of liquid from a bowl."

Bikaropin snarled. "And the bowls are probably being filled from a rather familiar looking yellow bottle."

Bonarain pointed. "On the other side of the huts…three more catapults."

Soolchakan contemplated while studying the island inhabitants. He turned to Chyning. "Chyning, the time is now. Go back and get your fighter. Then go and cut that shuttle-ship in half."

"Or quarters," said Chyning with a smile. "I'll make those *bimyocks* swim to this island."

"Ouch," said Bonarain. "They'll freeze to death while swimming." She looked at a gage on the console. "According to this, the water temperature is 6 degrees Abfar."

Kiyalee frowned. "Water freezes at 8 degrees. How come the ocean water isn't frozen?"

"Because it is all *salt* water," said Soolchakan patronizingly. "You have to have a temperature *way* below freezing before you get any ice. And that ice is usually fresh water that is formed into ice on top of the salt water."

Kiyalee just looked off to the side with her face flushed.

Chyning shrugged. "Oh well, that's not my problem." She vanished.

Soolchakan sighed. "Okay, let's go down and investigate this island."

Bikaropin shook his head. "Heyyah, Perek, Fastern, Tekaylath-Sar and Galsino. *H'oolyach*, what a mixture!"

Bonarain landed the shuttle. "I'm going to have to Jump this thing back to the Chok ship. I don't have enough power to take off again."

Kiyalee smiled. "We can both go back and get a shuttle that is still at full power. Plus we can get some weapons." She looked at Soolchakan expectantly.

"Do it," said Soolchakan flatly.

Soolchakan and Bikaropin stepped out of the shuttle. Bonarain Jumped the shuttle as soon as they were out.

Bikaropin looked around. "Where do we start?"

"You go see if you can find out who is in charge. I'm going to go see if there is something in the head of that big Turgon. The one that's feeding the others. If he's smart enough to handle a bowl, he's smart enough to have a sentient thought."

Bikaropin nudged Soolchakan and cleared his throat.

"Uh…*she*…not he!"

Soolchakan frowned. "What? She?" He looked down the body of the big one. He raised his eyebrows. "Oh, it is female." He nodded. "A matriarchy! Interesting!" He headed toward the female Turgon and signaled Bikaropin to go to the huts.

As soon as each Turgon finished lapping up the contents of the bowl, they momentarily stopped yipping and looked around as if they were seeing things in a totally different perspective, for the very first time. Each one was then let out of their cage.

The big female was called "Queen" by all of the Heyyah and Elf people on the island. Queen seemed a lot smarter than any of the other Turgons. As Soolchakan delved deeper into that mind, he found out that she was given two bottles of the intelligence elixir each day. No wonder she was so much more intelligent than the other Turgons.

Once she had fed twelve Turgons the intelligence elixir, each one was let out and the "Team" was now taken over to one of the catapults and given instruction on how to use the weapon. The instructions were given three times as they launched practice loads off the west end of the island. Then the Turgons would try it. The Team got it right the first time. Now, they simply had to wait until the shuttle-ship got back and the Team would be taken to the mainland with their own catapult.

Soolchakan chuckled. **"Chyning, have you been able to blast that shuttle-ship yet**?"

"No, I just got back. I forgot what I should landmark on. I had to think about that big sail. Once I

got that, I arrived. Did you want me to hold fire?"

"Sink it!"

Chyning hit the trigger on her 459 cannon. **"We have a big slice right through the platform! We now have major panic and pandemonium. Going around. Slicing right through the nose of the ship, right down the middle. Everybody in the front is now in the water. Slicing through the aft section**." She giggled. **"The only thing that's still intact is the rudder...and that's just floating away**."

Bikaropin was walking back to Soolchakan. "Did we really need that play by play?"

Soolchakan shrugged. "At least we know that the thing is never coming back here."

The one seat fighter was now flying over the island.

"Did you want me to blast anything on the island?"

Soolchakan snickered. **"Not yet, just land and we'll decide later**." He looked around confused. **"Bonarain! Where are you**?"

Kiyalee responded. **"We had to power up and supply a different shuttle. We'll be there shortly**."

Bikaropin shrugged. "Do you want the briefing now?"

"No, wait till everyone is here. That way you only have to give it once."

The shuttlecraft finally appeared overhead. They came down slowly for their landing. Once on the ground, the side door opened. Bonarain and Kiyalee stepped out holding weapons. Soolchakan cringed while worrying about Kiyalee holding any form of a weapon.

Bonarain shook her head. "Turgons running loose among several different races of Elf and some Heyyah and no one is being attacked and eaten. I never thought I'd see the day. That brain elixir is incredible."

At that moment Chyning did another low fly by in her fighter.

Soolchakan snarled. "**Will you land that thing? We have some things we need to discuss**."

The fighter came back to the island slowly and landed next to the shuttle. The canopy opened up. Chyning sat there looking disgusted. "I can't have any fun can I?"

Soolchakan snarled at her. "You already had some fun! Get out here."

She stuck her tongue out at him as she climbed out of the fighter. She walked up to the group. "Okay, what're we looking at?"

Soolchakan sighed. "From what I'm seeing, they seem to have a rather large supply of the intelligence elixir that the Teltermak manufactured from the brains of the Owlamites they murdered. Currently, they're using it to make these Turgons smarter. Smart enough to understand how to use a catapult, here.

It seems to wear off before they can utilize them at the wall. They have enough smarts to get the things there, but, they forget how to use them or even what they're for."

"That doesn't help their cause very much," said Kiyalee. "If they can get it there but not be able to use it...that means that they'll have to have more elixir in order to do something with the catapults."

"They've got plenty of elixir here on this island," said Bikaropin. "The big hut has a very large refrigeration unit in it... along with a generator that keeps it working. Where they came up with that technology is another mystery. They've got thirty unopened cases of elixir in there. There's one opened case. There's a place behind the hut where they've burned some empty cases. How many have been burned...I don't know." He sniffed. "There are twenty-four bottles per case." He looked around. "There seem to be a lot of abandoned and empty yellow bottles."

Bonarain groaned. "That's still 720 bottles...plus the ones in the open case that haven't been used yet."

Bikaropin nodded. "It makes one wonder just how much they started with. I did a little figuring and according to that vulgar recipe the Teltermak had for the elixir, they should've been able to make at least 97,000 bottles of the stuff."

Soolchakan looked up and shook his head. "We've already destroyed many thousands of bottles of that *stuff*. We sent over four thousand on that ship with Ootgreeg. How much more could possibly be here on Hardooth?"

"We can destroy the thirty cases that are here," said

Bikaropin. "The bigger problem is that no one here, not Fastern, not Perek, not Galsino, not Heyyah and not any Tekaylath-Sar has a clue as to what they're doing with this arming of the Turgons. They know that it is some kind of diversion, but…the people here don't know why."

Bonarain scoffed. "Beautiful tactic! Send a group here to cause a diversion. Don't give any of them the bigger picture about what the real goal is. That way, if any of them are caught…they can't tell you anything…except specifics about their diversion." She snarled. "They cannot tell you why somebody wants their attention on the Turgons."

"Other than the fact that this is a diversion," said Kiyalee. She huffed. *"Chogos!"*

Chyning snickered. "They're not gonna be able to get those other three catapults to the peninsula. The four quarters of that ship all went under. The only thing there now is the rudder and floating dead." She shrugged. "If any of the dead are still floating."

Bonarain raised her eyebrows. "So they did freeze to death?"

Chyning nodded. "Very quickly."

Soolchakan chuckled. "These people here have a bigger problem. That big female has learned some subterfuge. From the thoughts I got from her, as soon as the last catapult is loaded on the shuttle-ship, the Turgons were going to be ordered to attack and eat all of the – as her thoughts put it – food things on this island."

Chyning looked perplexed. "Food things! That is all they think of when they think of us…food things?"

"They think using a lot of pictures of nouns." Soolchakan folded his arms across his chest. "The bottles of elixir are funny rock things with funny tasting water in them. The catapults are throw things. And all of the non-Turgon inhabitants of this island are food things."

Bikaropin shook his head. "Wait! If she was going to order an attack on all of the food things…after the last catapult is loaded on the shuttle-ship…why would the rowers on the shuttle ship bother taking the last Team of Turgons to the mainland?"

Soolchakan grunted. "I said she's deceptive, I did *not* say that she's brilliant."

Bikaropin flushed and chuckled. "Sorry for that misunderstanding."

Kiyalee smiled. "Let's get rid of all of the funny tasting water and the problems for the non-Turgons will heat up *real* quick."

Soolchakan chuckled. "Good idea."

Bonarain looked at the hut. "Where should we send those thirty cases?"

"Dimension #45," said Soolchakan nonchalantly. "I can't think of any reason why they should be in this dimension."

They went to the big refrigerator and hopped all of the cases out of their misery.

Bikaropin looked at the pens where the other Turgons were still imprisoned. "I think that we can make things even more interesting here on the island."

Soolchakan looked at him suspiciously. "How?"

Bikaropin had an evil grin. "Let the un-intellectualized Turgons free."

Kiyalee looked aghast. "Let me out of here before you do that!"

Chyning looked puzzled. "Why? You haven't puked over anything for quite a while now. Why should this make a difference?"

Bonarain looked thoughtful. "You're right. She usually lost it just over one drop of blood." She looked at Soolchakan accusingly. "Do you know anything about that?"

Soolchakan huffed and looked off to the side with guilt written all over his face. "I try...I do everything I can to...not interfere with...the lives of others. But...it seemed like...every time something happened...she made a mess. Yes, in her case, I used the *Voice of Power* to give her a stronger stomach."

Bonarain looked very upset. "What other things have you done to her...or me...or *us*?"

The three women surrounded Soolchakan with their arms folded across their chests while glaring at him.

He snarled at them. "Don't push it! I could make every one of you forget this conversation ever took place. I merely made it so that…we didn't have to step around her puke, every time we went into a battle…and injured someone."

Kiyalee sighed and her shoulders sagged as she dropped her arms. "I guess you could say that he did help me." She gave him a dirty look. "I'll forgive you on that one, but don't you dare make a habit of it."

Soolchakan smiled in a patronizing manner. "Can we get back to the subject at hand?"

Bikaropin had wandered over to the pen where the other twenty-four Turgons were imprisoned. "Ready when you are."

Soolchakan shrugged and sighed. "Do it!"

Bikaropin hopped the big cage into Observation dimension. Suddenly two dozen (still ignorant and hungry) Turgons saw no barrier between them and the food things. As soon as a Tekaylath-Sar Elf got his throat ripped out, it was now Bonarain who looked as if she were going to lose her lunch. The slaughter and battle was on.

The Fastern were very tall and had huge fangs. They could bite back. The Perek were rather short, however, they had retractable claws on both their feet and hands and were able to do significant damage to the Turgons. The Galsino also had sharp claws on their talon hands so they were able to rend their enemies fatally…very quickly. The Tekaylath-Sar were even shorter than the Perek. They had no natural bodily self-defense mechanisms. The Tekaylath-Sar were fighting a lost battle for survival. All they could do was run to the ice-cold water because they knew that the Turgons feared stepping in any water at all. The big female was smart enough to get over her fear and so she plunged into the mild surf after the unfortunate Tekaylath-Sar. After killing at least three of them, they overwhelmed her with numbers and shoved her face underwater until she stopped kicking.

Bonarain headed for the shuttlecraft. "Can we get out of here now?"

Soolchakan followed her. "Yeah, I think we've done enough damage here."

Kiyalee ran into the shuttlecraft as well. Chyning hopped in her fighter and Jumped it to her parking spot in the Chok ship in #45. Bikaropin simply Jumped back to his apartment in the gorge.

Bonarain Jumped the shuttle to the normal parking place in #45. She turned to Soolchakan. "So what do we do now?"

Soolchakan leaned back in his seat. "We have some good clues now. The four races of Elf that we saw on that island, all are indigenous to North and South Chilamte. The Fastern live in the far eastern peninsula. The Perek live in the south, central portion. The Tekaylath-Sar live just south of the Perek. The Galsino originated in North Chilamte. I don't know where they're living now. I know we ran them out of their original home, but…they could still be living on either continent, somewhere."

Bonarain nodded. "So we find a place where all four of them have some meeting ground and…hope we can then find out what is going on."

"Right now, we need to go to the Turgon Wall," said Kiyalee.

"Why," asked Bonarain?

"Let them know that this catapult thing is just a diversion and that the danger is now over."

"That's reasonable," said Soolchakan.

"I wonder what they'll think about this blind diversion," said Bonarain.

Soolchakan just shrugged. "It should get their attention off of the catapults and let them all start investigating in other areas, regarding the question: What is really going on and why this diversion?"

Bonarain scoffed. "The diversion is meant to get all of the attention here. We have to look elsewhere...for anything funny or sinister going on."

Soolchakan simply nodded and grunted in disgust. "Could be anywhere."

4

Soolchakan was in complete agreement that they needed to go to the Turgon Wall, however, he felt they needed to go there and get the attention of all of the people there with some grand or outrageous entrance. He put the question to all Owlamites: How do we make a spectacular entrance that leaves all of the inhabitants in awe?

There were several ideas about some kind of pyrotechnic show or coming down in a spacecraft. He did not want to put on a fiery show and he did not want to show others any of their sophisticated technological equipment.

After five days of bad, inane, counterproductive (and some completely stupid) ideas, the first quartet was sitting in their dining room eating a meal. Dining with them were their three youngest children, Sonotana, Piykroom and Nondaza who were nearly twelve years old.

The three children listened while Soolchakan looked over the latest list of rejects.

Nondaza looked up at Chyning. "Momma, why don't you do what we did in that place you call Beasties?"

Chyning looked a little puzzled. "What was that?"

The girl grinned. "You remember! We rode those big Guard Eaters."

Chyning snickered a little. "*Gourd* Eaters."

Kiyalee was horrified. "You...rode on the backs of those beasts?"

Chyning shrugged. "They're very docile. You don't have to break them like you would those stubborn equines. They don't mind having someone, or something, riding on their back."

Bonarain joined the protest. "But you got on the back of a Gourd Eater. What happens to you...when they jump?"

"That's the real fun part," said Nondaza with a big grin. She looked up at the ceiling. "They jump *real* high. You have to hang on *real* tight."

Soolchakan let out a frustrated groan. "That sounds interesting, but how do we control them? The only thing they're interested in is eating those gourds...and mating."

Bonarain smiled. "I remember a picture I saw one time. A Heyyah was riding on one of those equines. He had a vegetable on a stick that he hung in front of the beast. The beast was following that food. He could steer it by moving the stick one way or another."

"That's all well and good," said Soolchakan. "How do we keep the Wall inhabitants from noticing that we're steering stupid animals with food?"

Bonarain grinned. "We hop the gourd, the stick and the eyes of the beasts into Spy dimension. We can make them go anywhere we want because that'll be the only gourds the hungry beasts see."

Soolchakan looked around in complete disbelief with his mouth hanging open. He shook his head. "That is just stupid enough to work!" He then shook his head. "No, we'd have to have them stabled while we're discussing things with the guardians at the Wall. How do we keep them in the stable stalls while we're discussing business at the Wall? They seem to want to eat... gourds constantly."

"We don't," giggled Chyning. "As soon as we ride them into the stable, we hop them back into their dimension and let them chow down."

Soolchakan rolled his eyes. "What do we tell the stable-master?"

Chyning leaned back looking superior. "We tell whoever it is that they don't want to know where the things are. If they give us any guff, then they'll find out *the hard way* where the beasts are."

Soolchakan snickered. "That sounds good, but...just the four of us...won't make that big a show."

Bonarain smiled. "Then we don't have just four. How many men were on the ships in that flotilla, to and from, Oosam?"

"One hundred and fifty," said Soolchakan.

"That should make a grand show," said Kiyalee.

Soolchakan sighed. "Mercy, we're getting vicious and outlandish!"

After a long silence, Chyning leaned forward. "Well?"

Soolchakan chuckled. "Okay, we'll do it that way." He picked up his fork. "Start contacting all of the ones you want riding Gourd Eaters."

Soolchakan looked at the ones seated in the auditorium. All men. He turned to Bonarain. "What is wrong with having a few women on this flagrant escapade?"

Bonarain flushed. "They all want to stay behind, watch and be with their children. I mean, this isn't like we have to defend our children from some outworld invader."

Soolchakan raised his eyebrows. "What about you three? Each one of you has a very young child."

"We can always get Mahanee to take care of them while we're gone," said Kiyalee.

"You know how she loves being with children...any children," said Chyning.

Soolchakan just moaned and shook his head. He turned back to the men in the seats and gave them the briefing.

Each one was to go to Beasties, find a Gourd Eater and a gourd. They were going to ride the Gourd Eater, holding the gourd out in front, hanging from the tip of a spear, so that the Gourd Eater was chasing the gourd. In order to make their disguise look complete, the gourd and the eyes of the Gourd Eater were to be hopped into Spy. That way only the Gourd Eater would see the gourd and no one would know that it was chasing a gourd. Anyone else would only see someone riding on the back of a huge unidentifiable animal, in formation, headed for the Turgon Wall.

They were going to have to keep this up for quite some time because since the Wall had been used as a prison, several villages had sprouted up in the area. They could not just Jump to a spot near the Wall and ride in. They had to ride through three villages as well.

They were going to make a grand entrance at the Turgon Wall, riding in formation on the nasty looking beasts. They were going to ride all of the Gourd Eaters into a stable. After entering the stable, they were to hop their steeds back to Beasties – with their gourds. Exit the stables and leave any caretakers of that stable completely in the dark as to what happened to the animals.

Most of the men were sitting there chuckling.

Sunok stood up. "What's the purpose of this ruse?"

Soolchakan replied: "We make a grand entrance to the Wall area. We shock everyone to get their attention. Once we have their attention, we let them know that the catapults are nothing but a diversion. We don't know, yet, what their attention is to be diverted away from, but, we're working on it. We'll let them know at the earliest possible moment. Meanwhile, those catapults were never a danger to anyone on the wall."

Waybar stood up. "When is this going to happen?"

"As soon as we can get everything aligned and set up," said Soolchakan. "It may be a few days so don't get impatient. Just remember the spot you first grabbed the Gourd Eater. When we send them back, we don't want them all going back to the exact same place. That could be disastrous."

Bonarain addressed the group. "You might want to go to Beasties and practice riding one of the Gourd Eaters. They're very tall creatures and they can run *very* fast."

Each one went to Beasties and grabbed a gourd. They found that it was easy to entice one of the Gourd Eaters with one that was on the ground. They also found that it was easy to ride on the back of the big beasts without any complaint from the creatures. The one thing that you wanted to avoid was a female with a calf. She might get a little temperamental about someone being near her calf, plus you might have to bring the calf with her. A female could also be in heat and that could mess up the formation rather awkwardly. They all decided to go with male Gourd Eaters. They were going to have backpacks with extra gourds – just in case the ride was longer than anticipated.

Soolchakan had them go to a place just south of the most southern village by the wall. He placed them all in the formation that they would be riding into the outer gates of the Turgon Wall. Each one landmarked their position in the formation.

The formation was spread out for quite a long way because of the size of the Gourd Eaters and the number of men involved. Soolchakan decided to communicate mentally. **"The time has** arrived. **I need all of you to go find a gourd and Gourd Eater. It'll probably be best if you grab one just after it finishes a gourd. That way, the thing won't be so ready to grab another already, but they'll still follow it.**" He turned to Bonarain. "When they start coming back, we'll need a roll call."

Bonarain sighed. "Of course."

Soolchakan smiled. "**Everyone, go get your Gourd Eater now.**"

As each one obtained their mount and Jumped back to the road with the bewildered beasts in tow, they all called in and Bonarain checked them off. It took longer than expected to get them all there and some of the first ones to arrive had to give up a gourd in order to keep the beasts in line.

Finally they were all there.

Soolchakan mounted his tall steed by Jumping up on the back. "**All right, we're ready to go. Hang the gourd on the end of your spears, hop the gourd into spy and hop the eyes of the Gourd Eater into Spy.**" He shook his head. "**Onward and forward.**"

The procession got off to a rather shaky start, however, with some manipulations of the proper placement of the gourds in front of the eyes of the always hungry Gourd Eaters, they were actually able to get the formation *in* formation.

They rode through the main street of the first village and scared the daylights out of every citizen (and animal) that saw the tall, gruesome looking beasts. It was not that long a ride before they got to the second village because the long legs of the beasts they were able to run very fast and did not seem to tire very easily. The results were the same there. The third and final village achieved the same results.

Now, the only thing in front of them was the eastern wall. This wall kept the prisoners in and was also billeting for all of the guards at the Wall as well as most of the others who were higher in the chain of command. They got closer.

Kiyalee looked up at the people on the east wall. "**They've got all of their archers up there. They're planning on repelling us. What do we do**?"

"**Hop the whole formation into Ghost**," sent Bikaropin. "**That way we can make an even bigger splash and still be safe**."

Soolchakan chuckled. "**That should work. Everybody do it. Hop to Ghost. We'll go right through that closed gate**." He did not really want to give away the existence of Ghost dimension, however, he did not feel like getting pin-cushioned by a hailstorm of steel-tipped arrows.

A guard that was standing on the top of the wall hollered at them to stop or they would shoot. The Owlamites ignored the order and the running Gourd Eaters swiftly made up the ground between them.

Another man looked both ways at all of the archers. He looked back at the running formation. "ALL ARCHERS...!" He pointed at the Owlam formation. "...LOOSE!"

Approximately eighty arrows came flying toward the front of the formation. All of them harmlessly stuck in the road or the ground near the road.

Kiyalee grimaced. **"That's a little unnerving."**

"Just remember that you're in Ghost," sent Bonarain.

"Thank the Great Maker," sent Chyning.

"Right through the gate," sent Soolchakan. **"We'll keep on track and head for that big stable just to the north of the gate."**

Daykon huffed. **"You're the one leading the way. We're following you to...wherever or whatever...and why ever."**

Two more volleys of arrows were wasted on shooting holes in the ground. Some of the archers panicked and ran. Others just stared in shock. Others looked to their leader for some guidance. He was one of the ones staring in shock and confusion.

Soolchakan and Bonarain were in the lead. **"Here we go...right through the gate,"** he sent.

The leaders rode through followed immediately by Kiyalee and Chyning.

"That wasn't so bad," sent Chyning.

Kiyalee chuckled as she saw some of the archers beating a hasty retreat. **"The archers. Some of them, their pants are now yellow and brown, instead of light tan."**

Bonarain shook her head. **"Mercy! I'm glad we can't smell that.**"

"You must be holding your nose," sent Soolchakan.

Bonarain suddenly grimaced. **"You're right! I forgot! We're not in Observation.**"

The entire formation of 154 Gourd Eaters came through the closed gates. The gatekeepers just stood there helplessly slack-jawed. They had their swords up and ready for...what... they did not know.

Some of the archers who were still up on top of the wall looked back out at all of the arrows sticking out of the ground and shook their heads in wonder.

Soolchakan sent a private message to Bonarain. **"You do have that list of the Elf races working at the Wall don't you**?"

Bonarain shook her head. **"I gave it to Shalam for safekeeping.**"

Soolchakan nodded. **"That works.**" He moved his spear to the right in order to steer his steed. **"The stable is just over there. As soon as we get through the doors of the stable, Jump your beast back to Beasties and then we'll all leave the stables together.**"

Soolchakan and Bonarain went through the doors and Jumped. Kiyalee and Chyning were directly behind them. Each one Jumped their beast to their specific spot in Beasties. They then Jumped back to their assigned spot in the stable.

The Stable Master and all of his hands ran in terror and hid behind troughs or other barriers as the big lumbering Gourd Eaters passed through the closed stable doors like ghosts. All 154 of them into a stable that might hold twenty normal sized equines cramped.

Soolchakan watched the formation continue through the doors from inside the stable. "**Who is in the last row**?"

"**Lojuk and Jodatak**," sent Bonarain.

Soolchakan nodded. "**Lojuk and Jodatak, let me know when you're nearing the stable doors**." He continued watching as more and more of them came through the doors and Jumped.

Kiyalee shook her head. "**I didn't realize we had this many**."

"**We had to make a grand entrance**," sent Chyning. "**I think we managed to do just that**."

Lojuk called in. "**We're making the last turn. We'll be there in two shakes**."

Lojuk and Jodatak finally came through and Jumped.

Soolchakan gave a sigh of relief. "**Everyone get your money out. Time for phase two of the grand entrance**."

Kiyalee huffed. "**Why are we giving them this much money? The cost of stabling an equine is 10 laten. We're paying them a full pasel for each beast. That is ten times the price**."

Soolchakan grinned. **"Big tippers are remembered. Cheap ones are as well. Which one do you want to be remembered as...big or cheap?"**

Kiyalee just snarled. **"I don't like wasting money."**

As soon as Lojuk and Jodatak had Jumped back to the stable from Beasties, Soolchakan headed for the stable doors. He shoved them open and led his entourage out of the stable. He flipped a pasel coin to the Stable Master. "For your troubles, Sir. Don't worry, they don't need much care."

Kiyalee shook her head as she flipped her pasel coin to one of the stable hands. 'Ten times what their worth,' she thought. 'Plus we're not even stabling them here.'

The Stable Master dropped several of the coins. He quickly retrieved them as the stable hands were gathering up other fallen coins. All of the stable crew were staring in wonder. One – the fortune that they were receiving. Two – what are those big ugly beasts? Three – *where* are those big ugly beasts?

Once again Lojuk and Jodatak were the last ones in the marching formation. They both looked back inside the stable.

Lojuk walked directly up to the Stable Master. "Don't worry. As he said, you don't have to care for them that much."

One of the stable hands had gone to the door to see exactly how that many of those huge beasts could possibly fit inside the stable. He looked back at Jodatak. "WHERE ARE THEY?"

Jodatak smiled. "You don't have to worry about that. But if you mess with us...you'll find out where they are...the hard way." He gave an evil grin. He turned and fell back in line with the marching formation.

All of the stable crew walked into the stables. Each one looking around totally mystified, terrified and awed.

A young boy shook his head as he looked down at all of the strange paw prints. "Where are they?"

Another one was spinning around trying to see if any of them were still here. "What are they?"

The Stable Master looked down at the fortune in his hands. He looked up. "Who cares? Someone wants me to…not take care of…something I can't see…and pays me…to not worry about it. I don't care!" He continued stuffing the big coins in his pockets. He still looked around rather baffled. He again looked down at the fortune in his hands and his demeanor changed from confusion to greed.

They had created quite a stir coming in through a closed gate and then running their steeds through another closed door. There were several people of different races pouring out of the doors of the Headquarters building. Most of them were armed with all kinds of weapons.

Chyning tried to stifle a laugh. **"What is that over to the right? Those three have pink hair."**

"They're Argaman-Or Elf," sent Bikaropin. **"Pink hair is normal for their race."**

Chyning cleared her throat to keep from further laughing. **"Is that their normal skin color…uh…what would you**

call it?"

"**Lavender**," sent Bikaropin. "**And yes, that is their normal skin color**."

Several tall Wokig Elf men stood in front of the Headquarters group with bow and arrows. They pulled back on their bows. One of the Wokig hollered for the formation to halt.

Another tall Elf man with a bird beak came forward. "Who are you? What is your purpose here?"

Soolchakan stopped. "**Might as well let them know that we're here peacefully – in spite of our *fabulous* entrance**." He held his hands up to show he was unarmed. "I am Soolchakan! Drey Sssorg of the Owlam nation!"

The bird beak opened his beak wide and squawked. He took a few steps forward of the archers. He signaled the archers to lower their weapons. They complied.

The bird beak regained his composure. "I am High Commander Finfot Sheej. I'm the primary leader here at the Turgon Wall." He clasped his hands in front of his chest. "It has been a very long time since we were visited by any member of the Owlam nation…here at the Wall."

Soolchakan nodded. "Yes, it has been…a very long time since we were here."

Finfot nodded. "Since none of us, here at the Wall, has ever seen an Owlam, first hand, I must require some…proof…as to who you are."

Soolchakan smiled. "**Oops**!" "Such as?"

Finfot waved his hand at someone behind him. One of the Argaman-Or walked up behind him with a large binder. Finfot took the binder and opened it. He looked down at the open page in front of him.

"Who was your Supreme Officer, at the time the Turgon Wall was established as an international prison?"

Soolchakan felt a lump in his throat. "**Does anyone remember who it was**?"

The three women almost felt some panic.

"**This is Rintokam. I just Jumped to a spot behind the beaked one. According to what I see written here, it was Nakalak**."

"**Sneaky**," sent Chyning facetiously while trying to stifle her giggling.

Soolchakan smiled. "Obviously, High Commander, it was Nakalak."

Finfot nodded. He shrugged. "I was wondering how you pronounced it." He turned to another page. "Who were the first of the T'Mor race to greet the Owlams…in our original home?"

Rintokam sent the information to Soolchakan.

Soolchakan smiled warmly. "Yitok Ocho was the Group Commander on your home wall. He was gallantly leading a fight against a wave of Turgons. After our ancestors joined the fight and assisted in defeating the Turgons, they were introduced to Noybiy Unk, your Exalted Commander…at the time. Paka Tay was also there. She was an Over Commander, I believe." Soolchakan clasped his hands behind his back. "And I also recall that Commander Chocho Sah was the very first top T'Mor leader here at the Turgon Wall."

Finfot had to look down at the pages and search through the writings. He found it and looked up wide-eyed. "Quite correct!" He flipped through several other pages till he found what he wanted. "It was not long after that, the Owlam people disappeared. Before they vanished, they gave the Kalash a recipe. The recipe was shared by the Kalash with us and all other Elf races at the Turgon Wall. Who was the one race we were instructed to hide this recipe from?"

Soolchakan thought quickly. "That has to be the *Tuzine*. You were told to keep it secret from the Teltermak."

"**Very good**," sent Rintokam. "**Get ready for the ingredients**."

"**Oh, *h'oolyach***," sent Bonarain. "**Does anyone remember that**?"

Rintokam groaned. "**It is right in front of me! Don't worry**!"

Bonarain sighed in relief.

Soolchakan snickered. "**Bonarain, if they ask, you get to list the ingredients**."

Bonarain was about to make a terse comment. She stopped when Finfot asked for the ingredients. Rintokam started listing them off.

Bonarain stepped forward and smiled. "The shoonshook weed – deep roots only. The idimberry – berry peeling only. The vohososk plant – leaves only. Mychelik herb – the entire plant. Zoyga plant – roots only. Fendelik plant – young leaves only. Finally, the poolhatha vine – only the small leaves near the blossom." **"Oh, please don't ask how all of that *h'oolyach* is mixed!"**

Finfot slammed the binder shut and broke down in tears. "The Owlam people have returned! The ones who saved the T'Mor race from complete extinction!" He shoved the big binder back in the hands of the Argaman-Or (so hard that it nearly knocked him over) and ran to Soolchakan with his arms wide open, sobbing the entire time.

Soolchakan was afraid he was going to get bowled over by the tall T'Mor. At the last moment the T'Mor dropped to his knees at Soolchakan's feet and hugged the knees of Soolchakan.

"Welcome, saviors of the T'Mor people! Welcome, welcome, welcome! Why did you stay away so long?" He was in tears.

Soolchakan felt a little embarrassed as he pried the man from his legs. "*Please*, my friend, get up! We're not ones to be worshipped. Our ancestors did what was necessary to save a people who were not our enemy." He sighed. "And from what I've read of the history of that time, friends were scarce, enemies abundant."

The Wokig archers all put their arrows back in the quivers.

They held their bows down at their sides.

Suddenly there was a crowd of T'Mor coming out of the building, all running to the Owlamites making strange sounds that only someone with a beak could make. The tall T'Mor did everything they could to embrace the shorter Owlamites in friendship.

After the thirtieth hug, Soolchakan held his hands up. "PLEASE! The reason we're here is because we've heard about this strange thing with the Turgons suddenly having sophisticated weapons."

Finfot looked surprised. "You heard about that? Unfortunately, it is very true. The Turgons started pushing catapults up to the wall…uh…many years ago and…then they seemed to forget why they brought them here."

Soolchakan tried to look surprised. "Really?" He nodded. "Where are these catapults? Have they used any of them against you…yet?"

Finfot pointed at the west wall. "They're very close by. I'll let the watch up there, give you a briefing on what happened with the catapults." He did some kind of bird chitter for a moment. "Would you like to see the catapults now or…after you've had some refreshments?"

"The catapults could be a problem," said Soolchakan. "Refreshments can wait."

"Of course, my friend. As you wish." Finfot started leading the way. "Follow me, my exalted friend."

Heromon was looking around at all of the T'Mor. "**Did you really save all of their lives**?"

Bonarain responded. "**If it hadn't been for us, there would be absolutely no T'Mor still living. We had to move...what was left of them in the city, out here, east of the Turgon Wall.**"

Chyning had to get her thoughts in. "**Then we kicked the *piddleeyanks* out of the Sodle.**"

The contingency of Owlamites stood on the Wall looking over the field of abandoned (and somewhat rotting) catapults.

Soolchakan was puzzled by the lack of any Turgons walking around the weapons. They had been in abundance before. Now there were none. The only sound was the footfalls of all the people on the wall and the wind. "Why did they leave them?"

A Cowpa Elf, named Hozoozook, was one of the Sector Leaders in this area. He walked up to the edge of the wall.

Chyning was having a difficult time keeping a straight face as she looked at the pale brown skin and dark blue hair that was racial characteristics of the Cowpa.

Hozoozook pointed at one of the weapons. "That was the first one they brought. It was around ten years ago...I think...or maybe even...a lot longer." He looked off in thought. He waved it off with his hands. "Anyway, they brought a total of fifty-three catapults over the years. They would bring them here and...then wander around and among them. A few years ago...they stopped their aimless wanderings and then attacked the Wall...in their normal way. They completely forgot about the catapults and have not done anything with them since. All of it is a complete mystery."

A reptilian skinned Saraff-Or Elf shook his head. "That was a mess. That was one of the biggest attacks on the Wall... ever. There were many trophies taken that day as we killed over six hundred of the beasts." He looked over at a memorial on the back of the Wall. "We also lost twelve of the fighters that day as well – some to death and some to crippling."

Soolchakan gave Chyning an evil side glance. "Did any of them ever fire one of the catapults?"

The Saraff-Or laughed. His laugh sounded more like canine barking. "There were three times that they were able to prepare the weapons for hurling. All three times they did trigger the things – twice with fatal results – to the Turgons."

"Really," said Chyning? She looked at some of the many tails that were hanging from different belts and wondered which one was the specific one that should be hanging on her belt.

"Yes," continued the Saraff-Or. "The first time, one of the stupid beasts was sitting in the thing. He was hurled up here at the wall. The aim was a little low and...he hit the wall. I think he died immediately when he hit the wall but..." He pointed at a Kafal-Shan Elf. "Moolkrok there smashed the things skull anyway... just to make sure."

'And got *my* trophy,' thought Chyning with clenched teeth.

Hozoozook chuckled. "The other one…was not aimed at the Wall. When the catapult was triggered, one of the Turgons was a little too close and…it tore off an upper appendage. As is the way of the Turgons, when that one was injured, the others attacked and devoured him…very rapidly." He pointed to one of the far catapults. "That one back there. That was the other firing. There was no payload in the thing so…the triggering was a waste of time to talk about."

Soolchakan nodded. "Why haven't you done something about the catapults…since the Turgons are not here right now?"

Hozoozook huffed. "No one wants to go down there. I doubt that any of us could outrun or out-climb the Turgons if they were to suddenly show up."

Soolchakan turned to the Wokigs. "I understand that you people are supposed to be very good with the bow. Why don't you prove it by shooting a few flaming arrows at the things?"

One of the Wokigs leaned down with a somewhat sinister look on his face. "We *are* very good with the bow and arrow. *No* living creature is better." He stood back straight. "The problem is that the flame on the arrow doesn't burn long enough to catch that wood on fire."

Bikaropin looked up at him with a smile. "Then put a bottle of oil on the end of an arrow, shoot it at a catapult. When the bottle shatters, before the oil evaporates, you hit the puddle with a flaming arrow. See if *that* will catch the thing on fire."

The Wokig looked startled. "That just might work." He turned to another Wokig. "Go get a bunch of bottles and some oil. I'd absolutely love to try this plan. It might not work but...I haven't heard anything else useful...as far as destroying those catapults."

The second Wokig pointed at an Arba-Kara Elf. "You! Go get some bottles, a lot of bottles...now!"

The Arba-Kara fell to all fours and took off running – very fast. He ran down the staircase to a window in a small building. He stood up and started talking to someone inside. He received four small bottles which he stuffed in his belt. He turned and ran to another spot where a Heyyah woman was sitting next to a large vat peeling some tubers. They had a brief conversation. The woman looked up at the people on the Wall and spread her arms as if she were asking a question. The Wokig did a very exaggerated nod of affirmation. The woman shrugged and filled the four bottles from a spigot on the side of the vat. The Arba-Kara placed the bottles in his belt, dropped to all fours again and ran back up to the Wokig on the Wall.

Kiyalee shook her head. "I've heard that they were fast when running on all fours but...I've never seen it until today." She shook her head. "They are...*very* fast."

The Wokig smiled. "Very useful when you need messages delivered, quickly."

Kiyalee guffawed. "Really!"

One of the Wokigs stuck an arrow in the bottle. "How do we keep the oil in the bottle...on the fly?"

Loov reached in his vest pocket. "I usually use this to

exercise my hands." He pulled out a ball of clay. "Put some of this around the opening and…it should hold the oil in long enough."

The Wokig took some clay and used it to clog the opening around the arrow shaft. He looked at one of his colleagues. The other Wokig placed his arrowhead in a torch until it caught fire. The first Wokig aimed his arrow and fired. His arrow hit one of the catapults and the bottle shattered. The second Wokig immediately loosed his flaming arrow. He hit true in the middle of the oil. The oil caught fire.

"Now," said Soolchakan. "We'll see if this'll catch the whole thing on fire and end any chance of those beasts ever using those weapons."

They all stood there watching the flames as the oil burned. It took several moments, however, the fire started burning the area around where the oil had been. Soon a quarter of the catapult was on fire – then half – then eventually the entire thing was engulfed in flames.

"It works," said Finfot triumphantly. "We're going to need a lot more bottles of oil to accomplish this task."

"You'll also need a lot more clay," said Loov. "I don't think I have enough to stopper another fifty-two bottles." He huffed. "See if you can get our Arba-Kara runners checking for all of the necessities throughout the area."

"Done," said Finfot!

Back in the Headquarters, Soolchakan gave a briefing to

all of the upper echelon of command at the Wall.

"We've done a little reconnaissance of our own. We followed the coastline beyond the Wall. We found a place where… somehow, they had Turgons that they could communicate with and…they were supplying the Turgons with the catapults."

"They communicated?" Finfot was totally shocked. "With Turgons?" He looked around at some of the other people in the room. "Uh…who is…*they*?"

Soolchakan looked at Bikaropin. "Who all was there?"

Bikaropin pulled a small piece of paper out. "There were Heyyah, Fastern Elf, Galsino Elf, Perek Elf and Tekaylath-Sar Elf."

Soolchakan looked back at Finfot. "We captured several of them and after a few bouts of torture…" He looked off to the side with clenched teeth. "…they admitted that they were doing it as a diversion." He shrugged. "As to why they were diverting attention to the Wall and those catapults…none of *them* knew. They were just obeying orders by creating the diversion."

Finfot groaned. "Very good strategy! Don't tell them why…in case of capture. Just tell them enough to get that job done. Only the ones at their Headquarters know the full picture." He huffed. "Excellent strategy." He shook his head. "I've heard of that intelligence elixir before. Didn't believe a thing about it, but, you seem to have confirmed the existence of that stuff." He grunted. "Wasting something like that on Turgons…so deplorable."

Another T'Mor spoke up. "But…where's the Headquarters? You've named four Elf races…two who are located at totally different places on this continent and two from South Chilamte. You named Heyyah who…are everywhere on both continents… on all continents. Where are they Headquartered?"

"A very good question," said Soolchakan sadly as he shrugged.

Bonarain looked up from what she was reading. "Do you have any idea where the Galsino are living? The last thing I heard was that they were on the run. They abandoned their home city because of attacks on them by us and the Kalash."

Finfot now looked confused. "Where have you been? The Galsino moved back into their original home…centuries ago."

"We've been attending to other things that were more important to our personal survival," said Soolchakan with a smile. "The Galsino were rather…unimportant."

Bonarain smiled. "We did have a few problems with those nasty Teltermak. We had to hide from them in order to survive… until they all died off."

Finfot nodded. "Yes, it has been quite some time since I have seen or heard of a Teltermak." He looked up in thought. "I wonder what happened to them."

Bonarain shrugged. "Who knows?" She cleared her throat. "We were in a situation where we had to kill them in order to defend ourselves. It has been a very long time since we saw any of them." Again she shrugged.

5

The Owlamites had to go back to the stables and start Jumping their steeds back. They departed with the same grand show as when they had arrived. They once again left many of the regular troops, officers and several stable-hands completely baffled as to where the giant steeds had vanished to and where they had reappeared from...or what they were.

By the end of 5488, the population of the Owlamites had risen to 9,982. The hallways of the top two floors of apartments in the gorge was constantly filled with playing children. By the end of 5489, the population was 9,993. The three children on the twelfth level were brought up to the first or second level to be with the other children in order to keep them in touch with children of their age – even though most of them were of different generations.

The first quartet was still too hard-headed to move. They liked being in one place. They had lived there for more time than they could remember. They had no desire to move – ever again. They had their banner from when they were Team 7016. They had all of the patches they took victoriously from other Teams. This was their home and only the Great Maker himself would be the force that would make them move. Plus there was just too much stuff. It would take months (if not years) to move all of their possessions.

Chyning went back to the island to find out who won the battle for that sand bar. She saw the three decaying catapults still sitting where they had been before. She saw one starving Turgon searching through the huts and chewing on old bones. She was a little flabbergasted that this one Turgon had been able to survive as long as it had. Just exactly what it had been eating was a mystery. She wondered if any of the other Elf races or Heyyah had come back and seen that one starving Turgon. They might be waiting until it died to go back and start the mess going again. Or they might go back to claim the unused bottles of intelligence elixir. Either way, she did not have time to wait and see. Whoever did it would now be the ones where the attention would be drawn to this diversion that they had originally set up to divert the attention of others.

Bikaropin and a few others were very busy in the control room for quite a while. They were moving satellites from one orbit to another in order to see any or all of the area where the Fastern, the Galsino, the Perek and the Tekaylath-Sar were living. They were trying to see if there was some main meeting place in each one of their claimed areas where all of the races got together to discuss plans.

Bonarain looked at all of the results of the searches. "I

think we're going to have to go back to what we did with the Algothons." She sighed. "We have to get someone into each one of their tribal areas and start looking for the ones who are planning… what that wretched diversion was supposed to be hiding."

Soolchakan cleared his throat. "Are we going to go with just men doing this spying? Or are we going to include the women in it as well?"

"Oh come on!" Kiyalee looked disgusted. "When Neenatha and Holla and Wymini and Plykatha were the Supreme Officers, none of us had any children. Now, since we do have children, none of the women want to leave their children unattended…no matter what their age."

Soolchakan closed his eyes and snarled. "We're going to be in Spy dimension!" He opened his eyes and looked angrily at the women. "When we were doing our spying from Spy dimension… did anyone get killed? Did anyone get injured? No! You can take your children with you and…teach them dimension hopping and a few other things while we're at it."

Chyning felt rather disturbed and embarrassed by his chastisement. "Okay, if we send someone to the Galsino city or the Fastern city…how do we decide who the Teams are that'll be assigned there?"

Soolchakan shrugged. "Families. So far, that, has worked with all the other endeavors we've pulled…especially against the Wizard Cliques."

Kiyalee gave Soolchakan a dirty look. "Are you going to assign the men as the Team Leaders?"

Soolchakan sighed and shook his head. "No, it'll be the eldest member of that family. I believe that Hisang is married to Faroog. Hisang is definitely older than Faroog so...she's that Team Leader."

Bonarain shrugged. "That's fair. Good old seniority."

"We also change them out more often," said Soolchakan. "Our population is just under 10,000. Keep them rotating every three days. Make sure that the outbound Team gives the inbound Team a full briefing as well as any notes taken by others who were there before them. All other Teams assigned to that area will be given all briefings as well. That way, even though they're not spending that much time there, they'll still be fully informed."

Kiyalee rolled her eyes and turned to Bonarain. "You're right. He has gotten smarter. I didn't think it'd happen."

Bonarain and Chyning giggled. Soolchakan just gave her an evil glare and shook his head in disgust as he walked away.

In 5490, Maheska of the Seventh was born. She was number 10,000 on the list of living Owlamites.

It was almost at the end of the year 5490 before they finally found something significant. Jashalo of the Eleventh came to apartment 12-562 and started hammering on the door.

Soolchakan was rather surprised and nearly spilled his juice. **"Whoever is knocking on my door...haven't you heard of communicating mentally? It is much easier on the knuckles...and the ears!"**

"**I'm sorry, Drey Sssorg! I was just so excited I... wanted to tell you...but I didn't know if you were here in your apartment.**"

Soolchakan looked at his family. Bonarain, Kiyalee and Chyning were equally as perturbed as he was. The three children were all fourteen years old, however, it had startled them as well.

Soolchakan clenched his teeth. "**You still haven't told me who you are.**"

"**So sorry! I am Jashalo of the Eleventh. I am here with my three wives: Chaya, Quakee and Joosha.**"

Soolchakan smiled sardonically at Bonarain. "Finally got an answer." "**Come on in and tell us what this wonderful news is.**"

The four appeared on this side of the door with three children close to the ages of Soolchakan's youngest.

Bonarain turned to her daughter. "Why don't you keep their children company while we discuss business?"

The six children all went off to the side.

Jashalo almost ran to Soolchakan. "We were following some of the Perek. They got on a ship in Joktel. They took that ship all the way to Blasinigan."

Soolchakan closed his eyes. "How is this significant? Blasinigan is the capital city of South Paselter and one of the largest cities and seaports in the world. Why should that be so unusual?" He opened his eyes and gazed at Jashalo expectantly.

"They were couriers," said Jashalo. "They had several dispatches. They had no idea what was in those dispatches, but, they were headed for a certain rather large building in Blasinigan. This specific building is one where the nobles of South Paselter usually go to attend any and all meetings called by King Dolomon." He leaned forward. "We followed them into a secret meeting. They gave the dispatches to another Perek who read them. He called a Perek runner who called a meeting for (Ahem) all concerned."

Chaya broke in. "The other people attending this meeting were some higher ups from the Fastern, the Galsino, the Tekaylath-Sar, as well as the Ikogo, the Pryato and the Zaberd."

Kiyalee looked horrified. "What, in the flames, brought all of those Elf races together?"

Jashalo smiled. "This is the entire thing. All of those Elf races are scheming with King Dolomon. There're a few nobles of South Paselter who were there as well, but, all of them are there to plan a strategy for reuniting all of South and North Paselter, back to one kingdom, with those Elf races having a very strong influence in the new government of the reunited Paselter."

Chyning gave a side glance. "What's supposed to happen to King Dolomot of North Paselter?"

Jashalo shook his head sadly. "They're planning on killing him and his entire family. King Dolomon of South Paselter will be crowned King of all Paselter…but…he'll only be a figurehead. He has no intellect, desire or capability to be a King. He likes his position, but he doesn't want the responsibility of making any kind of important decision. The intelligence and decision making is left up to his advisors."

"Most of which consist of members of the seven races of Elf who were in attendance," said Quakee.

Soolchakan leaned back in his chair. He closed his eyes and thought for a few moments. "Do we know what kind of a leader King Dolomot is?"

Bonarain huffed. "They're twin brothers but...beyond physical similarity, they're totally different. Everything I'm hearing from the Turgon Wall says that Dolomot is a very good leader. Most of the races of Elf in North Paselter have anything bad to say about him."

"He is also not a fat slob," said Joosha. "You'll have no difficult time telling the two apart. Dolomot has kept himself in very good shape. He practices with sword, spear, battle-axe and the bow almost every day. He also goes about his home walking briskly and staying in shape. Dolomon has stayed very close to the dinner table and now...he weighs four times as much as his brother."

Soolchakan looked down at his glass of fruit juice. "I think...we need to get to the capital city of Sontor and...inform King Dolomot. We should inform the people at the Turgon Wall as well. They deserve to know what's going on." He took a drink. "Call all of the other Teams. See if they've observed any of their Elf races sending dispatches to this...meeting place."

Jashalo bowed. "At once, Drey Sssorg." He signaled to his children. "We'll depart and get the message out."

All seven of the visitors vanished.

Bonarain sighed. "First it was the Heyyah with the Fastern, the Galsino, the Perek and the Tekaylath-Sar. Now we add the Ikogo, the Pryato and the Zaberd."

"Sounds almost like old times," said Kiyalee bitterly.

Chyning shook her head. "Nah! Before, we had that horrid problem of not being able to read the minds of the Teltermak. I don't remember any problems with any of these other races."

Bonarain raised her eyebrows and smiled at Soolchakan. "So how do we explain to King Dolomot that his twin brother is the main conspirator against him?"

"Very carefully," said Soolchakan. He looked around at all those in the room. "And we better have a lot more valid, physical evidence before we do present any of the information. Otherwise, the consequences could be disastrous."

Kiyalee huffed. "How do we go about that?"

Soolchakan shrugged. "They said that those couriers had some dispatches. All we need to do is get in there and obtain some of those dispatches."

Bonarain stirred her juice. "We need to make sure that we get the most revealing ones that we can find."

Chyning frowned. "Revealing what?"

Bonarain smiled. "Who is involved, how far they're willing to go, what their timeline is, when are they going to attack, how they plan to attack, where they plan to attack and...why?" She bit her lip. "And…who they plan on killing. Basically, anything we can get our hands on."

"That's a mouthful of information," said Kiyalee.

"Right," said Soolchakan. "We need to contact Jashalo and get as many people in that conclave of conspiracy as soon as possible. Gather *all* of the dispatches. There's no telling which one will be the most valuable."

Bonarain sat there with her eyes closed.

Kiyalee tapped Bonarain on the shoulder. "What are you doing?"

Bonarain looked at Kiyalee scornfully. "Contacting Jashalo." She closed her eyes again.

Kiyalee grimaced, flushed, turned away and clasped her hands in her lap.

Chyning sat there giggling quietly.

In a very rapid manner, all Teams that were assigned to spy on any of the conspirators were now in Blasinigan. They would wait in the secret meeting room of that very large government building for any new information. There were times that no new information came in for at least three weeks. Other times it was just the next day.

The conspirators would brief everyone on their setups and spies that were infiltrating the North. They would then burn all written dispatches. Bikaropin devised a method of switching the documents just before they were put to the flame. That way, the

Owlamites had the unblemished reports (even though they might be slightly singed on a corner of the page…and a little wrinkled).

The Owlamites found they could afford to be patient. The conspirators were not ready to pounce yet. It would still take some time before they had everything in place.

Right now, several of them were wondering just exactly how their diversion at the Turgon Wall had gone so badly awry. They no longer had all of that attention on the west side of the Turgon Wall or the western sector of North Paselter. This setback had slowed their plans by at least one year before they could do a few other secret maneuvers. Part of the slowing down was the investigation of just exactly how the diversion had gone so badly wrong and now attempting to set up some other massive diversion.

They were now planning another diversion. The problem was that the diversion had to be something that attracted all of the attention to the north. They wanted something that was coming in from the ocean. The problem there was on the east coast the countries of Cheseet, Eang, Ithagum and Tabrow took most of that coastline away from North Paselter. They might be blamed for some incursion and all that would do is give the Army of North Paselter some first-hand experience in actual combat. This could end up a negative because it might hurt the current lives of many of the conspirators in the North.

In the west, there was nothing but Paselter coastline and open seas until you got to the Turgon Wall. If they did anything major there, the North Paselter Navy would be able to stop anything by halting and searching all ships along the coastline.

To the north there was nothing that was financially feasible. From Tabrow to the Turgon Wall, it was all tundra. During the winter, it was mainly covered in snow and ice. During the summer, the ground was just too soft to support any kind of major movement of troops or equipment.

The east coast also now had the handicap of a lot of coast watchers in a very small Paseltern coastal area between Cheseet and Eang. The catapults had been identified as coming from Bertheel. That small patch of Paseltern coastline was only four days sailing away from the island nation of Bertheel. The conspirators would have to go around the peninsula where Eang and Ithagum were located in order to find more Paselter coastline in the east. This still left only a small coastal area between Eang and Tabrow which could be very tricky during the winter.

The Owlamites were finding it rather humorous listening to all of the complaints and bickering of the conspirators. Each party wanted and needed more assistance from the other parties to the scheme. Each party was complaining that they were overburdened with what they currently had and still needed some ideas for a new spectacular diversion.

Ispino of the Tenth reported in to Soolchakan. She had uncovered some internal plots. Of the seven Elf races trying to accomplish this conspiracy and takeover, the Fastern, the Galsino, the Perek, the Pryato, the Tekaylath-Sar and the Zaberd all wanted to be the primary rulers of this new kingdom with all others subservient to them. Only the Ikogo were willing to share the power with the other races. The Heyyah were not aware of the fact that all Heyyah were supposed to be completely subservient to all

Elf races once the takeover had been accomplished – primarily as lackeys with a few of them being obedient figureheads.

Soolchakan looked over all of the paperwork that had been amassed in the uncovering of these subplots. He groaned in frustration. "I understand that you're still acquiring more information to prove this?"

Ispino nodded. "Oh yes. My husband, Oss, is still there with my sister wives, Quezza and Shysang. We seem to be accumulating more information daily."

He nodded. "Have you informed all of the other Teams about these…subplots of traitors betraying traitors, treason against treason and sedition against sedition?"

Ispino grinned. "Oh absolutely. Tolahair of the Eighth and Barlar of the Fifth are doing a lot of the coordinating of who watches who and when."

He looked up rather upset. "Why wasn't I informed of this earlier?"

Ispino shrugged. "We wanted to make sure of what we had."

He stood up looking rather angry. "You've just handed me over 500 documents with all of this information!" He leaned forward. "Dontcha think it might have been a bit more expedient to get this information to me when it was less than 100?"

Now Ispino looked defensive. "We weren't sure…about the Ikogo." She cleared her throat nervously. "We wanted to make sure that…you were getting…accurate information."

He walked around the table. He placed his right hand on the back of the chair she was sitting on. "Information is always timely. It can always be updated as you find new information – even if it is contradictory." He leaned down, placed his left hand on her right cheek. He moved his mouth up close to her left ear. "Leak some...or a lot...of this information to the Ikogo. Let them look at it for a while and...then sit back and see what happens."

She sat there for a moment, wide-eyed in shock. She placed her hands over her mouth and started snickering. "That would... cause all kinds of...mayhem." She looked up at him. "Should we...leak the information...to the other Elf races...as well?"

"Yes, and to the Heyyah. Get all of them wondering about all the other factions."

She nodded. "Give all of them all of this information and..."

He grabbed her lower jaw with his left hand to stop her. "No! Give each one of them a few tastes of the information. Don't make it a flood...yet. Start the suspicions and then...once we've got them mistrusting each other...then we give them further confirmation of...underhanded activities...by all the others." He grinned.

She grinned back. "Lovely idea." She giggled. "We'll have all of them looking to kill all the others. It could destroy the entire plot...before King Dolomot even knows about any of this mess."

Soolchakan stood up and sighed. "King Dolomot is already aware of the fact that there were catapults on the wrong side of the

Turgon Wall. If we suddenly shut off all intelligence data, he and the Elf races at the Turgon wall will wonder what *we* are up to."

Ispino sighed. "That stinks."

The reaction by the Ikogo was immediate. Two Heyyah nobles from South Paselter were assassinated. There were five different high leaders of the Fastern, the Galsino, the Pryato, the Tekaylath-Sar and the Zaberd who were assassinated as well. The Owlamites leaked certain information to the Galsino and the Zaberd as to who had committed the assassinations. Within three days there were five different Ikogo leaders who were murdered. The Galsino and Zaberd gave the information they found to the Perek and Tekaylath-Sar - five more Ikogo leaders ambushed and killed.

The alliance turned into chaos. Each of the Elf races returned to their sanctuaries to rethink the entire process. As each one tried to decide whom they could trust, the Owlamites gave more information to all of the Elf races. The trust dissolved even further and there were several more mangled bodies, of various races, littering the back alleys of Blasinigan or floating, face down, in canals and cesspools.

As the Owlamites investigated further, it was found that the vast majority of the assassinations were committed by the Ikogo. They are an amphibious race. They have ebony skin and gills. They can hide underwater without needing any breathing tubes. They come up out of the water at night, when their ebony coloring acts as camouflage. After doing the deed, they retreat back to the water and hide again...until their next attack.

Now, no one trusted anyone in the former alliance. In order to make any attempt at reestablishing an alliance whose purpose was to take the Paselter Empire and reunite both north and south in an empire that would aim for global domination, they had to sign all kinds of treaties that guaranteed there would be no more secrets from the different races. Everything would be in the open. Each one grudgingly signed the pacts. Each one held back information anyway. The Owlamites started gathering this withheld information in order to strike back at a later date and restart the confusion.

In order to make an attempt at keeping the new alliance intact, there were two other Elf races brought in on the conspiracy. The Feeror from Aerisau and the Filkont from Ficara. They were brought in on the hope that they could assist in maintaining some kind of order. They were also brought in because it was hoped that they would not try anything stupid because of their short stature. Both races were just over one teckist in height. The Owlamites were rather puzzled by this because one of the original Elf races involved in the conspiracy – the Tekaylath-Sar – were even shorter than the Feeror or the Filkont.

Another confusing issue was that there were envoys sent to the far southern portion of Aerisau in an attempt at bringing the Orek-Karaw into the fold. This is a very tall Elf race. Short stature does not help here.

Another set of envoys risked their lives going to a place in Eang to contact the Tendixive and try to bring them into the alliance. The Tendixive are just as short in stature as the Tekaylath-Sar, however, these people can spit venom…with deadly (and most times, fatal) accuracy.

Each time some kind of move was made by the shaky alliance, the Owlamites cataloged and filed each tidbit of information for further use (or abuse) against the alliance.

They also wondered how much of this information they should share with their allies. Someone might start asking how they were obtaining the information and that could cause some sticky situations about questions they did not want to answer. It seemed better to cause chaos among the enemy alliance rather than give a lot of information to the friends.

Soolchakan was getting even more tired of political intrigue. Who is your enemy – today? Who is your friend – today? Who do you trust and how far – today? Who trusts us – today? Who knows what about us – today? What will they know – tomorrow? Can I trust them – tomorrow? Will they trust us – tomorrow? If this enemy is exposed – today, do I turn that one into a puppet or just kill them?

Bikaropin came to Soolchakan with a suggestion.

"Why don't we get some information out…to certain Elf races about all of this plotting and conspiracy?"

Soolchakan looked at Bikaropin in disbelief. "You want to add more fuel to this fire? You want to add more players to this silly game?"

Bonarain was sitting there listening in. "You want to bring the Tsaylaw-Ozen in on this...why?"

Bikaropin pointed to the map. "This is the area where the Tsaylaw-Ozen have their homes. This is also on North Chilamte. Now, the current conspirators have brought most of the other Elf races of North Chilamte in...why not the Tsaylaw-Ozen?"

"Because they have poisonous spikes on the tips of their ears," said Bonarain. "They don't like anyone entering their area and they usually deal with any intruders with fatal results. They like to be left alone. They're totally xenophobic. What makes you think they'd be interested in getting involved?"

Bikaropin smiled. "These conspirators have involved most of the reclusive and nasty Elf races from North and South Chilamte. They went on to include other reclusive and nasty Elf races from other continents. What would happen if the Tsaylaw-Ozen were to find out that they've been left out of something like this? It could cause even more chaos among the conspirators."

"It could also add an ally," said Bonarain bluntly. "*That*...I don't like."

Bikaropin shrugged. "I just put something out there to think about. I'll let you ponder it...while I go get some lunch." He vanished.

Bonarain looked at Soolchakan. "Are you really going to consider it?"

Soolchakan sighed. "I will think long and hard on it before I bring those sneaky little *bimyocks* into this mess." He smiled at her. "Long and hard…in order to make sure we're making the right decision."

Bonarain shook her head. "Thank the Great Maker for computers. Can you imagine how much of a mess this would be if we had to keep all of this on loose documents?"

"We've been spoiled," said Soolchakan.

The years had gone by as the conspirators were kept in a state of mistrust, chaos and disruption. There were problems with any of them making any agreements. Every dirty little secret that one of them would try to keep from the others was exposed by the Owlamites. No one could figure out who the spies, double agents and triple agents were. This prevented them from making any kind of an assault on North Paselter. All of the Owlamites felt that it would be best to do everything to stop any armed confrontation. This would be a civil war and those usually end up being the absolute worst kind of situation.

Another reason the Owlamites wanted to keep the conspirators in complete chaos was because several of the allied factions were from different continents. If they were able to reunite Paselter through conquest, that would give them the courage to conquer the other six countries on the North Chilamte continent. Then they would go on to other continents. The South Chilamte continent was not that far from North Chilamte and High Country, where the Owlamites now lived, just might be one of the first ones attacked in spite of the Dragon Force that defended the country.

In late 5494 ATUT, Krijolo and Mimamay of the Twenty-First became the parents of the first set of quadruplets born to the Owlamites. Four baby girls who brought the population up to 10,076. For the time being, Krijolo and Mimamay were excused from any spying operations because, for the next few years, they would be rather busy.

By the end of the year 5495 ATUT, the Owlam population was 10,098. There were very young children and babies all over the top three levels of apartments in the gorge. The Year 5496 ended with the population up to 10,150. No one was complaining about all the noise from the young children because it meant that there were children and the Owlamites had a growing future – even though no Owlamite had died since the year 4861 ATUT... and they had those mysterious stones worn by the first generation.

While still keeping the conspirators in a constant state of mistrust, in 5498 ATUT, the three wives of Soolchakan got their maternal instinct going again. Their current youngest children were only 22 years old and suddenly all three of them wanted another child. Very early in 5499, all three became mothers of brand new babies. Bonarain had a new son named Entornok. Kiyalee had a new daughter named Whikena. Chyning had a new daughter named Quorza. Soolchakan did not try to understand this maternal drive, he just remembered that he really did not wish to perpetuate any more lies to or on the women – *any* Owlamite women. He sat down and looked at the roll call. He was now the father of twenty-two children ranging from newborn to Shalam whose age was 5,483 years old.

By the end of the year 5500 ATUT, the Owlam population was 10,377.

They were no closer to stopping the conspiracy. For some reason the stubborn conspirators were determined to start a conquest of the continent and then the planet. They were determined that it had to start with the reuniting of Paselter. No other nation could claim to be as powerful as a reunited Paselter. They were continually making a new pact even through all of the secret plots that each race was hatching against all of the others. Certain personnel were picked out of each ethnic group and executed for treason against the alliance. Then the plotting would go on…as well as the subplots and secret backstabbing.

The Owlamites were always there to find information and deliver it to the wrong people in order to create more havoc among the conspirators.

6

"All these years and those *bimyocks* keep plotting," muttered Chyning bitterly. She then looked down and smiled at her youngest daughter as the small baby suckled on her breast.

"We have to do something," said Kiyalee. "Somehow, each of those plotters keep going back to trusting each other. Even though we keep exposing all of the hidden plots, they keep going back to it."

"We keep King Dolomot informed but…he still hasn't done a thing," said Bonarain. She shook her head.

All three women looked at Soolchakan with accusing glares while still attending to their young babies.

He grunted in disgust. "Do you want me to try controlling him? Should I make him attack his brother? Should I cause a civil war between North and South Paselter?"

"The civil war is already there," snarled Kiyalee.

"No hostile blow has been struck yet. No blood has been shed," said Soolchakan sternly! "Dolomot has been kept up to date on everything that Dolomon is doing and he still chooses to wait."

"Dolomon isn't doing anything other than stuffing his fat face," said Chyning with complete disdain. "You rarely find him anywhere other than at the breakfast table, the lunch table or the dinner table."

"He waddles off to the bathroom or bedroom... occasionally," snickered Kiyalee.

"True," said Bonarain. "If Dolomot attacks, he won't be attacking his brother Dolomon."

"But he *will* be attacking forces of South Paselter and that would still put blood kin relatives against each other," spat Soolchakan. "King Dolomot has openly stated that he doesn't want that. He wants some sort of peaceful resolution to this problem...if that is possible."

Shalam had been listening to the arguments. "Why don't we talk to some of the military commanders?"

Soolchakan looked at Shalam expectantly. "What've you got in mind?"

Shalam shrugged. "I don't think any of them want a big mess on their hands. So far, none of them want to be the one who orders the first strike...even if it comes as a command from the King...either King."

Soolchakan sighed. "Should we tell them to disobey a royal proclamation?"

"No, just have some of the top commanders from the north go talk to the top commanders of the south...uh...any of them that are not part of the plot." Shalam smiled. "Maybe they can work something out…where they go after the conspirators and not the military forces of the other half of the empire."

"That sounds like something worth discussing," said Bonarain looking thoughtful.

Soolchakan shrugged. "All right. Let's find the top army and navy commanders. See if we can arrange this meeting and… see if we really can find some kind of peaceful solution to this mess." He looked around the room at all the faces. "Maybe we should arrange this meeting to take place in a neutral location… like the city of Galgatam."

Bonarain frowned. "Why in the capital of Cheseet?"

Shalam smiled. "It just happens to be half way between Sontor and Blasinigan. It is also on the same continent as Paselter. I'm sure that the people of Cheseet are just as eager to see a peaceful solution because a big civil war between the Paseltern north and south could easily spill over into Cheseet."

Kiyalee pursed her lips and looked a little coquettish. "If they're not willing to host the meeting, maybe the people of Varnast would welcome the meeting in Kagigan."

Soolchakan looked thoughtful. "Maybe we could have meetings in both capitals. Both countries could suffer badly from a nasty civil war that would take place on their borders."

"So we send someone to Galgatam and Kagigan," said Bonarain. "Whom shall we send?"

"Shalam thought of it," said Chyning with a big grin.

"Our other best choice is Bikaropin," said Kiyalee.

Soolchakan looked at Shalam and smiled. "Choose! Do you want to go to Galgatam or Kagigan?"

Shalam smiled weakly. "I guess...I'll go to...Galgatam."

Soolchakan nodded happily. "And Bikaropin goes to Kagigan."

"I'm sure he'll be thrilled with that news," said Shalam sarcastically. He sighed and then looked with contentment at the new babies that were in the room. One of them had just made some cooing sound and it was rather pleasant to hear. He thought of his own children. Eight of them had been born then killed in the first Teltermak war. All eight brought back in the grand mass resurrections. Now two new ones born just 24 years ago. He smiled while doing his contemplations. He headed off to give Bikaropin the news.

Bikaropin stared at Shalam. "Whose idea was this?"

"It was mine," said Shalam with a shrug and a wan smile.

Bikaropin looked down at his mug of kwatha. "I hate being a diplomat." He started spooning for lumps. "I'd prefer to ambush from a hidden spot and worry about the consequences later. Talking to any career politicians always seems to be a waste of breath. The only thing that a career politician wants is...*what is in it for me?*"

Shalam snickered. "Yeah, but the way we can hide or

Jump, we don't have to worry about getting caught."

Bikaropin nodded. "That's one reason why I don't worry about consequences."

"But we do have to worry about results."

"True." He brought up a large lump. He popped it in his mouth and chewed slowly. "Kagigan eh?" He shook his head. "It's been a while since I was there. I don't even know who is in command militarily or…who is on the throne in Varnast."

Shalam chuckled. "That's why we do a little spying…in Spy…before we introduce ourselves."

Bikaropin nodded sadly. "I know the drill." He put a spoonful of the broth in his mouth then licked the spoon. "How soon do we have to get this done?"

"By the calendar, we just started a new century. This is now the beginning of the year 5501 ATUT. I think that we should have this done sometime before *this* year ends. Besides, all we're going there for is to set up a meeting place. The guests are going to be the tough part."

He grunted. "It can still wait until I'm finished with my kwatha. This is a really good batch." He went back to spooning for lumps.

It was only four days later that Shalam and Bikaropin reported back to the first quartet.

"The people of Galgatam are more than willing to host

a peace conference," said Shalam. "They're terrified of the consequences of a war between two powerful military entities like the ones in North and South Paselter."

"The people of Varnast are equally thrilled at hearing of a peace conference," said Bikaropin. "Their military is extremely small because they were depending on the Paselter military to assist in their defense. No one would want any hostile force getting a toe-hold on North Chilamte, even in Varnast. They're very amicable about a conference in Kagigan."

Soolchakan chuckled. "Everybody wants peace. They like their status as it is and they don't want any form of ambitious *bimyock* coming in and messing up their nice little lives." He sighed. "Now, we have to figure out who the best people are to attend these meetings. We're going to have to delve into a few minds and choose the ones least likely to lose their temper and cause any problems at the meetings."

Bonarain walked back and forth rocking her youngest child. "The main problems are the ones in South Chilamte. They're the ones that are conspiring with those nasty Elf races."

Chyning chuckled. "Yeah! So far, at least four of the high ranking nobles, who are still alive, of South Chilamte have been recognized as conspirators...by us. How many of them should have fatal accidents?"

"As many as it takes to keep the peace," grumbled Soolchakan. He grunted. "We've already exposed sixteen of them and they have mysteriously disappeared. Why any of the other nobles want to be involved in this conspiracy is beyond me."

"Blind and stupid ambition," said Bikaropin flatly. "If something does happen, they want to be a part of the winning team in order to keep their exalted positions."

"We still have to find a way to keep the meetings secret from any of the conspirators," said Bonarain. "Otherwise it'll all be for nothing."

Soolchakan shook his head. "Why is peace always harder than war?"

"Because of nasty, ambitious *bimyocks*," said Kiyalee.

"Don't forget to call them greedy as well," said Chyning smugly.

"Use all the adjectives, synonyms, declaratives or obscenities you want," said Soolchakan. "It all adds up to the same thing."

"A mess," said Bikaropin. "The main mess is trying to figure out which is friend and which is foe."

Bonarain hung her head. "That sounds painfully familiar."

"I remember some of the former Drey Sssorg having the same feelings about war," said Soolchakan. "They're tired of fighting but have no desire to give in to ambitious conquerors."

The next few days was a flurry of finding as many military commanders, of both sides, as possible. Read their minds and find out where they stood as far as any kind of civil war and loyalty to their King. Then arrange for them to go to either Galgatam or

Kagigan, or both, to meet with their counterparts.

Part of arranging the meetings involved getting the ones who wanted a peaceful solution and giving them the information about the traitors to Dolomon, South Paselter as well as North Paselter.

The Owlamites were being hounded as far as how they knew this information and how they knew of the accuracy of it. They were simply told that if that was divulged, there were many lives that would be in grave danger (namely Owlamites). They were also informed that the Owlamites were still trying to figure out who they could or could not trust. The Owlamites mainly informed the commanders that the meetings were badly needed in order to make some kind of plan to thwart the conspirators in a manner where there were as few casualties as possible.

The first meetings took place. All of the military commanders were in agreement about peaceful solutions. They were all still very suspicious as to how the Owlamites were able to readily obtain all of this information.

Most of them only partially believed the Owlamites. Many of them were thinking that this was a plot to weaken the forces of both North and South Paselter and then the Owlamites would come in and take over. The main stumbling block to that thought was that the Owlamites were only suggesting an attack on the Galsino, the Ikogo and the Pryato. Considering the numbers of these three Elf races living on North Chilamte, any attack on any of them might give the Paselter military an interesting afternoon…or two.

Any attack on the Fastern would require some kind of diplomatic meeting between Paselter and Ithagum. True the Fastern were a race living on North Chilamte, however, they were the only race of Elf that did not have a territory inside Paslter. Hopefully Ithagum would be agreeable in crushing any form of revolution by knocking the Fastern down before any major war was started.

The Perek and Tekaylath-Sar were from South Chilamte. Any knocking down there would require some other diplomatic envoy departing the continent. The same thing would happen with the Feeror from Aerisau, the Filkont from Ficara and the Zaberd from Cifpasica.

The prime hope was that if they could stop the entire thing on North Chilamte, then the entire plot would die...hopefully.

Soolchakan looked over the reports he was getting from all of his different Owlamite spies. He shook his head in frustration. He looked up at Shalam. "Hasn't anyone found anything on the Teltermak potions yet?"

The six men sitting in the main room at apartment 12-562 all looked around at each other in confusion.

Zormun was the first to speak. "Were we supposed to be looking for...potions?" He smiled nervously as he glanced around at the other members of the meeting.

Soolchakan dropped all of the paperwork and glared back at the six. "What makes you think that you were *not* supposed to be looking?"

All six sat there with anguish, consternation and red faces.

"I don't remember you saying anything about it," said Bikaropin. "We got rid of all of the bottles that were on that island…south of the Turgon area. What makes you think that… there are still more?"

Soolchakan was now glaring angrily at them. "What makes you think that there are NOT?" He stood up and walked among them looking at each one with irritation on his face. "There were several cases on that island. Somebody had to have them stored *somewhere*…for who knows how long. Whoever that somebody is…there might be more potions in their possession." He went back to his seat. "A *lot* more potions. The other horror of this is that there might still be some Teltermak running around here as well." He snarled in disgust. "Either way, we need to find out *something!*" He looked at the six who were still staring at him in fear. "NOW!"

Shalam, Monaha, Peldom, Baktim, Zormun and Bikaropin all Jumped out of there, heading out to get with all the others and start this ball rolling – NOW.

Soolchakan was now sitting there alone. He spoke to the air. "How long has it been? How long have we been trying to obliterate this silly plot? The whole time they should've been looking for the potions as well!" He shook his head. "*H'OOLYACH!*"

Bonarain walked in. "Is something bothering you?"

He shook his head. "You don't wanna know."

Kiyalee was right behind Bonarain. "I think we do wanna know."

Chyning came in from a different direction. "What do we wanna know?"

Soolchakan sighed and informed them of the blunder. All this time, no one was attempting to find out anything about any possibility of remaining potions.

Bonarain rolled her eyes and groaned. "Maybe we should be the ones who do some of the looking for the potions."

"Speak for yourself," said Chyning. "Look at these three younglings that we've got here. You wanna take them on some spy trip with you?"

Bonarain smiled. "At least we'd know where they are."

"Give it a few days," said Soolchakan. "If they don't have any results by this time next week…then we go on a few missions of our own." He chuckled. "If for no other reason than to stay well practiced."

Monaha showed up with Bendarik and Sunok. Soolchakan looked up at the trio in a rather dull-eyed manner.

"We found some potions," said Monaha with an uneasy smile. "The Galsino have some potions hidden in underground vaults under their city."

Soolchakan chuckled. All this time and he had not really thought about all of the underground mazes under each of the cities in a long time. If the Galsino had rediscovered them, or remembered them all along it was no wonder that they would utilize them.

"There are four cases of brown bottles," said Bendarik.

"There are six cases of red bottles," said Sunok.

"There are at least fifty cases of white bottles," said Monaha.

Soolchakan frowned. "None…that are yellow?"

All three men shook their heads.

Soolchakan shrugged. "Maybe they had all of the yellow bottles on that island." He smiled. "Uh…where are the…many cases of other colored bottles…at this time?"

"They're still there," said Monaha.

Soolchakan closed his eyes in frustration. He sighed. "Show me."

Monaha touched Soolchakan on the shoulder and Jumped them both to the vault with the potions. Soolchakan gasped as he found himself inside a very large area filled with ice.

"Don't ask me how, but they've got some kind of refrigeration unit here," said Monaha. "Some…way…it survived all of these millennium and…they're able to keep the potions cold in here."

Soolchakan huffed at him. "You could've warned someone about this…*cold*!"

"Sorry," said Monaha nervously.

Bendarik pointed to a place on the wall. "Over there, they've got some recipes etched into the wall. They tell how to mix the stuff in order to manufacture the potions. I don't think the Teltermak informed the Galsino as to what the *special* prime ingredient for each one happens to be."

Soolchakan frowned as he hugged himself. "Why do you say that?"

Bendarik pointed at some tables. "None of their tools have been used in a long time...if ever. All of them are covered with several layers of ice."

Sunok chipped at the ice on one of the work tables. "In here, you find a lot of ice on the tables. In another vault, that's not quite so cold, they have some ovens." He looked up at Soolchakan. "All of the ovens are covered with dust...inside and out."

Soolchakan felt a little better about the situation. "That would mean that the Galsino obtained the recipes...without finding out what the primary ingredient is." He chuckled. "Otherwise, they might be looking for us...in the same stubborn manner that the Teltermak were doing. The Teltermak knew that it was our internal organs that were the prime ingredients for all the potions. For some reason...they kept it a secret...all the way to the grave." He looked up and grinned. "Or outer space."

Sunok picked up a red bottle. "What do you want us to do with these?"

"Destroy them," said Soolchakan flatly. "Get them on a

shuttlecraft and drop them into the atmosphere of either Ragath or Rogoth."

Bendarik looked a little apprehensive. "Once we've destroyed these bottles, should we keep looking for potions?"

Soolchakan hung his head. "Unfortunately, yes. We had no idea that the Galsino had these and…some of the others could have some bottles as well. Until we're absolutely certain that all of them are…gone…keep on looking."

"We can do that," said Monaha.

"Meanwhile, we keep looking for peace between North and South Paselter," said Bendarik.

Soolchakan Jumped back to his apartment. The difference in temperature was incredible. He had to sit down for a few moments to readjust to the heavy humid air of the gorge again.

"There you are," said Peldom jubilantly.

Soolchakan was rather startled. He had not expected anyone to be here. "What did you want?"

"We found the potions," said Peldom with a big smile.

Soolchakan groaned and leaned his head back with his eyes closed. "Where?"

"The Fastern have some in their city in Ithagum."

Soolchakan shook his head and sighed. He lowered his head and looked at Peldom with a wan smile. "Show me."

Peldom had a flashlight in his hand. He turned it on, took

Soolchakan's hand and Jumped. Soolchakan saw, as soon as they reached the destination, the reason for the flashlight. They were in another sub-level vault with all of the local lighting turned out...and it was, once again, extremely cold in the vault. Farn and Korpem were there in the vault, each with a flashlight of their own.

Korpem aimed his light. "Over there. All of those crates against the back wall. All of those are the potions."

Soolchakan followed his beam. He slowly walked over to the stacks of boxes while mentally inventorying the collection.

Farn came up next to Soolchakan. "Eight cases of red, seven cases of brown, one case of yellow and twenty-six cases of white."

Soolchakan shook his head. "So they held back one case of the brain potion." He snarled as he hugged himself for warmth. "Somebody go find Bikaropin. Bring him here."

Korpem looked a little confused, however, he complied. He did a few mental communications and then vanished. Moments later he was back in the vault with Bikaropin.

Bikaropin let out a slight gasp. "Why is it...so cold in here?"

"That's what I'd like you to figure out," said Soolchakan without taking his eyes off of the potion boxes. "I thought that we were the only ones who still had any technology. Now, I find out that both the Galsino and Fastern have fully functional technological refrigeration units in their sub-level vaults." He turned to look at

Bikaropin. "How did we…and all of those outworld conquerors, who did everything they could to knock out any and all planetary technology miss it…for all of these millennium?"

Bikaropin blew in his hands to warm them. "The only thing I can think of…is…uh, do I have to stay here to check it out or can I go someplace warmer to test my theory?"

Soolchakan contemplated and sighed. "If your theory is better tested elsewhere, go and test it in any way you wish. Just… find something that can…explain this conundrum."

Bikaropin saluted and vanished.

At that moment all of the lights came on in the vault. They heard a door being opened at the other end of the big room. Two very tall Fastern Elf walked in wearing large winter coats. Their long white fangs stood out like a beacons against their dark brown skin. They both headed directly to the potion cases.

Soolchakan raised his eyebrows. "Interesting. Let's see what happens."

One of the Fastern pulled the flaps back on one of the cases of white bottles. "Which one is the open one?"

The other Fastern grunted. "It's the one with the red mark on the stopper, you *pevek*!"

The first one snarled back and pulled the bottle out. He pulled the stopper and inserted a tube into the bottle.

The second one growled as he talked. "Remember, no more than three drops."

The first one scowled back. "I know, you *kivots*! I've been doing this for a long time. Matter of fact, longer than you." He pulled a very tiny vial from one of the big pockets on his coat. He pulled the tube out of the white bottle and inserted it into the small glass vial. He carefully allowed three drops to fall from the tube. He placed the tube back in the white bottle and tapped it several times to free all of the cold liquid from the tube. "Done!" He put the stopper back in the white bottle and also stoppered the vial. "Let's get out of this cold."

Soolchakan sniffed. "This looks interesting. Let's follow them and...find out what they're doing...with only *three* lousy drops."

They exited the refrigerated vault and removed their heavy coats. They pushed a heavy sliding door into place, closing the cold unit from the musty heat in the hallway. They turned and headed away from the cold unit.

The two Fastern seemed to be in no hurry at all. They slowly walked the hallways to the staircase. They slowly ascended the stairs. It took quite a while because they were on the eighth sub-level under their city.

Soolchakan looked around as they took this journey with some consternation. They were walking on metal grating where the clangs of the footfalls of the two Fastern was all too familiar. There was electronic lighting above in all of the hallways. The staircase was lit as well. One light bulb was flickering slightly. Another one was buzzing. He shook his head. For people who seemed to have an existence without any technological luxuries above ground, there were certainly a lot of them below ground.

Soolchakan turned to Peldom. "Has anyone tried to find out how they have so much technology down here...but nothing up above?"

"I have," said Farn.

Soolchakan looked at him. "And?"

"They know how to replace a light bulb. They don't know how to replace wiring or any other parts of the setup. They've been trying to find anything in their archives that can act as some form of tutorial, but...all of that information has been lost to them completely because they've also lost all of their computers. They did not lose equipment."

Soolchakan shook his head in wonder and huffed. "That means that all the electrical components down here are...over 14,000 years old...and still working? That is definitely some high quality equipment."

They got up to the fourth sub-level and suddenly there was no more electricity. There were lit oil lamps hanging from the ceiling. They were low enough that the tall Fastern could reach them without ladders. The pungent smell of the burning oil was very prevalent in this area.

"We've gone back to pre-technology here," said Soolchakan. "I wonder why."

"All of the good stuff is fifth level or lower," said Farn.

"All the way down to the fifteenth sub-level," said Korpem.

Soolchakan was still awed by the difference. "Anybody know what is in some of those lower levels?"

Korpem laughed. "Most of the doors down there are sealed electronically. They haven't figured out how to get in them yet. Bashing down an iron door…doesn't work very well."

Soolchakan smiled. "Maybe, one of these days, we should take a look."

"Once we've solved a few other riddles and have some more leisure time for that kind of search," said Peldom.

The two Fastern stopped at the top of the stairs.

The first one smacked his hand against a door next to him. "I wish this lifting room still worked. It sure made things a lot easier getting up and down in these lower areas."

"Yes, it was nice," sighed the second. "Too bad."

They both leaned against the wall to catch their breath. They also took the time to wipe perspiration off their foreheads. After getting breath and strength back, they moved on. They went to a room where there were many different colored bottles on numerous shelves that lined all of the walls.

The first one placed the vial with the drops on a table in the middle of the room. The second one reached for a blue opaque bottle on a lower shelf.

"No, no, no," said the first one. "He said that he wanted it without the bitter taste. He doesn't want her to know."

The second one scoffed. "That's no fun at all."

The first one shrugged. "So what! That's his choice." He sighed. "Give the customer what the customer wants."

The second one shrugged as well and reached for a much larger brown bottle on a different shelf. "Just river water it is," he said.

The first one held the vial, with tweezers, over a funnel. The funnel was set to drain into a much larger clear bottle. Both of them got close to watch what they were doing. The second one slowly poured water directly into the vial. The vial was turned over to drain all contents and then turned upright.

"Still more in the vial," said the second. He poured more water into the vial.

Once again the contents were dumped and now both men smiled as they were satisfied that all of the potion was now in the lower bottle.

The first one picked the bottle up and started shaking it. "Come on you little beast – dissolve!"

The second one chuckled. "Got a stubborn one?"

"Yes, it doesn't want to give up the…ah…there is goes. Now, it is all in solution."

The second one placed the funnel in the top of a rather odd looking black bottle. None of the Owlamites were sure what the bottle was made from. It could have been glass, or wood or clay.

The contents of the clear bottle were poured into the odd bottle.

"Now we're ready," chuckled the second one.

They headed out of the bottle room and moved on down the hall.

"That is an incredibly diluted...and small amount of the potion," said Soolchakan. "As I recall...the white bottle has the love potion in it."

"You mean, it has some of our neck mucus in it," said Korpem?

"Yes," said Soolchakan. "And as I remember, the instructions were that...you had to consume the entire contents of the bottle in order for it to work."

Farn clicked his tongue. "Maybe the Fastern have found that you don't really need that much to get someone...*interested*." He smiled and raised his eyebrows.

Soolchakan shook his head. "I'd still like to see if it works – even with that tiny amount."

Peldom sighed. "Do we really need to go and have a peep show?"

"No," said Soolchakan. "You can go back down there and confiscate *all* of their potions." He snickered. "Ruin their business." He grinned. "That'll get their blood pressure up."

Peldom, Farn and Korpem all disappeared. Soolchakan continued following the new mixture.

The two Fastern went to a different room. Here they both donned odd looking dark, but colorful robes. They then proceeded to a place that looked like some kind of apothecary shop. Before they entered the back area of the shop, they both stooped over as if they were old and having problems standing up. They slowly walked into the shop. Soolchakan had not seen when it happened, however, the first one was using a cane and now had some kind of pronounced limp.

"Oh, pour it on thick, you fabricating *bimyocks*," scoffed Soolchakan.

There was a Heyyah man standing in the shop looking rather impatient. He was probably in his forties with a shock of blonde hair that stood straight up. He had a slight paunch. His clothing was definitely not from the best tailors in town. He turned when the two Fastern entered. He appeared very irritated. "Well it's about time! Were you able to make it?"

The first one responded in a creaky old voice. "Yes, it is made. Just as you asked."

The second one rubbed his temples. "It took quite a bit out of us, but we got it."

Soolchakan rolled his eyes. "Oh, *thicker* and *thicker*, you swindling *bimyocks*!"

"That will be twenty Gorpek," said the first one.

Soolchakan was shocked. "Twenty Gorpek? That is… expensive!" He tried to remember the conversion of this currency to another. He huffed and decided it was not that important.

The Heyyah pulled out his money pouch. "For that much, it'd better work." He counted out the coins.

"Oh it will," said the first one with a smile. "We guarantee results."

The Heyyah collected his merchandise and departed.

Soolchakan sighed as he started following the Heyyah. He did not like the idea of watching two people copulating, however, he just wanted to see if that minute amount did actually work. He felt that all he had to see was her reaction after consuming the drink.

The Heyyah was escorted out of the main part of the city that was populated by Fastern only. He then got on an equine-drawn two wheel cart to head back to his home. Soolchakan hitched a ride on the back of the cart. The ride was long and bumpy. Soolchakan was glad that he did not have to memorize any route. Once he had what he needed, he could Jump back to his apartment in the gorge.

They finally arrived at a rather isolated farmhouse. At this time of the year, the crops were just starting to show their first leaves above the ground. There was a smell in the air that told Soolchakan that this man was growing some kind of tuber in his large field.

While the man put his equine in the barn for the night, Soolchakan stretched his legs a little and looked over the farmhouse. It was a (predominately) white two story structure that looked rather weather beaten and a little rickety. It was badly in need of a new paint job. On the walls that he could see there were several patch jobs that had varied colors of brown or tan or... some color he could not identify.

The man came out of the barn. He pulled the bottle out of his pocket and smiled at it. He put it back in his pocket and headed for the house. Soolchakan followed him.

Inside, he saw that most of the furniture was in need of repair as well. The floors were in bad shape too. The smell of something being cooked wafted his way. He followed the man into the dining room.

A woman came out of the kitchen carrying a large bowl of something that was steaming. She gave the man a nasty look, snarled and placed the bowl on the table. She looked older than the man and she was definitely fatter. She had black stringy hair with streaks of gray in it. She was dressed in a shapeless threadbare dress that might have been colorful at one time…in the past…long ago. Her face was the type where she would be ugly, even if she was giving you a friendly smile. She went back in the kitchen.

The man pulled the bottle out and quickly poured the contents into one of the glasses on the table. He put it back in his pocket and then picked up a pitcher and filled both of the glasses on the table. He chuckled to himself as he sat down with the glass that had the "untainted" drink in it.

Soolchakan was a little disturbed. He shook his head as he thought to himself. 'He wants to…have sex with…*that*?' He sighed. 'No accounting for someone else's taste.'

The woman came back in carrying a platter with several bread rolls on it. She placed the platter on the table and reached for the pitcher.

"I've already done that," said the man.

She grunted at him. "For once you've done something positive. Do you want some reward for that?"

He started some return badmouthing. Soolchakan rolled his eyes and hopped to Observation. He decided he did not need to listen to their argument. He sat there and watched as each one ladled some of the stew into bowls, grab a couple of bread rolls and start eating…while still arguing. Soolchakan kept his eyes on her glass – so did the man.

The woman kept on complaining at him between mouthfuls of food. She took a roll and got as much of the gravy out of the bowl that she could and stuffed the roll in her mouth – between complaints. She wiped her mouth on her arm and finally reached for her glass. Soolchakan perked up and hopped back to Spy.

She took a long drink, put the glass down, belched and wiped her mouth with her hand. She suddenly got a look of horror and surprise on her face. She turned her gaze to him and now it changed to hate and anger. "YOU SNAKE! You did it again!" She stood up and leaned over the table moaning while grabbing her crotch with both hands. "Why did you do it?" She moaned again.

He leaned back in his chair and wiped his mouth with his sleeve. "It's the only way that I can get any kind of cuddle with you."

She looked up at him panting. "You could've probably got some harlot from that tavern for less than what you paid for this…" She closed her eyes and moaned again.

"If I got one of those harlots, I'd probably catch some

sex disease and then I'd have to pay even more for a healer...or medicine."

She clenched her teeth and glared at him. "Oh, what I'm gonna do to you in the morning...I..."

At that point Soolchakan had seen enough. He Jumped back to his apartment in the gorge. He was rather surprised that just three drops had done the job. The Teltermak had been terribly wasteful in what they had considered the dosage necessary to do the job. Apparently they made that part of the instructions in order to make people buy more of the stuff. Either that or they figured that they had a never ending supply, as long as any Owlamites existed.

Shalam came walking in. "I found the potions," he said happily.

Soolchakan groaned. "Where?"

"Would you like to see them?"

"No! Where did you find them?"

"In a sub-level vault in the home of the Ikogo. Wouldn't you like to see them?"

Soolchakan just shook his head. "No, just confiscate them." He sighed.

"You seemed highly interested...before."

"That was before we found some in cities of the Galsino and Fastern and now Ikogo." He shook his head. "How many of those rotten things did the Teltermak actually make?" He looked up at Shalam. "I wonder if they're going to find any in the home of the Pryato."

Shalam shrugged. "Don't know. I'll go confiscate the ones that I found."

"Thank you."

Shalam smiled and vanished.

Soolchakan shook his head. "At least we're not finding any Teltermak." He then looked to heaven in somewhat of a begging manner. "I hope we never do find any more of those...parasites."

7

Bikaropin smiled. "I think I found out why the outworlders didn't destroy a lot of the sub-level mazes under most of the cities."

Soolchakan looked at him wide-eyed. "I'd say that I'm all ears, but I hate mentioning the size of these beastly things protruding from the sides of my head."

Bikaropin chuckled. "When I flew some of those ships around Hardooth, most of them were able to find anything on the surface of the planet. Most of them weren't able to find anything under the surface, until they came a lot closer. Then and only then was I able to find *some* of the sub-level passages under *some* of the cities."

"How close did you have to get in order to find the really deep sub-levels?"

"In some cases, I had to land."

Soolchakan nodded. "That's why some of those places still have working passages." He shook his head. "Even though they can't understand the technology, they're still able to utilize some of it." He frowned. "I wonder how they were able to find all of those mineral deposits on Bri but...not sub-level hallways under…virtually every large city-state on Hardooth. I also wonder how there is still some power source in those lower levels…even after all of these millennium."

"I'm amazed at that myself," said Bikaropin while scratching his head. "A lot of the technology should've rotted away a long time ago." He shook his head. "As to why they find stuff on Bri but not Hardooth…I'm at a loss myself."

"Apparently, there are some things about those underground areas that we don't understand enough about it to…clear up the mystery."

"What do you mean?"

Soolchakan smiled. "Consider how magic works here on our planet in our atmosphere. This same magic doesn't work in other dimensions or on other planets in this dimension. Our inbred abilities work in all dimensions. How do we figure out what works where…other than experimentation?"

Bikaropin nodded while contemplating. "Just another mystery that may take some time to unravel. The only real thing that I can come up with on those subterranean levels is that, whoever the architects were…they were incredibly intelligent. I don't know if they designed the things with some kind of stealth technology that hides it from other types of technology…but I doubt that they had the forethought of outworlders coming here."

Soolchakan was reading some reports about how there were some very angry Fastern, Galsino and Ikogo. They had gone back to their refrigerated vaults and discovered that all of the potions were gone. Several investigations were going on in these cities, however, no questionings came up with any positive results, no matter how much torture was utilized. He put the documents down feeling somewhat satisfied.

"This is Rinnboz calling Soolchakan, can you hear me?"

Soolchakan looked up rather startled. **"This is Soolchakan, I hear you. What did you need**?"

"We're in the observation room. We've been looking at the monitors from Bri. It seems that there is some kind of outworlder orbiting the planet. They're looking at all of the mineral wealth of the planet."

Soolchakan shook his head. 'All of those outworlders with all of that technology. They can see all of the mineral wealth of Bri, but they can't see most of the sub-levels.' He shook his head again and then stood up in shock as he finally comprehended what Rinnboz had just told him. **"All Owlamites, we have another outworlder in our system. Everyone get to your fighter ships and let's get out there to the planet Bri**." He Jumped to his fighter which was parked on the big Chokchakchok ship.

Bonarain, Kiyalee and Chyning were there getting their spacesuits on. All three of them looked rather upset over this turn of events. It had been some time since the last outworlder had bothered them.

As each one finished donning their spacesuit, they climbed into their fighter and waited for Soolchakan to give the order for a mass Jump to Bri.

Soolchakan looked around the big fighter hangar. He watched as eighty other Owlamites all climbed in their fighters. He was the last to climb into his.

"All fighters, hop to Spy in Home and then Jump to Bri."

They all Jumped in the formations that were set up so that no one would "join" with another ship. The Jump took place and they were all now in an equatorial orbit of the planet Bri with Soolchakan leading the formation. They started looking for the ship that Rinnboz talked about.

The search did not take long. The outworld ship was parked over the area where the mammoth gold and platinum deposits were located. Unlike some of the other ships this one looked like a very long and large gray rectangle. The aft end was easy to spot because of four big exhaust cones. The bow was a jungle of different types (and lengths) of censors that all protruded forward. There was a triple row of round portholes near the top, on the front. There were numerous portholes from front to rear on the sides. None on the top or bottom.

"Let's do it the normal way," sent Soolchakan. **"It always worked before, I don't see any reason to change things now**."

"I wonder if anything has changed in all this time," sent Kiyalee.

"I doubt it," sent Bonarain. **"The laws of physics still

apply and that seems to have never changed."

Soolchakan watched as the three women steered their fighters to different locations in the big ship. **"Chyning, wait until we clear you before you start your thievery**."

Chyning sneered inside her helmet. **"*H'oolyach*!"**

Soolchakan and Bonarain headed for (what was their best guess) the bridge of the ship. Kiyalee headed for her best guess at the engine room. Chyning headed for the middle to just get nosy. All others waited outside the ship for orders.

The people inside were definitely new. Their clothing consisted of nothing more than white shorts with a black belt. Their skin was pale yellow with eight pale brown stripes on their back that ran parallel to the ground. The upper torso looked oversized for the rest of the body. Their arms and legs were incredibly skinny but very long. They had three long fingers and an opposable thumb on the end of their arms, however, they did not appear to have any hands. Their feet looked like flat round discs that had two great toenails protruding forward. They were hairless. Their round heads were on a very scrawny neck. They had no nose or nostrils that were visible. They had a wide mouth and two round eyes that did not seem to blink at all. Their ears looked like small nubs on the sides of the head. When they spoke, it was very high pitched and squeaky.

All of the bridge crew were looking at all kinds of graphs of the planet Bri. They seemed to be mapping all of the minerals that were on the planet (big surprise).

Soolchakan and Bonarain started reading some minds to

pick up their language. Kiyalee was doing the same in the engine room. Chyning was randomly trying to listen in on their thoughts, hoping that someone would mention something valuable on the ship that she could swipe (once she totally understood their language).

"**They call themselves the Tanmir**," sent Bonarain. "**They know about Hardooth being inhabited and are here just to map the minerals for future conquest. They're definitely conquerors. They're not here to make friends.**"

"**What a shocker**," scoffed Chyning.

Bonarain did a quick sending to get everyone a starting indoctrination on this new language of the Tanmir.

Chyning was looking around one of the crew quarters. "**Who is the head *bimyock* in charge?**"

Bonarain was a little puzzled about the question. "**Her rank is Toloken and her name is…about eight syllables. We'll just go with the first two syllables – Conksoth… why?**"

"**I think I'm in her quarters**," sent Chyning. "**She's got some gorgeous, uh, they look like candelabras. Not to mention some rather expensive looking dinnerware.**"

Soolchakan sighed and shook his head. He primed his 459 cannon. "**They're conquerors so…no point in trying to make friends. This is a forward recon ship and…they're exploring to get all of the fine details to set up an attack.**

Shalam, Monaha, get in position and knock out some of their forward censor arrays, just to see how they react."

Shalam and Monaha got into position. They charged their 459 cannons.

Shalam smiled. "Read this you *bimyocks!*" He fired. Numerous pieces of equipment were blown off of the front of the ship.

Monaha fired at the lower portion of the forward arrays.

In the bridge, several alarms went off as several parts were blown off of the front of the ship. There was a flurry of activity on the bridge as most of the Tanmir were now keying furiously on their keyboards. More alarms went off.

Soolchakan was shocked to see several of the Tanmir looking directly at his fighter and pulling, what appeared to be, some kind of sidearm out of a pocket in their shorts and aiming them at him. He pulled the trigger on his 459 and quickly cut a large circular hole in the front of the bridge. In less time than he could see, the entire bridge crew was sucked out the hole as the bridge went through catastrophic rapid decompression.

Soolchakan still sat there in his fighter in shock. "**They could see me!**"

"**I know,**" sent Bonarain. "**They were looking directly at me as well.**"

"**They're in Spy dimension,**" sent Bikaropin. "**We're out here getting shot at by their defensive weapons!**"

Soolchakan was half way to panic. "**Everyone Jump to the other side of Bri! We'll reset from there...after we figure out what happened.**"

They Jumped to the opposite side of the planet – most of them.

Chyning was looking around rather worried. "**Where's Kiyalee?!**"

"**I'm back on Hardooth,**" sent Kiyalee. "**When they saw me in the engine room, they fired at me and did some bad damage to my fighter. I set my 459 for overload and Jumped back to my bedroom. I'm going to another fighter. I haven't got there...yet, so I'll have to wait until later to go there...until you can tell me what happened?**"

Soolchakan felt a little anxiety. "**You...overloaded your 459?**"

"**There wasn't much else I could do. They'd already done some severe damage to my fighter.**"

Bikaropin broke in. "**If she overloaded her 459...in the engine room, then it must have gone off by now. It may have caused a catastrophic cascade in the engine room and...there might just be only debris...by now.**"

Soolchakan shook his head. "**Everyone turn on that... forward magneto shield on your fighters. We're going to go back around there...slowly. If that thing blew up... in Spy, then there's a lot of debris...in Spy.**"

Chyning was feeling some turmoil. **"How did they go to Spy? I've never seen that before."**

"I have no idea," sent Soolchakan. **"We may have to wait until a second ship comes here…before we find out anything about their capabilities."**

The formation headed around Bri, taking their sweet time. They all had their forward sensors on maximum, looking for any debris that was floating or flying by.

Bikaropin broke in again. **"I think we need to be in Observation! I was just thinking…that ship was in Spy and…all of the debris is in Spy and…it could be flying right through Bri. Since we're in Spy, it might hit us from the side. I suggest we go to Observation until we get back to where it was and then…take a quick peek in Spy…there."**

Soolchakan did not have to think long on that one. **"Good idea. Everybody do exactly that."**

They cautiously continued until they were in the area of the big deposits.

Soolchakan took several deep breaths. He turned his scanners on. He quickly hopped himself and his fighter to Spy and then quickly back. He looked down at the readings from the scanners. The readings showed that there were three very large chunks and thousands of pieces of varying sizes of small debris. Most of it seemed to be relatively motionless. Motionless – why? He hopped back to Spy and looked around. **"It appears to be somewhat safe in Spy. Everybody can come here and**

take a look. Keep your scanners looking for any fast flying debris."

All of the other fighters were hopped into Spy. They all noticed that the three large pieces of the intruder vessel did not seem to be moving at all.

Chyning looked around confused. "**What happened to that powerful gravitational pull of Bri? Shouldn't it be pulling all that stuff towards the planet?**"

Bikaropin checked a few readings on his scanners. "**Bri is in Home dimension. The Tanmir spaceship...er wreckage is in Spy. Until someone hops all that garbage back into Home, it'll do nothing but float around aimlessly...here in Spy.**"

Zormun growled. "**That means that we've got to clean this mess up. If we ever wanna come back here in Spy. We can't have all this floating junk in our way.**"

There were several mental moans and groans over that statement.

Soolchakan just shook his head. He knew that Zormun was absolutely correct. The planet Bri, especially in this location, was unavoidable and very tempting to all outworlders who came here to explore – then conquer. They had to clean it all up.

Bikaropin broke in again. "**We can get some of those stronger electromagnets and hook them up to some shuttlecraft. We gather up all of the small stuff with that. We hop the big pieces into Home and let them fall** to the planet."

"**No**," sent Soolchakan. "**If we allow that ship to crash on Bri, it'll only create more questions from other outworlders. We have to gather all of it, including the big pieces and drop them in either Ragath or Rogoth.**"

Jotsoom was looking at his scanners. "**We have another problem to worry about right now. It seems that there were sixteen escape pods that launched out of that ship, even after it blew up. I followed their trajectory. They're headed for Denhahbon. I was wondering why, so I took a look at the scanners from there. It looks like there's another Tanmir ship orbiting Denhahbon. There are transmissions being sent out from the pods to that mother ship.**"

"**I've got it**," sent Zintom. "**That mother ship is moving towards the escape pods. They're probably going to pick them up and then do some further reconnaissance.**"

Soolchakan closed his eyes and growled in frustration. "**WE have to do some further reconnaissance. We have to find out how that ship was able to hop to Spy. These people may be more dangerous than we think. Let's get those electromagnets out here, collect the three big chunks and see if we can restart any of their computers and find out how they can hop to other dimensions.**"

Monaha sighed. "**We need to get all of that done before that other ship finishes rescuing all of the pods.**

It'll probably come back here to see if there are any other survivors."

Soolchakan clenched his teeth. "**Then let's get moving**."

All of the fighters hopped back to #45. They Jumped into their parking spots on the Chokchakchok ship. All of the Owlamites now scrambled to shuttlecraft in order to get out there and clean up the debris field. It took quite some time, however, they were finally able to hook several electromagnets to the bow of fifteen of the shuttlecraft. Once that was done, they were then all able to get back to the planet Bri in order to begin the cleanup.

Kiyalee had obtained a new fighter. She was able to rejoin the group at Bri.

Lorib attached the electromagnet on his shuttle to one of the big chunks. As soon as it was secure, he hopped to #45. Mayakton did the same with the second large chunk. Galem secured the third. Now the rest of the ten shuttlecraft were sweeping the area for smaller objects.

During the cleanup, all of the fighters in the area were watching towards Denhahbon. They had their scanners on maximum distance looking for that other Tanmir ship. Soolchakan decided that there was the possibility of the Tanmir ship coming in from the side, so they formed a very large semi-circle in order to sweep a much larger area.

Galem called in from #45. "**I found one of the *bimyocks* alive. He was hidden in an escape pod that malfunctioned. It didn't take off. He's stuck in the thing. What do you want me to do with him**?"

Soolchakan had been hoping for a prisoner. He was surprised at the way they obtained one, however, it was still a good thing. **"Bonarain and Bikaropin, get to dimension 45 and start some questioning on that prisoner."**

Bikaropin responded. **"What if they can find him in #45? Should we take some precautionary move?"**

Soolchakan sighed as he sat there thinking. **"Take the chunk with the prisoner to...oh...say dimension 220. That way if they can trace him, they won't find our treasure trove in dimension 45."**

Bonarain huffed. **"What do we use to interrogate him? We can't just leave him in that pod."**

Bikaropin came in. **"We can take a Jowfoonda ship with us. We still have some of them that are working. Get him and a few guards on that ship and he won't find out that much about us, unless he can read minds as well."**

"They didn't show that capability," sent Bonarain. **"We should be able to ask questions and read his mind for any answers."**

Yamang called in. **"We've finished cleaning up all of the debris. Or maybe I should say we've finished cleaning up all of the debris that stayed in this area. Any parts that were blown away from here...we have no idea where they are or which way they went...or how far."**

Soolchakan checked his scanner again. **"Okay, everybody in cleanup, get out of here. All fighters, hop to Observation. Hopefully, that Tanmir ship is coming in here in Home. I can't for the life of me think of how to hop to Observation and observe Spy."**

Monaha responded. **"They are in Spy. I tuned my scanners to see what the monitors on Bri were seeing. Remember, they're in Spy as well. They're seeing that Tanmir ship coming in and...I hope that the Tanmir are not looking for the monitors on Bri. If they are, then we might lose all of our monitors."**

"I've got my scanner tuned in to the Bri monitors as well," sent Bendarik. **"It looks like they've got some kind of scanner that can block some signals because... the monitors are getting a little fuzzy in what they're picking up."**

"Oh, _h'oolyach_," sent Monaha. **"They just shot out a monitor."**

Soolchakan snarled. They could not afford to lose the monitors on Bri. That was one of their best warning systems for any outworlder. **"Monaha! Bendarik! Line up for a kill shot from the side on that ship. Everyone else, line up with Monaha and Bendarik. Everybody get your 459 cannons ready to shoot. When I give the signal, everyone hop to Spy and open fire on that Tanmir ship. I doubt that their magneto shields can withstand the sustained fire of this many cannons."**

They lined up with Monaha and Bendarik. They lined up in a stacked formation where there were three levels of fighters. This way, several of them could aim for the same spot and drain any of the shielding that the ship had very quickly. Then they would just filet the entire ship, while hoping the enemy could not perform any kind of deadly return fire.

Soolchakan looked around. He took a deep breath. **"Everyone ready? Move to Spy...NOW!"**

All the fighters hopped and opened fire. Only a few of them had to make adjustments in order to hit the Tanmir ship. There were a few feeble attempts at return fire, however, they were totally ineffective. There were several explosions throughout the ship as the giant rectangle started breaking up.

Suddenly a long cylindrical object shot out of the bottom of the ship near the stern. It was moving at a rather rapid rate as it flew away from the ship.

"Leave that cylinder alone," sent Kiyalee! **"That thing is the engine that makes them go faster than light. If we blow that up...we're all in trouble**."

The Tanmir ship broke up into at least thirty large pieces. There were several escape pods that started launching out of pieces of the ship.

"Go chase those pods," sent Soolchakan. **"I don't want any of those *chokwads* getting away**."

The fighters all stopped shooting and started chasing the escape pods. All fighters except one. Soolchakan sat there looking at the devastated ship. He sighed. **"Get those electromagnets back here and collect the remains of this ship as well. We don't want to leave anything that someone else can find…as evidence.**"

All of the "evidence" was taken to dimension #220. There, along with Bonarain and Bikaropin, they listened to the questioning of the first prisoner.

Nineteen more prisoners were taken in captured escape pods. They found that the Tanmir had some very interesting technology at their disposal.

Each time Bonarain would ask a question, there were several Owlamites who sat there reading the minds of the prisoners. The prisoners all tried to remain stubbornly silent, however, without them knowing, they were giving everything away. She asked a question and each one would think about it.

Baktim and Bikaropin were in a portion of the first ship where some of the computer banks were (somehow) still intact. The others in the questioning area were relaying the information to them. They were able to obtain fourteen different passwords into the system. They were able to get into many different areas of the computer system. They found a very interesting program that identified how they were able to go to different dimensions as well as how to identify which dimension they were in.

"Look at this frequency thing," said Baktim. "I don't understand how each dimension gives off a different frequency, but…this silly thing can tell them apart."

Bikaropin nodded. "We need to get this back to the Chokchakchok ship so...we can get them out of this..." He looked around. "...messy remains of a ship."

Baktim shook his head. "No, Soolchakan doesn't want any of this stuff in dimension 45, just in case the Tanmir are able to find this specific stuff, they won't find our treasures that are hidden there."

Bikaropin grunted in frustration. "Then we'll have to bring one of the Chokchakchok ships here."

"And hope that no one comes along, who belongs in this dimension, and tries to claim it," chuckled Baktim.

"There," said Bikaropin happily. "I found it."

"Found...what?"

"Information about their home planet." He grunted. "They call it Tan!"

Baktim rolled his eyes. "So we have the Tanmir from Tan."

"Yeah."

Soolchakan sat there listening to Baktim and Bikaropin.

"We've found a way to identify each one of the dimensions that the Tanmir have found," said Bikaropin. "We didn't know it before, but each dimension gives off some kind of frequency. We can pick it up on their machines." He huffed. "We can pick it up on our equipment…we just never looked at it, or for it, before."

"We need to make one of our own machines perform just this frequency finding," said Baktim. "We can't risk using theirs, because if they have some way of communicating with it, or finding it, even though we hid it in dimension 220, they could get all of the 239 dimensions that we know of and…they'd be all over those places."

Soolchakan nodded. "How many dimensions are they aware of?"

"22," said Bikaropin. "Again, we have the frequencies of all of these 22, but, we don't know which goes with which because we've never chased after frequencies. We just hop from one to another without worrying about any frequency – just imagery. We do it naturally, they do it technologically."

Bonarain leaned forward in her chair. "Is the imagery anything close to the frequency?"

Baktim shook his head sadly. "From what we've seen… not related at all."

Chyning decided to get in on the fun. "Is there something about the frequency that aides them in getting to the different dimensions?"

"Absolutely everything," said Bikaropin. "They get the frequency and they feed it into their computer. The computer does some kind of search to find that frequency in outer space and then…hop. There they are in a different dimension."

Kiyalee smiled. "Need help in making this…*just* a

frequency finder?"

Baktim smiled back. "Any help we can get will be greatly appreciated."

Kiyalee shrugged. "Let's get to work."

It took eight days to fabricate their own frequency finder. Bikaropin fed the 22 different frequencies into their machine.

Kiyalee groaned. "Now all we have to do is go to all 239 dimensions and...see which ones match the ones in the machine."

"Let's hope that they're in the first 30," said Baktim. "Otherwise it is going to be a *long, long* day."

"Or week," said Bikaropin glumly.

They climbed into a shuttlecraft.

Kiyalee sighed. "Here we go." She hopped the craft into #2. She looked at Bikaropin expectantly.

Bikaropin shook his head. "Did you really think that we were gonna get that lucky?"

"I was hoping," said Kiyalee. She sighed. "Your turn to hop."

Baktim hopped the craft to #3. "There's always hope!"

Bikaropin snickered as he read the graph. "Nope! Not this...uh...wait."

Kiyalee and Baktim both frowned at Bikaropin.

Bikaropin looked up chuckling nervously. "I didn't think of it but…this one is good. This is one of the dimensions that the Tanmir found. The crazy thing is…it was the tenth one on their list. They found these things in a different order."

The realization hit Kiyalee. "We didn't number them in order of difficulty originally. We had names for them for when we found them."

"Right," said Bikaropin. "Dimension 3 was originally called *Bonarain 7*. That means that it was the seventh dimension that she personally found."

Baktim looked hopeful. "Should we go back to Dimension 2? Is it possible that you missed that one on your graph?"

Bikaropin shook his head as he looked at the readout. "No. There wasn't any sign of that one. Besides, I did record it and just checked it with the other twenty-one. No such luck. Dimension 2 is unknown to the Tanmir."

#4 through #16 turned up nothing. #17 (originally called *Chyning 8*) showed up as the first dimension the Tanmir had found. The next one to show on the graph was #19 (originally called *Amtosha 1*) as the seventh one found by the Tanmir. *Bibitaya 1* or #22 came next as the fourth dimension for Tanmir. When they got another hit with #25, they became hopeful that it would be a faster process than they're hopes had been. Wrong. They did not get another hit until #34. Then #40, #51, #53 (Spy), #63, #72 and #91.

Bikaropin looked tired. "We found twelve in the first ninety-one. Only one hundred forty-eight more dimensions to go to find the other ten."

Kiyalee and Baktim groaned.

The next three were #119, #122 and #136. Their hopes were still there even though they were getting a little tired. #142, #154, #166 and #175. Nineteen down – only three to go – among 64 more known dimensions. #189 was a hit. The next hit was #201.

Baktim looked up. He, like the other two, was exhausted from all of the rapid hopping. "Only one left to find. Should we continue or…go get some rest?"

Kiyalee looked up through bloodshot eyes. "I don't wanna start over again tomorrow. Let's get this done! Only one left to go…among thirty-eight others. Let's move! Whose turn it is to hop?"

Bikaropin shook his head. "Who cares?"

Kiyalee grunted. "I'll take the next hop."

The last one was finally found as #212. The three of them smiled at each other, in relief and satisfaction, having found all twenty-two.

Bikaropin groaned. "We still have to record the rest of them."

Kiyalee shook her head. "You can record the other… however many there are, tomorrow. I'm spent. I'm going to bed."

"Same with me," said Baktim.

Bikaropin shrugged and accepted the inevitable. Tomorrow would be good. Only twenty-seven left to record. No more searching the different parts of the graph. Just hop and record.

All three of them headed to their beds. The next day they recorded the frequencies of the last few dimensions.

Bonarain continued the interrogation of the prisoners. The prisoners remained silent and smug. They thought that because they were being asked the same questions, over and over, they were giving up nothing. Their attitude was obvious from what was being read in their minds. All that Bonarain was doing was confirming any information that someone asked for or bringing out new information as they found out more and more from the prisoners.

Kiyalee came back with all the information they had on the dimension shifting capabilities of the Tanmir. "These *bimyocks* have come up with a way of trailing things into other dimensions. Apparently they came across someone or something that had dimension hopping abilities before and the Tanmir found a way to trail them."

Soolchakan raised his eyebrows in surprise. "Trail? How?"

"It has something to do with the actual hop," said Bikaropin. "Their computer can somehow observe something moving from one dimension to another and then follow it. It picks up the frequency of the new dimension and then simply shifts their entire ship to that new frequency." He sighed. "That's how they found our Spy dimension."

Bonarain groaned as she mulled it over. "Is there any weakness in this computer program...that we can exploit?"

Bikaropin looked hopeful. "The only thing that I can find, it takes a good three count for the computer to find the trail, analyze it and then hop. We can hop in less than a single count. What that means is...when we face them, if there are others coming here, we have to prepare the imagery for at least four or five hops. Once we do the first hop, don't hesitate on to the second, third, fourth or fifth. If you hesitate, they can follow."

Soolchakan scoffed. "We could teach them all kinds of new dimensions if we do that."

Bikaropin chuckled. "Not if the first two or three are dimensions that they already know. We give then nothing. It still takes the three count for each one of their hops, no matter which one it is."

Chyning snarled at him. "They already know those dimensions, so what stops them from shifting before we can get out of range?"

"It still takes a three count," said Bikaropin adamantly. "We hop to two or three that they know and before they can make the adjustment, we've gone to one they can't find."

"At first," said Bonarain. "If we have to go through an extended war with this bunch, they'll learn which ones we're going to and…hop to the third one before we go to the fourth."

Bikaropin shrugged. "If that happens, we'll simply have to adjust our list. We may give up a few dimension, but in the long run, we'll still leave them behind us."

Chyning looked at the list that had been supplied by Bikaropin. "Why don't you have these dimensions listed in order?"

"That's the order in which the Tanmir found those dimensions," said Kiyalee. "Unfortunately, we were the ones who gave them Spy dimension."

"We'll have to watch them from Observation," grumbled Soolchakan. "We don't ever give them that one. If we do, we'll have nowhere to hide from them."

"Then I suggest that until we get rid of this pestilence, we hop all of the apartments in the gorge to Observation," said Bonarain.

"We'll worry about that if they start coming in mass attack formation," said Soolchakan.

"They are," said Bonarain. "Those two that were here were definitely a forward reconnaissance team. The escape pods gave the second ship the frequency to Spy dimension."

Kiyalee looked a little frightened. "Do you think they were able to send the information back to their attack armada… about Spy dimension?"

"For security purposes, treat it as if they *were* able to send it out," said Soolchakan. "I'd hate to be sitting in Spy and... they're on us before *we* know what's happening."

Chyning hung her head. "*H'oolyach*! Those candelabras were so pretty. Now they're just part of the debris."

Kiyalee scoffed. "There are a lot of things that are just debris now. We lost all of their weaponry, so we can't study it and don't know a thing about it."

8

Soolchakan was feeling like he was being stretched in ten different directions. "Do we still have people looking for those rotten potions?"

"Yes," said Bonarain. "They learned their lesson on that one. So far, no one has found any more potions, but, who knows what the future holds?"

Soolchakan nodded. "Are the peace meetings still going on in Varnast and Cheseet?"

"Yes," said Chyning. "They're not getting very far because they're still waiting for some decision from either King Dolomon or King Dolomot..." She scoffed. "As if the one in South Paselter could or would make a decision...but, they're at least still having discussions on how to, hopefully, end the situation peacefully while still keeping their meetings a big secret from the conspirators."

Soolchakan looked rather glum about the next one. "What about watching for the Tanmir?"

"That's gonna take a *group* of people to do that," said Kiyalee. "We have to have someone go to dimension 3, then hop to Observation and watch for them. We'll also have to have someone go to dimension 17, then hop to Observation and watch for them. We'll also have to have someone do that for all of the twenty-two dimensions that those *chokwads* know about."

Soolchakan shook his head in disgust and frustration. "Do we have anything regarding a landmark...for any place on their home planet?"

Kiyalee shook her head. "We destroyed too much in their computers. We've got all kinds of landmarks but we don't know what is where. We think they've conquered some sixteen star systems...that we know of in this dimension. If they've done any conquering in the other dimensions...that could add to our problems, as far as totally defeating them...or even determining which dimension they're originally from."

Soolchakan sighed. "So many things to do...and still protect our children from..." He closed his eyes and hung his head. "Question the prisoners again. See if you can find out which dimension they are originally from. That should narrow some of it down."

The interrogation gave them the information. The Tanmir are from Home dimension. That was the only new item that came from the new inquisition.

"That does narrow it down," said Kiyalee. "Should we ask them about some of the landmarks that we've seen? Maybe they'll think about them and give us a clue as to which planet those landmarks are on."

That interrogation was not that fruitful. Several of them had not been born on the home planet of Tan. They had been on other conquered planets for such a long time, they felt that those were their home planets (partially because some of them had never been able to set foot on Tan). It was difficult to determine which ones were telling what about the term "home planet". They had a very abstract way of thinking.

Yamshono called in. "**I'm seeing an armada of Tanmir box-ships coming in. They're in dimension 122.**"

Soolchakan growled. "Why can't all of these *bimyocks* leave us alone?" "**Yamshono, can you tell how many ships are in this group?**"

"**There are forty-seven of them coming in.**"

Bonarain looked skeptical. "Forty-seven ships? That doesn't sound like the entire fleet of a group of space conquerors."

"No, it doesn't," said Soolchakan sadly. "But it's still forty-seven headed our way. We have to confuse or destroy them… completely." He closed his eyes. "**Does anyone else see any of the Tanmir ships coming in, in any other dimension?**"

There was no affirmative response.

Soolchakan sadly gave the order. "**Everyone who is capable of flying a fighter, get to it and let's meet this armada.**"

Yamshono called in again. "**That armada hopped to Home dimension and is gathering around Weeloow. They're doing nothing. They're just orbiting the gas**

giant."

Over 1,000 fighters hopped to Observation and then Jumped to Weeloow. They saw the Tanmir ships flying in two lines orbiting the gas giant.

Soolchakan shook his head as he looked at the formations. "**Can anyone see anything that would indicate which one is the command ship**?"

"**We're just going to have to look at each one, one at a time in order to determine that**," sent Bikaropin.

Bonarain came in. "**The sooner we start, the sooner we find it**."

The Command ship turned out to be the fourteenth one that was checked. Soolchakan, Bonarain and Bikaropin all went to the bridge to read some minds and determine exactly what was going on here.

Kiyalee and Baktim were in the engine room. Again, Kiyalee could see very little that was different here as to how they were able to obtain flight faster than the speed of light. The only difference was the design of the combustion chambers in which the reaction took place.

After finding the individual who was in command (the rank was called Miftonij and was fifth from the bottom), the Owlamites zeroed in on all of the thoughts of that one along with any that appeared to be the top staff of the commander. They found that this was a forward group, awaiting the arrival of the main invasion force. The main force was commanded by someone with the rank of Makapa. There was only one military rank higher than Makapa and that was the Cholkomy.

"I have an idea," sent Bikaropin. **"It takes them three mith in order for them to find the frequency of a new dimension...according to what we're finding in their computers. If we contaminate the mixture in the light speed engines, it creates a catastrophic explosion in only one or two miths. We're in Observation, we could dump some debris in the light speed engines, all at the same time, and this bunch would never know what hit them."**

"That sounds like a good plan," sent Soolchakan. **"The main difference – we'll hop to Spy before we dump the debris. As soon as we dump the debris and start that rapid, disastrous chain reaction, we hop to dimension 3. Any questions?"**

None.

Forty-seven people were assigned to the different ships. Once they were all in place, Soolchakan gave the countdown and the command of execution. All forty-seven of the Tanmir ships blew up, practically at the same time. The fighters that were watching the attack occur then watched all of the debris quickly get caught in the gravitational pull of Weeloow...including several escape pods that somehow had been able to launch from the crippled ships. They were hoping that the escape pods were empty and had just been launched by the ship functions.

Soolchakan ordered all personnel to return to their

assigned areas and watch for any other Tanmir ships coming in to the Hardooth system.

Two days later, Zizhonim called in. **"There are thirty-three Tanmir ships coming in. They're in dimension 25."**

Yohwell called in. **"I see forty-five Tanmir ships coming in. They're in dimension 63."**

Bruss called in. **"There are thirty-eight more Tanmir ships coming in, in dimension 91."**

Quimdant called in. **"I see fifty-one ships coming in. They're in dimension 3."**

Clardon called in. **"There are forty more ships coming in. They're currently in dimension 166."**

Soolchakan sat there, half-dressed, in his bedroom staring off into space. *"H'OOLYACH!"* He closed his eyes and sighed. **"Everyone, get to your fighters."**

All fighters headed for a showdown somewhere near the planet Afkoth.

Soolchakan was preparing his 459 for some deadly combat. He sat there patiently waiting for the call that the armadas were all close enough for confrontation. They all knew that it was still a few mithist away.

Bikaropin suddenly appeared in his fighter, nose to nose, directly in front of Soolchakan. **"I have an idea. One where**

we can use the Tanmir against themselves."

Soolchakan frowned. He wondered what dirty little trick Bikaropin was cooking up. He shrugged. It was worth a try if it could, in some way or another put the odds in favor of the Owlamites. "**Whatcha got in mind?**"

"**They're all coming in from the exact same direction. They're all in almost the same position. They're coming in from five different dimensions to try to confuse us or not let us know their numbers. What I've got in mind, we'll have to give up another dimension to them, but, in the long run it'll work for us.**"

He sent a private thought message to Soolchakan as to what the specifics of the plan would be. Soolchakan shrugged and told him to go ahead. Even if it did not come up with the destruction that Bikaropin was predicting or hoping for, it would still hurt the Tanmir and cause some massive confusion...hopefully.

Bikaropin closed his eyes and made the general mental callout. "**Zizhonim, Yohwell, Bruss, Quimdant and Clardon. Show yourselves to the Tanmir. Let them chase you. When I give you the signal, all of you hop to Dimension 2. After two miths, then you Jump to an orbit around Bri.**"

Yohwell responded. "**They don't know about Dimension 2. We'd be giving them another dimension.**"

"**There is a purpose to it,**" sent Soolchakan. "**Go with the plan, as instructed, and find out what happens.**" He waited for a moment. "**Any questions?**"

All of the 1,000 fighters at Afkoth hopped to Dimension #2, then hopped to Observation. They waited to see if the plan would work.

Bikaropin called out to the five that were standing guard. **"Hop to Dimension 2…NOW!"**

All of the fighters saw the five Owlamites appear on their scanners and almost immediately disappear again. All two hundred and seven Tanmir ships appeared in Dimension #2 at practically the same instant – in the same area – going the same direction – at approximately the same speed. Now the Owlamites saw some massive explosions on their scanners as one ship coming in from Dimension #25 *joined* with a ship coming in from Dimension #63. Another *join* collision as a ship came in from Dimension #91 and *joined* with a ship coming in from Dimension #3. Two hundred seven ships coming in from five dimensions without any form of coordination. The collisions and *joinings* were all over the place and extremely destructive. One ship would *join* with the engine room of another. The part of the ship inside the light speed cylinders would upset the mix and cause the catastrophic chain reaction. Before any of them could react, the results were a complete disaster for the Tanmir.

Bikaropin watched his scanners with hope that his predictions would come to pass. He had hoped that the Tanmir would lose at least 30% or their total fleet and that the confusion would stop them, or at least slow them while they were rescuing people from damaged ships.

His estimate was not close at all. In the initial collisions, one hundred sixteen ships were completely demolished. Of the remaining ships, forty-four were completely crippled, seventeen were badly damaged and ten others were fired upon, hit and damaged by their own because of the chaos caused by the situation. The remaining twenty ships were now forced to stop what they were doing and start rescuing thousands of survivors from the other one hundred eighty-seven ships. They were in no position to attack anyone or anything.

Soolchakan saw the mayhem that had been created by the collisions. **"Let's go in there and make them sorry they ever heard of us."**

Shalam responded. **"Are we going to kill them all?"**

Soolchakan thought for a moment. **"No, we're going to damage all of the ships that are undamaged. Then we'll give them the ultimatum that if they ever return...then none of them will be allowed to live."** He growled as he hit the throttle in his fighter. **"Hop to Spy before we get there. Don't hop from Observation while we're there otherwise we'll be giving them another dimension."**

While performing the rescue of any and all escape pods, they had to drop their defensive magneto shields. This made them easy prey for the Owlamite cannons. The Tanmir could not shoot back because of all of the escape pods in the area (and the fact that the Owlamites were hopping to Spy after each strafing run and the Tanmir could not hop as quickly). The Tanmir also could not hop to the other dimension while engaged in accepting the escape pods.

After accidentally destroying one of the surviving ships, Soolchakan called for a cease fire. He then got on his communicator and called the Commander of the Tanmir fleet. "This is Soolchakan! I am Drey Sssorg of the Owlam people. The destruction that you have suffered in this attack is only a small part of what will happen to you if you do not turn around and leave us alone...FOREVER!"

A response came back. *"This is Makapa Fiy Noochoon. Ranking Officer of the Fleet. We hear your warning. You have proven yourselves to be a formidable foe. We will leave and I will inform the Cholkomy of your words. Will you now stop shooting at us, so that we may rescue our personnel?"*

Soolchakan cleared his throat. He wondered if he could trust the Tanmir Makapa. "Finish your rescues and then leave... as quickly as possible."

"Thank you. Makapa Noochoon...out."

"He's lying, that deceitful *bimyock*," sent Monaha. **"He's already informed some of the other officers that they're going to return as soon as they can build up the fleet again**."

Soolchakan clenched his teeth. "Why can't anyone ever learn the first time that they've been burned? Why does everyone have to be so stubborn?" **"Is there any way to find out how big their fleet actually is...at this time**?"

"I watched them check on that very information," sent Monaha. **"There were only thirty-seven ships that didn't take part in this invasion. With the nineteen that**

received minor damage, that gives them a total of fifty-six. According to this Makapa Noochoon, they're going to need at least three hundred ships."

"Which they're probably going to start building those ships immediately," sent Peldom.

Soolchakan shook his head. "We're going to have to follow these *doovofts* back to their home planet. We're going to have to cause them no end of grief, there, in order to get them off of our backs."

Monaha called in again. "They're going to go home. They have no choice. All of the nineteen ships are overloaded with survivors from the wrecked ships. They're going to need as many living crewmembers they can get in order to staff all those ships. I'll get their headings for their home planet as soon as they're ready to leave."

Soolchakan nodded. "Meanwhile we have to get back and find out how the meetings in Varnast and Cheseet are going." He chuckled. "See if they're getting any positives that we can all live with." "Shalam and Monaha, take the first shift in riding along with those *bimyocks*. We absolutely need to have some landmark on their home planet."

Soolchakan Jumped back to the Chokchakchok ship to park his fighter. He arrived there and turned his 459 cannon off. He took the battery out of the 459 and hooked it up to a charger. He looked around the hangar. "I hope we don't have to cause a mass cataclysm like that in Paselter in order to stop a war." He sat there watching as several other fighters came Jumping into the hangar bay. He stripped off his spacesuit and hung it up. He Jumped to his bedroom in the gorge.

It was nineteen days later when Shalam and Monaha checked in. They had stayed with the badly diminished fleet all the way to their home world. They now had a huge landmark in the capital city and could hardly wait to show it to the first quartet.

Soolchakan was ready to go just about anywhere to get away from the bickering bureaucrats from North and South Paselter. Both sides wanted to end the mess peacefully between the governments. They both wanted the other side to be the primary to attack the different Elf factions who were attempting to cause all of the commotion. No one could decide on how the attacks were to take place or when. They were both of the same mind in that all nine Elf races should be attacked and punished for what they were doing. Again, some of the races were not indigenous to North Chilamte and therefore it would require some foreign diplomatic maneuvers in order to attack or punish those races.

Shalam and Monaha got all of the first quartet in a circle. They all hopped to Observation and Jumped to an incredibly large meeting place in the capital city of the Tanmir on their home world.

They were on a raised platform that was round and surrounded completely by circular rows of seats. The thick carpeting on the platform was dark purple. The carpeting in the aisles between the seats was deep red. The seats were all made of some light colored wood. There were a few seats made of dark wood that were scattered among the plethora of seats. The entire room had a moldy smell of unwashed armpits. Soolchakan stopped counting the rows of seats when he got to thirty. There were many rows beyond that.

"This is their great meeting hall," said Shalam. "I think they set it up to hold about sixteen thousand spectators but, from what we can find in some of the archives we've stuck our noses in, the largest crowd they recorded was just over four thousand."

Bonarain looked around in shock. "You're saying…that there are sixteen thousand seats…surrounding this stage?"

"We didn't bother counting them," said Shalam. "We just went with what we could find from the original construction."

Soolchakan frowned. "Just how long were you nosing around, in this place, before you contacted us?"

"Eight days," said Monaha flatly.

"We wanted to know as soon as you found it," scolded Bonarain. "We wanted to get several people here. The more eyes we have here, the better. This also means it'll be a lot faster that we find out any and everything we want to know about these *doovofts*."

Both Shalam and Monaha stood there with helpless smiles on their faces.

"We can go back and get somebody now," said Shalam.

"No," said Soolchakan. "Shalam goes back and gets some more. Monaha stays here and gives us a little more information about what you've found so far." He looked at the women. "I suggest that we get off of the stage because Shalam will be bringing others back and if he chose the center of this stage to be his landmark, I don't wanna be here, when the next group arrives."

Monaha led them to a set of stairs. There were eight sets of stairs, equally placed, around the stage. "We can sit down while waiting for reinforcements," he said.

Chyning sat down and shook her head. "I need to sit down. Have any of you bothered to look up? How does that…ceiling keep from collapsing on this place? I don't see any columns holding the roof up."

Soolchakan sat down in the first row and looked up at the center ceiling. "Oh grief! I see what you mean." He looked at Shalam.

"That is a dome," said Monaha. "It is an incredibly high dome, as a matter of fact. The central part of it is about seven floors up and I have no idea why they built it that high."

Kiyalee had to slouch down in the seat in order to be able to look straight up. "Is there anything up there…other than a high dome?"

"Nothing," said Monaha. "There are walkways up there but no offices or any facilities of any type. I think that the only reason for someone to go up there is to clean the interior and exterior of the dome…without using any scaffolding."

"A big high hollow…dome," said Chyning incredulously.

Soolchakan huffed. "What an incredible waste of space!"

Shalam appeared with Peldom, Baktim, Zormun and Bendarik. He pointed to one of the staircases. "I have to bring others to this stage so…vacate the area while I go get some others."

The four men proceeded without hesitation.

Bendarik looked around. "You think this building is big enough for a town meeting," he asked facetiously?

Baktim scoffed. "Depends on the size of the town."

Zormun looked up in the dome. "If we go up to one of those walkways up there, is it possible to get a good look at the city?"

"No," said Monaha. "Most of the surrounding structures are taller. You'd have to go to the top of one of them in order to get a good look at the city."

Chyning gave him a dull gaze. "You're saying that this place…with the high, waste-of-space dome…is one of the smaller buildings?"

Monaha smiled, shrugged and nodded.

Shalam reappeared with Zorkeen, Banama, Ashak and Poolkiy.

"That's enough for the moment," said Soolchakan. "Give the ones here a briefing on what you've got and…we'll see if we need to bring some more here, in the near future."

Kiyalee snickered. "Could you imagine if we dug a hole this big in the gorge?"

"It'd end up as a sinkhole," said Bonarain glibly.

"Just a big unstable bowl," said Kiyalee.

Soolchakan huffed. "I still say that a dome is a horrible waste of space...unless you put floors up there and have offices, homes or some kind of storage space. Then it'd be functional. No floors...no purpose. All you have is just a bunch of air that's trapped inside." He looked up in the center of that huge dome again and shook his head. "Waste!"

"You have to admit that some of their murals are kinda pretty," said Chyning.

Soolchakan just hung his head and groaned. "So what!" He Jumped back to his home in the gorge.

Bonarain and Kiyalee both gave Chyning a condescending look. Chyning hunched down, flushed and looked away.

Shalam and Monaha gave the newcomers a briefing on some of the things they had found already. They also gave briefings on where certain things were that were of high interest.

Chyning got bored listening to the briefings and decided to take a look around for herself. She remembered that if you do anything, do not come in from Observation dimension. These Tanmir could trace where you came from and that would give away their one advantage over the enemy. This enemy was going to be very frustrating because she was not going to be able to purloin anything at her whim. She could not use Observation.

Bonarain and Kiyalee got a little bored with the briefing as well. They both Jumped back to the gorge to check on their youngest children.

Five days later, Chyning walked in to the main dining area in their home. She was dressed in her special green uniform shirt and black cape – the type that they wore when going out on some mission to meet other people. She had a big grin on her face, her youngest daughter in one arm and a huge golden goblet in her other hand. "I found a way to mess with the Tanmir and they can't do anything about it."

Soolchakan looked at her in terror. "What'd you do?"

Bonarain and Kiyalee stopped feeding their infants and looked up equally in fear.

Chyning smiled. "I thought about what was said about their hopping capability." She placed the big goblet down. "According to what we know, it takes about three miths for them to be able to analyze, computerize and then accomplish their dimensional hop. We can do it a lot faster. What you have to do is plan ahead."

Soolchakan looked suspicious. "And…?"

"Get the imagery for…oh say…five different hops in your head. Then…you reach through each one with your arm…grab something of theirs and…then go back through the same five as quickly as possible. You can do all five hops in less than two miths. By the time they analyze, computerize and hop to the first one…you're already gone and whatever that trail is that they're following is gone as well."

"But you're giving them a new dimension on their first hop

when you do that," scolded Bonarain. "We can't give them any more new dimensions."

Chyning adjusted her hold on her child. "No, you don't understand." She walked over and sat down with the other two women. "The first one that they're looking for is one they already know. You can even use the second one as one they already know. Their computer has to analyze the trail and even if it finds a dimension that it knows, it still takes about three miths. By then... you've gone through about four other hops and it can't find the trail to the next one yet because...somehow, the hopping trail is already gone." She smiled triumphantly.

Soolchakan still looked suspicious. "You're sure of this?"

Chyning looked back at the goblet and grinned. "I brought that thing here without fear. I tried it several times with some other things. When I swiped this big mug off of some kind of holy altar, I thought they were gonna have a real fit." She looked off to the side pondering. "No, they *did* really have a big fit." She smiled. "I sat there in Observation and watched what they were doing." She giggled. "Some *bimyock* did the hop to dimension 3, with the aid of some device he had, and...seeing as how he hopped to the void of outer space...he ain't comin' back...ever." She giggled. "They brought someone else in there with a spacesuit...and some strange box. He hopped and...he came back...a little while later. He still had that box with him. He said that he couldn't find where I was in the other dimension because the trail had degraded completely."

Bonarain looked indignant. "Was that the end of the experiment?"

Chyning laid her sleeping baby on the table. "Nope! I tested it again while that *bimyock* was there with the box. It still took three miths for them to hop to dimension 3. The next one for them to go to was dimension 17. They couldn't find it. The trail goes dead before three miths is up."

Bonarain looked over at Soolchakan. "It'd be nice if we could get hold of one of those..." She looked at Chyning. "... dimension hopping boxes."

Chyning grinned. "We do. I gave one to Bikaropin."

Kiyalee was aghast. "What about me? I'm the one who taught Bikaropin a lot of what he knows about electronics."

Chyning giggled. She pulled a strange looking silvery, square gadget with several buttons and lights on it, out of a pouch in her cape. "I thought you might like one as well." She pulled a pamphlet of some kind out of another pouch. "I thought you might like the instructions as well."

Kiyalee snarled. "I should slap you." She adjusted her hold on her baby. She picked up the box and gave it a once over. She picked up the pamphlet and looked over the first page. She sighed. "I'll get with Bikaropin as soon as possible."

Soolchakan finished his drink. "Chyning, did you inform Shalam, Monaha and the others there on the Tanmir home planet about your...stunt?"

Chyning looked a little startled. She snickered and gave him a silly, guilty grin. "I guess I should've done that. I didn't. I'll let them know about it...right quick." She looked at Bonarain.

"Can you take care of Quorza for a little while?"

Bonarain looked down at Chyning's daughter. "Call Mahanee. She doesn't mind taking care of children…in herds."

Chyning shrugged. She leaned her head back and closed her eyes.

There was a knock on the door.

Chyning smiled. "Come on in, Mahanee."

Mahanee appeared inside the door. "What's the emergency?"

Chyning picked her daughter up and walked towards Mahanee. "I need you to take care of Quorza for a little while."

Mahanee smiled and took the sleeping babe in her arms with a smile. "No problem. You know where to find me when you get back," she said while rocking the baby. She vanished.

Chyning turned and gave the others in the room a little wave. She vanished.

Kiyalee shook her head. "She might've actually done something positive here."

Soolchakan shook his head and Bonarain just sighed.

"She could've given something away," sighed Soolchakan.

"Like another dimension," said Bonarain.

"So she just got lucky," said Kiyalee.

"Right," said Soolchakan.

Chyning came back from the Tanmir home planet. She had informed all of the men there about the procedure she had used to hide her location from the Tanmir. She was sitting in the main room feeding her daughter. She looked up as the other three walked in.

Soolchakan smiled with no enthusiasm. "Are you ready to show us a little more on how you did it…especially since I see four more of those golden goblets?"

Chyning giggled. "I had to give them some good examples of how it works. Before I came back, they were causing no end of grief to those Tanmir people."

Bonarain shook her head. "Are they doing that…only in that big city?"

"They've added two more major cities to the ones that they're victimizing," snickered Chyning.

Soolchakan sat down with a disgusted grunt. "We're not there for simple harassment. We're there to stop them from ever attacking us again. They don't know that we're the ones harassing them."

"We hope that they don't know that it's us," said Kiyalee.

Bonarain scoffed. "How many other populations have they gone against who can do any dimension hopping?"

Soolchakan groaned and hung his head. "Hopefully, they'll find out where the Tanmir are building their new ships and we can stop them from building an entire armada."

Bonarain shook her head. "Hopefully."

"We have," said Bendarik.

All four of them were startled because none of them knew that he had Jumped in.

Soolchakan snarled at Bendarik. "Call first or knock first. Don't just enter at your own whim."

Bendarik smiled weakly. "You're right. Sorry about that."

9

"The Tanmir have five different ship building facilities," said Bendarik. "Each one is in a different dimension." He smiled. "Yes, we have all five of them pinpointed and landmarked."

"That's one very positive accomplishment," said Soolchakan.

"This is Bikaropin, calling Soolchakan. Can you hear me?"

Soolchakan sneered at Bendarik. "That's how it's done." **"Yes, I can hear you. What did you need?"**

"Can I come in?"

"Of course you can."

Bikaropin appeared in the main room. "Good, I see that Kiyalee is here as well."

Kiyalee frowned. "Is this important?"

"Yes, it is," said Bikaropin. "I hope you haven't used that dimension hopping box of theirs yet."

Now Kiyalee looked concerned. "No, I took it apart. I haven't put it back together again…yet. Why, is there a problem?"

"Because they're all hooked together, somehow. If you use one to go to another dimension, it sends a signal to all of the others. If you have one, that's turned on, when you go to another dimension, it sends a signal to all of the others." Bikaropin shrugged. "We have to destroy both of them before we give everything away. I don't know how to disconnect the two that we have from any of the others."

Kiyalee looked around with some trepidation. "I'm glad I didn't use it. I was still studying the components." She shook her head. "You know where my work desk is. Go get it and destroy... please."

Bikaropin smiled, bowed his head and disappeared.

Soolchakan turned to Bendarik. "Now, about the Tanmir work stations...where are they?"

Bendarik looked at his list. "They're in dimensions 1, 22, 40, 136 and 175. The Tanmir seem to have been able to find a planet like Bri in each one of these dimensions. Each one is in a star system in those dimensions."

"What do they have, a space station or just some kind of port?"

"Each one is a full space station *and* manufacturing port. Each one has the capability of building five ships at the same time...and they are...building five at the same time."

Bonarain hung her head. "Those things must be absolutely mammoth."

Bendarik smiled. "That's a good word to describe them."

Soolchakan was a little distressed. "That'd take an incredible amount of workers to build five ships at five different locations…I just can't imagine how many people that'd take." He looked off to the side. "Massive workforce."

Bendarik sighed. "Mostly slave labor. The technicians who work on the ships are Tanmir, but the ones mining and processing the ore are slaves."

"That's an awful lot of people to send back to their original homes…if we can find their homes," said Chyning looking more distressed than Soolchakan.

Bendarik shook his head. "They're better off dead. The conditions in the mines and smelting plants…are horrible. They're all worked to death. They have transport shuttles that brings new slaves in from other star systems in those dimensions. They shove as many of them as they can in the cargo hold of the shuttles and then move them to the mines. Over a third of them die before they get there."

Bonarain clenched her teeth. "Then they probably just jettison the dead, like trash, as they're going along."

Bendarik looked up at the ceiling. He looked rather nervous. "No…they don't jettison." He looked at Bonarain. He looked as if he was nauseous. "What do you think they feed the ones who're still alive?"

Kiyalee looked a little sick. "Do…they know it?"

Bendarik frowned. "Does…who know…what?"

"Do the enslaved know what they're eating?"

"The Tanmir don't bother cooking *anything* for the slaves. They also feed the worker slaves the bodies of the dead slaves."

Soolchakan was now looking rather queasy. "They *are* better off dead. Cannibalism on the way there. Nothing but back-breaking, never ending work and cannibalism when you get there. Their sanity would be highly questionable." He closed his eyes. "Those monsters have no conscience at all."

Bonarain held her youngest child close. "We can't let them get us. We have to destroy them…before they turn us into…their kind."

"We still have a large supply of some really nasty weapons on that big Chok ship," said Kiyalee. "How many of them should we use?"

Soolchakan was staring at the floor. "However many it takes to destroy those despicable things." He sucked in a deep lungful and let it out slowly. "Get everyone into the auditorium. We're going to have to plan this one very carefully. Those monsters have dimension hopping capability and we don't want to give them any more information than we have to before we destroy them."

The meeting was not very good. There was a general call out, asking for any suggestions as to how to defeat the Tanmir. They all decided that they had to go back home and think about it.

Several months later, Kankoo of the Fifth, came up with a suggestion for the problems between North and South Paselter.

Soolchakan was ready to listen to any suggestion – even a stupid one. Bonarain was skeptical. Kiyalee and Chyning were slightly interested.

Soolchakan smiled at Kankoo. "What did you have in mind?"

Kankoo smiled back. "Just tell King Dolomot to go ahead and ride into the capital city of Blasinigan. King Dolomon isn't interested in leading anything. The Elf races and the nobles of South Paselter are all doing everything they can to get him to order an attack on North Paselter. He is afraid to make any decision at all. Once Dolomot rides into the capital city, what is Dolomon going to do? All that fat boy is interested in is his next mouthful of food."

Kiyalee scoffed. "And what is supposed to keep him from being assassinated by one of the factions on the way through the city? That is one huge city and it takes quite a while to ride from the main gate, all the way along the King's Highway to the palace."

Kankoo cleared his throat nervously. "Us. We have our people going ahead, along the way, in Spy dimension. We check any place that we can think of where an assassin would be hiding. We read minds of as many people as we can and listen for some kind of nasty plot."

Kiyalee looked a little stunned. "My boy, you may have come up with a plan that is so ridiculous…it just might work."

Bonarain snickered. "I think you're right. We go to those peace meetings and tell all of the military. So far, no one in the military has given us any indication that they want war. Neither side has voiced any desire to conquer the other."

Soolchakan nodded. "We send Dolomot in, with his entourage of guards. They ride along the highway...lined with South Paselter military and...no one makes any hostile move. They salute him the same way they'd welcome any visiting foreign dignitary, especially since he is the brother of their King."

Kankoo shrugged. "When he gets to the palace, he confronts Dolomon and...they decide between them...right then and there...with a little help from us...what the next move will be."

Chyning frowned. "Should that entourage consist of all of his top military commanders as well?"

"I don't see why not," said Soolchakan. "All of the top ones along with their aides. That should make quite a pretty procession."

Bonarain frowned. "Pretty?"

"Yes, pretty," said Chyning. "When you consider all of the snazzy, colorful garbage that top officers put all over their uniforms, it becomes very showy."

Bonarain nodded with no expression. "I see what you mean. We've seen enough of that gaudy *h'oolyach* on the uniforms from outworlders as well."

Soolchakan snickered. "All of those frills and ostentatious nonsense. Serves no purpose other than to show off just how many worthless embellishments you can hang all over any uniform."

Kankoo smiled. "Do we suggest it to the ones at the meetings...first, or do we tell Dolomot...first?"

Soolchakan stood up. "Kankoo, my boy, you are the one who gets to go to the two meeting places and give this suggestion. Most of those Commanders know that Dolomon is just a deadbeat anyway. He's no King – whereas Dolomot is." He shook his head. "For identical twins...they are very much...*not* alike."

Kankoo smiled. "I've got to let Taysham and Ginata know where I'm going. Then I'll get to those two meeting places and let them know the plan. I'm sure that King Dolomot will agree. He'll get to talk to his brother face-to-face and hopefully solve the whole thing peacefully."

Chyning giggled. "While all of the conspirators sit there just...seething."

Kankoo came back four days later.

Soolchakan looked at him and smiled. "What did you accomplish?"

Kankoo beamed. "All of the military personnel and King Dolomot are completely ecstatic about the plan." He chuckled. "They're rather embarrassed about the fact that they didn't think it up. They're all going to be dressed up in all of their frilly superfluous uniforms...just to show off."

"How garish," said Chyning flatly.

Kiyalee cuddled her youngest child a little. "When's it

supposed to happen?"

"Whenever they arrange it," said Kankoo. "They've already obtained permission to lead their procession from Sontor, by the most direct route possible, through both Cheseet and Varnast, then on to Blasinigan. They're going to pick up the Imperial Minister of Cheseet and the Grand Sovereign of Varnast on the way and lead the entire procession into Blasinigan."

Chyning looked off to the side cross-eyed. "When I said garish, I think I vastly understated it."

Bonarain sniffed the air and looked down at her youngest son. "I really think the whole procession just might be like his diaper." She picked him up. "Excuse me." She headed off to change some linen.

Kiyalee snickered as Bonarain departed. "Are we going to be part of that procession?"

"No," said Kankoo. "We'll be looking around for any covert act by any of the conspirators."

Kiyalee grinned. "That means that we can do some nasty things to them without them knowing what happened. We can do nasty things to some Galsinos."

"Only if they're planning something malicious," said Soolchakan. "If they aren't doing anything nasty, we don't nasty them. If they try to do something nasty…then we do whatever nasty, rotten, filthy or despicable thing we want to them."

Chyning had an evil grin. "Yeah!"

Soolchakan looked at Chyning. "Sometimes, you worry me. I think you're getting a little too…I don't know what. You're becoming…evil."

Chyning looked mortified. "Becoming? I've been there for quite some time now." She grinned, closed her eyes and stuck her nose in the air.

Soolchakan just grunted and shook his head. "Marvelous influence on your children," he muttered sardonically.

King Dolomot left Sontor, with his entourage and headed south to Cheseet. It took three days to get to Galgatam where they rested for one night. They continued south with the Imperial Minister and his entourage to Varnast. Four days later they were in Kagigan. Here they had to stay for two days because the pace they had been keeping was wearing out all of their equines as well as the marching armies. They then continued south, now with the Grand Sovereign of Varnast and his entourage. All of these leaders were there to show unity and the hope for peace…no matter what. They slowed their pace so they could all get used to each other and make sure that all of their mounts were not lathered with sweat when they rode into Blasinigan. The last day of travel, they camped in a forest, just out of sight of the watchtowers of the great city. Once they started out in the morning, they knew that it would not be very long before they arrived at the King's Gate.

Kankoo met King Dolomot in the encampment before he went to bed. The King looked rather nervous.

"I was wondering when you were going to show up," said

Dolomot. "I've heard nothing from you or your people during the entire trip here."

Kankoo smiled. "Don't worry, Your Majesty. All of my people have been in Blasinigan all this time. They're watching for any foul act that might be perpetrated against you or anyone in your group. You won't see any of us. We're hiding in the shadows and anywhere else we can think of, watching out for all of you."

"Do you even know who to look for?"

"Oh, yes. The enemy is very well known to us."

"May I know of the conspirators and traitors?"

"We'll give you that information at the appropriate time. Right now, it'll be much more fun to thwart any of their illegal plans against you. Plus, if we catch someone in the act…it will be further proof of their treasonous activities."

Dolomot looked rather irritated. "I'm not here for *fun*… yours or mine."

Kankoo nodded. "I agree - bad word. What I really mean, is that it will assist us in identifying traitors that we didn't know about and confirm, or clear, ones that we aren't sure of yet. There is a list of those that we are very sure of…" He reached in a pocket and pulled out a slip of paper. He smiled as he handed the paper to Dolomot. "This is the list of the traitorous nobles, that we're *very* sure of."

Dolomot took the list and read it with an angry look on his face. He shook his head. "The last name on this list…is the *last* one that I would've ever expected." He looked up. "You said that you *are* sure…of all of these people?"

Kankoo nodded sadly. "When you're ready to start any trials for treason or sedition, we'll supply you with itemized lists of what they've done and are doing."

Dolomot closed his eyes and clenched his teeth. He opened his eyes. "This last name on the list…I grew up…playing with his sons. Dolomon and I have some wonderful memories of…" He looked off to the side and cleared his throat. "All that time together and it now means…nothing," he snarled through clenched teeth. He looked at the list again. "There had *better* be some solid proof to this list."

Kankoo nodded again. "I assure you, your Majesty, that we have kept some very careful records of everything we found. I see that it pains you but…some people are just too ambitious for their own good." He sniffed. "I'll see you at the palace after you've had a talk with King Dolomon." He vanished (into Spy dimension).

Dolomot sat there startled. He looked around somewhat aggravated. "How do they do that?" He huffed. "No wonder they can identify conspirators without the conspirators knowing they're being watched."

Soolchakan shook his head. "I don't like the idea of letting them know some of our powers, but…every now and then, it seems necessary."

"It was necessary with those royals in Oosam," said Kankoo with a shrug.

"I know," said Soolchakan quietly with a sigh. "It does tell him that we can do some serious investigation, without being seen, however, I just don't like showing off our skills…to anybody. Let's get to our places in Blasinigan." He grunted. "They might start demanding favors."

Kankoo smiled and nodded.

The Owlamites were waiting all along the King's Highway inside the city. They were looking everywhere they could and reading all minds that they could, searching for any kind of mischief.

Voozim of the Eighth found a Tekaylath-Sar archer, hiding on the second floor, in a burned out building. The ebony skin of the Tekaylath made it easy for him to hide in the charred remains. While Voozim kept an eye on the small Elf, the wife of Voozim, Whishim, looked around for any sign of a co-conspirator at this location. She found a tall Fastern Elf on the other side of the highway, hiding in plain sight. He was waiting there to signal his co-conspirator and see if the Tekaylath-Sar was able to do his job.

Whishim read the mind of the Fastern. She smiled and sent out a message. "**It seems that Voozim and I found the first of nine traps for King Dolomot. There's a Fastern sitting here who was thinking about how, if his Tekaylath-Sar friend misses with his arrow, there are eight others waiting somewhere along the highway between here and the palace**."

"**I've already found one of them**," sent Inahasin of

the Tenth. **"I've got a Filkont here who seems to think that he's pretty good with a spear. Looks like there's a Zaberd waiting to see what happens here**."

Soolchakan felt a little worried. Supposedly there were nine deadly ambush points along the way and so far they had only found two. As long as the road was, from the gate to the palace, it would take half the day for Dolomot to take that long ride. The other seven traps could be anywhere on the long road in any number of buildings.

"I found another one," sent Yozhazo of the Fifteenth. **"This one is a very nasty looking Heyyah. He has an arrow that has some kind of blue syrupy liquid dripping off the arrowhead**."

Bonarain looked at Soolchakan and scoffed. "Arrows, spears and poison. Where do all these monsters come from?"

"If I knew, I'd find them when they're real young and try to teach them the difference between right and wrong," snarled Soolchakan.

Kiyalee grunted. "And if they don't listen…kick their teeth in, until they do."

"I found another one," sent Klonbeer of the Seventeenth. **"She's a Perek with some poison tipped darts. My wife, Puff, found her lookout on the other side of the street. He's a Feeror that's acting as if he's drunk**."

"That makes four of the nine," sent Soolchakan. **"Everybody keep looking. They might not be in place**

yet. This could be a long day."

Aqueron of the Ninth called out. **"The parade is at the King's Gate."** He mentally chuckled. **"There're several soldiers up here who're part of the conspiracy. The Commander of the Gate Watch is on our side. He ordered all of the troops to stand down with the weapons and open the gate. He just called them all to attention and he's saluting King Dolomot. There's a lot of confused and scared conspirator troops up here, but they're obeying the orders. Now...the entourage is officially inside the walls of Blasinigan."** He mentally chuckled again. **"You wouldn't believe how many people are with this... parade."**

Yalpar of the Twelfth called out. **"There's some *bimyock* sending flag signals. He's about one teckist east of the King's Gate. I can't tell who is receiving the signals. He's finished sending signals and now he's grinning real big. Maybe he thinks that nobody can save King Dolomot."**

Memen of the Thirteenth called out. **"I've got the *bimyock* who was receiving the signals from the wall. She's a Filkont Elf. She's getting ready to send some signals from her position. None of the people on the wall can see her."** She stopped sending for a few moments. **"Now, no one can see her. I just sent the conniving *doovoft* to Stink. She's got something else on her devious little mind now."**

Soolchakan sent out. **"That means that there was someone close enough to the wall to see her. Everyone get ready, wherever you are. These schemers could be anywhere along the route."**

"Got one," sent Ahemeni of the Fifth. **"He was lining up with a longbow. Now, he's floating around in dimension #45. I can see this Heyyah who looks a little surprised that no arrow has come out of a certain window yet."**

Pabon of the Fifth called out. **"I got Ahemeni's watcher. He's not feeling too good right now. He got a whiff of Stink and...oh, what a mess he's making right now. He must have had a *big* breakfast."**

Soolchakan called out. **"One down – eight to go. Keep alert."**

Peldom and Jada of the Third took care of the next attempted assassination. A Zaberd, with his longbow, now dead. Her watcher was an Ikogo – who was now dead as well. Two down – seven to go.

The procession continued and so did the sneak attacks on the ambushers by the Owlamites. There were people, all along the route, who were counting on King Dolomot being killed long before any of the royal visitors arrived at the palace who were visibly shaken, rather disturbed and very upset at the failures of all of the assassins.

King Dolomon did a waddling retreat to his bedroom when he heard that King Dolomot was still very much alive and going to be in the palace very soon. Dolomon was pacing (or rather waddling) from one table to another. On each of the four large tables, in his bedroom, there were platters full of delicious pastries. He would grab one pastry and eat it while he walked to the next table. He would then stand, looking over the pastries on the next table while sucking icing off his fingers. He continued in this circle while worrying about what his brother was going to do when they met, for the first time, in several years.

Dolomot finally arrived at the palace where the gates were opened and all of the guards bowed to him and the other visiting nobles in the group.

Soolchakan was beginning to get worried. They had found and ridded the world of eight sets of assassins along with fifteen people who were signaling with flags. They still had not found the ninth set. That could only mean that the ninth set (or possibly group) was actually in the palace itself. There were now over four thousand Owlamites wandering around inside the palace, reading minds, attempting to find this last set of hired thugs.

Dolomot arrived at the main doors to the main building. He was wearing his finest field plate armor and needed help dismounting. He dismounted along with many others and headed for the throne room. On the way there, he met one of the military commanders who had assisted in arranging this meeting. He was informed that Dolomon was in his bedchambers.

Dolomot looked around sadly. "It is nice to be back, but… not under these circumstances."

"I understand, your Majesty" said the Commander. "However, now that you're here, maybe we can rid ourselves of these wretched evil Elf people and get back to some kind of normal existence."

"You're sure that my brother is in his bed chambers?"

"He either went there to hide…or fret…or stuff his face with more food, your Majesty."

Dolomot closed his eyes and sucked his lips in. "Is he really that…fat?"

The Commander sighed. "His waistline is much greater than his height, your Majesty."

Dolomot snarled. "Thank you. See to the comfort of our guests while…I go have a *chat* with my dear brother."

"Yes, Majesty." The Commander walked away from Dolomot with a smile on his face as he warmly greeted all of the visitors. He ordered some of his aides to start finding sufficient quarters suitable for all of them.

Dolomot did not need a guide. He had grown up in this palace. Only when his father died had he been placed as King of North Paselter with the capital city of Sontor. Now back here in Blasinigan, in the palace, nostalgia flooded his mind, along with disappointment in his brother. He arrived at the door to the bedroom.

Eight of the King's Guardsmen stood there at the door. They all bowed to Dolomot. Dolomot gave them a signal to give him room to pass. Four went to one side, four to the other and they stood at attention as Dolomot walked to the door and opened it.

Dolomot saw his brother stuffing something in his mouth. "Good day, brother."

Dolomon stood there with a look of terror on his face as he silently chewed on the pastry. He was perspiring heavily. He swallowed and looked around at the four tables where each of the platters were located. He looked back at his brother fearfully. He then started licking some of the sticky sugars off his hands.

"**I found one of the *bimyocks*,**" sent Fissok of the Sixth. "**He's hiding in a closet, waiting for the moment to take the best shot at Dolomot.**"

"**Got another one in another closet,**" sent Okondak of the Tenth. "**The Tekaylath-Sar are some sneaky little monsters.**"

"**Just get rid of them and check all of the closets in this room...as well as any other room in the palace,**" sent Soolchakan. "**Check any and all of adjoining closets as well. I don't want to find out, the hard way, that we missed somebody. Walk through the walls and see if there are any hidden passageways as well.**"

Eight more assassins were dispatched to various dimensions. The Owlamites did not stop seeking out other possibilities as well. They started spreading out over all of the palace, especially after Sumakim of the Thirteenth found one noble who was trying to set up a bottle of wine for both Dolomon and Dolomot that was full of poison. That bottle mysteriously disappeared...leaving one very surprised and upset nobleman, who was wondering just who and how many people were going to die from drinking from that bottle…as well as when.

Dolomon started whimpering. He slowly sidled over to another table, grabbed a pastry and stuck it in his mouth.

Dolomot snarled in frustration and stomped his foot.

Dolomon was startled and fell down backwards as he made a feeble attempt at fleeing. All of the regal finery that he was wearing hindered him in any kind of escape. He rolled around on the floor, trying to get on his side and then on his stomach. His huge cape was an equally enormous problem. It kept getting in the way of any attempt to get up. He tried pushing his mountain of flesh up. He grunted, groaned and panted heavily as he made the attempts to get up. He crawled over to one of the tables with perspiration covering his face. He reached up and tried to pull himself up. All he did was upset the table and spill some of his precious goodies on the floor. He quickly stuffed two of them in his mouth then crawled over to the bed while chewing and panting. The sweat was dripping off his nose and chin as he crawled to the bed. Again, it took several attempts and some strange manipulations with his arms and legs in using the bed for assistance, however, he eventually pulled himself back up to a standing position. He stood there panting while more perspiration dripped off his chin. Now, he just silently stared, terrified, at his brother.

Xakantolo of the Fifteenth found another Galsino who was trying to set up some messages to other Elf people to try setting up some more assassination attempts. That Galsino spent the rest of his life in Stink.

Dolomon again looked at his brother in fear. Without saying anything, he waddled back over to one of the tables and quickly shoved three more pastries in his mouth. He said nothing. He just whimpered…while chewing.

Dolomot looked off to the side and shook his head. "You're a disgrace," he muttered sadly. He looked back at his brother. "The kingdom is being taken over by evil Elf clans and traitorous nobles and all you can do is…*eat*…like a foolish glutton." He shook his head again. "Like *the* foolish glutton that you are." He scoffed. "That cape you're wearing could make blankets for at least three of my soldiers." He huffed.

Dolomon hung his head looking rather guilty. His guilt did not last long. He made another trip to one of the tables and grabbed another pastry.

Dolomot sighed. "I don't care what our father said. From this day forth, the kingdom is united back together. There is no longer a north and south. Now it is just one country…called Paselter. It is now under *my* reign." He clenched his teeth. "You are no longer fit to reign as a King. You can continue to eat yourself to *death*…and I don't care." He smiled. "Any objections to me taking over all of Paselter…without any bloodshed?"

Dolomon stood there with his lower lip quivering as if he were going to cry. He turned his gaze and sniffed. Then he walked over to another table and slowly ate all of the pastries from the big platter without looking up at his brother.

Dolomot was even more appalled. "You have nothing to say. You just stand there and continue…filling your face." He snarled. "Disgusting!" He left the room.

Jozodon of the Ninth called out. **"We have several different Elf and Heyyah who're leaving the palace... with great haste. Should we follow any of them?"**

Soolchakan sighed. **"If they do nothing but get out of the city, let them leave. Make sure that we have all of their names. If they try to get some meeting together where they're planning more mischief...Stink still has plenty of room. Read their minds and find out their destinations."**

Kiyalee looked around the bedroom where Dolomon was still sniffling while stuffing pastries in his face. "Now can we put all of our attention on the Tanmir?"

Soolchakan shook his head sadly. "Unfortunately we can't. Until the Elf people who planned all of this intrigue are convinced that they've lost, we're still going to have to keep an eye on them." He grunted in frustration. "Excuse me, but I've got some important papers to deliver to King Dolomot." He vanished.

Soolchakan and Kankoo were standing in a hallway waiting for Dolomot. When the King turned the corner into the hall he was a little startled at seeing the two Owlamites. Four guards that were acting as an escort were stopped from aiming their spears at the two Owlamites with just a slight wave of the hand by Dolomot. Upon recognizing Kankoo he casually walked up to them.

Dolomot smiled. "Are you ready to give me some more pertinent information?"

Kankoo held up a valise. "I wish I could be giving you some good news, your Majesty. This, however, is a longer list of conspirators, where they have worked against you and your brother and all of the notes kept at their meetings."

Dolomot hung his head. He looked up and sighed. He took the valise. "Thank you."

"There are several more on the list that might shock you, however, the notes will prove themselves accurate," said Soolchakan. "The last thing that I want to see, on this planet, is the destabilization of the largest and most powerful kingdom that currently exists."

Dolomot raised his eyebrows. "I wonder...just exactly which is the most powerful. Is it your domain or mine? You've come up with all of this evidence and...I don't even know where you come from...or are returning, after this mess is over."

Soolchakan smiled. "We hide because our numbers are small. We have ways of hiding that keeps us in the shadows and *that* is our protection. If we were to reveal ourselves, numbers or locations, I fear that our enemies would come down on us in droves."

Dolomot opened the valise and looked at the amount of the papers inside. "Again, thank you for what you've done. There is nothing quite as wonderful as a bloodless revolution." He hung his head. "If you forced to have a revolution."

Soolchakan cleared his throat nervously. "After you've read all of those documents, it won't be so bloodless. The headsman's axe will probably be *very* busy."

Dolomot smiled at them. The two Owlamites vanished. Dolomot grunted in frustration. "I wish they'd quit *doing* that." He placed the valise under his left arm and purposefully headed for the throne room. He looked all around him as he walked, wondering if those pesky Owlams would appear out of nowhere again.

The royal guards were all looking around confused. They followed Dolomot obediently, however they were still very worried as they glanced everywhere, trying to figure out where those two strangers had gone.

10

Several years went by and several Elf races were punished severely by the Paselter military. The Galsino were now being watched very closely as their city was surrounded with a permanent military presence. All persons, regardless of race, were checked going in and out of the city of Galsino. The Ikogo received the same treatment. The Paselter military could not do much about any of the Elf races that were located in other countries or on other continents, however, local appropriate authorities were informed of the plots that had been hatched by those people. Hopefully someone was doing something. As predicted, the headsman's axe was kept very busy in Blasinigan. Numerous other conspirators were dancing on air from the gallows as well, all over Paselter.

The years went by as all of the Owlamites were brooding over a way to get past the dimension hopping boxes of the Tanmir. They felt they were running out of time because they could not come up with any feasible plan. They were stumped.

Meanwhile, in 5513, Inbrun and Jentooa of the Seventeenth announced the birth of Glemiqua of the Eighteenth. Glemiqua became number 11,000 of the living Owlamites. In 5516, Omharn and Zebba of the Eighteenth married and took the last apartment on the third level of the gorge. In the same year, Eezhton and Conayna of the Eighteenth became the first couple to start populating the fourth level.

The first quartet still remained completely stubborn about staying in the home that they had live in since…well…whenever it was that they moved to the gorge so many centuries ago.

In the year 5518, Soolchakan called all Owlamites to the main auditorium. He was becoming extremely frustrated over all of the lack of ideas coming from everyone he talked to about the dimension hopping technology of the Tanmir. It was equally frustrating that the Tanmir were rapidly building up their armada in the planning of the all-out attack against Hardooth and the Owlam.

Once everyone was there, Soolchakan stood up center stage. "The time is getting short and…no one has come up with anything that seems practical or possible when it comes to defeating their technology. They can follow us and…they can find us if we try to plant some weapon there." He looked out over all of the Owlamites and shook his head. "Is there…*anyone*…who can make a decent suggestion?"

There were a lot of them who were looking around at each other. There was a little bit of murmuring back and forth between some of them.

Finally one woman stood up. Soolchakan felt a chill in his spine, a glimmer, hoping that there was something that would come out of her mouth that would end this stagnant situation.

"I'm Lenyen of the Eleventh," she said. "I have an idea… but…I'm wondering if you'll really listen."

Soolchakan was momentarily taken aback by that statement. He cleared his throat and shook his head to clear out any cobwebs. "My child, why should I, or would I not listen to you? I'm here to listen to *any* suggestion."

She folded her arms across her chest. "My husband, Yonsav, said that you weren't ready to listen to any woman."

Soolchakan was once again shocked at what he heard. "Well…uh…Yonsav…is completely wrong. What made anyone say that?" He looked over at Bonarain, Kiyalee and Chyning and got nothing but some very accusing glares.

Lenyen huffed. "All the time, you listen to Shalam and Monaha…and Bendarik and Bikaropin and Jotsoom…and Zorkeen and Bymin…"

"I also listen to Bonarain, Kiyalee, Chyning, Mahanee, Hisang and many others, when they have something intelligent or profound to say. I don't know why Yonsav came up with the idea that I won't listen to women. Several of the Drey Sssorg before me *were* women." He shook his head. "There were many women, in the Owlamite military, who outranked me…before you, my children, came along." He cleared his throat and looked around angrily. "Yonsav! Where are you? Why did you tell her that nonsense?" He was still rather confused. "If I ever gave the impression that…I would not listen to any woman, please accept any and all apologies that I am capable of rendering. I never had any intent of...intentionally giving that impression. Please, child, continue."

Yonsav was sitting very close to Lenyen. He stood up looking rather nervous. "Uh...almost every time...I saw you... listening to advice...it was from...Bikaropin or Bendarik...or Shalam or Monaha...or..."

"Well then you weren't paying attention all of the time were you?" Soolchakan huffed accusingly. "I've listened to advice from plenty of women - when they give it. I've also given plenty of advice to women - when they ask for it. I've also given and received from men. I don't have any problem listening to anyone...who has something intelligent to say." He cleared his throat to calm himself. "Now...Lenyen, what's your suggestion?"

Lenyen smiled and looked a little more zealous about her idea. She looked back at Yonsav and kicked him in his right kneecap. Yonsav sat down grimacing and holding his knee. "I read...in some of the history, that one time you destroyed some enemy computer by getting them to turn it off...in order to change something. While they had it off, you destroyed the entire building that the mainframe was in."

"Yes, I remember something of that escapade," said Soolchakan as he leaned forward for better hearing.

She smiled. "Why don't we do some mind controlling from Observation, on their main computer people, get them to do some, what they think is repair work, on the mainframe of those dimension hoppers of theirs and get them to foul up the whole system."

Bonarain was now standing next to Soolchakan looking very eager to listen. "How do you suggest that we foul the system?"

Lenyen seemed to be standing a little taller. "We make them put a false program in there. The computer thinks that the boxes are on, when they're really not. Then we can use all kinds of those powerful weapons that we've got stored on those Chok ships and blast every single one of their spaceships and space stations to pieces."

Bikaropin stood up. "At the same time, we could also destroy the mainframe of those silly boxes. That would strand all of the Tanmir in whatever dimension they're in."

Kaldon of the Sixth stood up. "Why would they be stranded? Couldn't they just rebuild those boxes and...start hopping again?"

"No," said Lenyen! "All of the boxes are controlled from one place. They get all of their information from there. They read the trail of some other dimension hopper, find it and send the information back to the mainframe. The mainframe then figures it out and sends the information back to *all* of the boxes. The first one that got the path now can take the path, while all of the other boxes now have the information as well."

Bonarain looked up with a grin. "Destroy the mainframe and you cripple the whole system." She looked at Soolchakan. "Just like we did it with those others."

"We could then, take our time demolishing all of the boxes that still exist," said Kiyalee.

Soolchakan was now very hopeful. "How many of those dimension hopping experts are there?"

"Fifteen," said Lenyen. "Those fifteen keep it in their family in order to keep control of their status in the empire." She grinned. "They don't like sharing with anyone outside of their special family circle."

Soolchakan started feeling even better. This could work. Later on, he was going to have some harsh words with Yonsav. "Let's get a crew to that…office of theirs and start learning about them and their computer programs." He smiled at Lenyen. "My child, I think that you'd be a good leader for that project."

All in the room (above the age of 50) stood up and cheered. There were over 100 volunteers who wanted to go to the home world of Tanmir, with Lenyen, and disrupt the entire operation.

The Tanmir currently had a fleet of 227 completed ships. Several more were under construction. They were also feverishly training new personnel in flying and maintaining those ships. Their plan was to get a fleet of at least 300 ships before the all-out attack on the Owlamites. The estimate of the date of the completion of ship number 300 was only a few years away.

Late in the year 5521, they finally had succeeded in gaining full control of (what was now) the seventeen specialists on the dimension hopping boxes. It took twenty days of coaxing (and mental manipulation) before they were finally able to make all of the Tanmir technicians go along with the bogus program. The program would make all of the other boxes think that everything was working correctly. It would give the personnel on the ships the false impression that everything was working correctly. The Owlamites were even willing to give up a few more dimensions in order to make them believe that everything was still working properly.

All of the dimension hopping specialists were in the same family. They kept the secret of the boxes and the programs a closely guarded family secret. The politics of the situation made them irreplaceable as far as this program was concerned. That family knew as long as they held the secret, they held power they could keep and stay outside of any high ranking inner circle of politicians. As long as they did not make any attempts at any other political aspirations, they were left alone to do their job because it gave the entire empire more places to conquer.

Soolchakan sighed with relief as he got the word from Lenyen that the task was completed and they could begin the destruction of the entire Tanmir fleet.

Another woman, Rodeta of the Nineteenth, had come up with the idea that the Tanmir transport ships should be destroyed as well. This would cripple the entire empire. Not only would they not be able to move from one dimension to another, they would not be able to move anything or anyone from one planet to another…in any dimension. The only thing that might be left, after the initial attack, would be a few shuttlecraft. Those could be dealt with leisurely.

Also in the year 5521, Bonarain got the maternal itch again and was now pregnant…with twins. Kiyalee followed suit two months later. Chyning decided that she did not want to be left out of the motherly thing, so she became pregnant as well. When the time came for the attack, the only one of the three who could still fit in her spacesuit was Chyning. Bonarain and Kiyalee were going to have to stay behind and assist in the coordination phase.

The Owlamites were getting everyone reeducated regarding the nuclear weapons when Koynala of the Eighth came up with another "old" plan. Since they were going to be destroying ships with those extremely volatile light speed engines, all they had to do was introduce some kind of debris into the mixing chambers and...boom! Gosh, did that sound familiar? The nuclear weapons should be used only on the spaceship building stations and the space stations.

Soolchakan was thinking about just stranding all of the Tanmir and their half-crazed slaves in the work areas where they were currently assigned. Nenola of the Twelfth came up with the thought that those people would still be in an area where they had all of the raw minerals, resources and factories - they could start building new ships immediately. The Owlamites would have to plant some nuclear bombs, in those places as well, for detonations both on land and in space. That way, the space station was destroyed and the raw ore was now contaminated with radiation for the next few decades.

During all of the preparations, Soolchakan was wondering how many other women had been stifled by men like Yonsav. Not just how many, but how long as well. He was receiving all kinds of good ideas from women, because they were no longer afraid of any repercussions for thinking. He made sure that *all* Owlamites were educated regarding the fact that *all* Owlamites were capable of sentient thought and that no one should be afraid to voice any intelligent idea. He wondered if the fact that he was the only Drey Sssorg that all of these Owlamites had ever known was him…was that why they thought he was a sexist?

The final day came. The Owlamites had given up dimensions #76 and #148. The Tanmir were distracted by trying to find out about the Owlamites in those two new dimensions. Now the bogus program went in and none of the Tanmir had any method of dimension hopping and could not figure out why.

One nuclear bomb was placed in Observation at the home station where the dimension hopping family was located. The Owlamites were going to steal all of the boxes before they blew up each ship. They were then going to take all of the boxes to #45 and dismantle them. This way, none of them would ever be found in any of the wreckage. No one would be able to put them back together again, just to figure out what they were and what they did. The mainframe (along with all of the programmers) was going to be at ground zero point of a nuclear blast, of one of the most powerful nuclear bombs they had in their arsenal, and all of the boxes would disappear forever.

229 attack spaceships, 635 transport vessels for slaves or cargo and 455 luxury transport vessels for Tanmir passengers for a total of 1,319 spaceship to be destroyed. 5 manufacturing space stations, 15 major space stations and 27 minor space stations totaling 47 space stations in several different dimensions.

There was one Owlamite assigned to each ship to grab the dimension hopping box from each ship, just before detonation. That was 1,366 Owlamites ready to grab a box and Jump to their home in the gorge. Immediately after the boxes were out of the ships and space stations, there was going to be some mass detonations of all space technology that the Tanmir had acquired.

The Owlamites were going to set off nuclear bombs and throw debris into the mixing chamber for the light speed engines – and then Jump back to the gorge just before detonation.

Soolchakan was sitting in his fighter, in Observation, orbiting the home planet of the Tanmir. There was one of the major space stations that was orbiting the planet and he just stared at the gigantic structure in awe. A tiny little box, that fit in his hand, could hop that huge monstrosity into another dimension in the blink of an eye. He hated the thought of destroying something like that, along with everyone on it, however, this was for the survival of all Owlamites and the end of a cruel conquering race.

Chyning brought her fighter parallel to Soolchakan. **"Once we blow that thing up, what's gonna happen to any big chunks**?"

He looked over at her. **"Some of them will probably be pulled down to the planet by gravity. Anything that's blown away from the planet…I have no idea where that'll end up**."

She giggled. **"Could I go to the surface and swipe a few more of those golden goblets? If there's a big enough chunk of that thing falling to the planet…it'll** smash any of them that are under it. Those things are made of gold and they are so pretty."

He scoffed. "Wait until after the detonation. If you do it before, they might be able to find you. If you do it after the detonation, you can go anywhere on the planet and steal anything you want, without them being able to do anything about it. They'll be in too big a panic to worry about any goblet. I suggest that you pilfer on the other side of the planet."

She sighed. "Okay, I'll wait," she thought dejectedly. She sighed. "In panic, there is profit." She looked around. "What're you waiting for? Why haven't you given the order to blast these *doovofts* back to a pre-industrial era?"

He sniffed. "I don't want to be on this side of the planet when that thing blows up. The fireball will be...incredibly intense and the debris will be going... everywhere."

The two of them gunned their engines and hastened their trip to the other side. Once on the other side, Soolchakan was ready to give the order.

He sent out a general message. "Is there anyone who is NOT in position yet?"

He received no responses. It seemed that they had all been in position for some time and were all getting a little bored waiting for the command.

He closed his eyes. **"Grab the boxes…NOW!"**

1,366 boxes were taken from the ships where they were installed. 652 spare boxes were grabbed from all the supply depots. Debris was thrown into the light speed engines of 1,319 spaceships. 47 nuclear bombs were hopped from Observation to which ever dimension the space station was in just a few heartbeats before they detonated. 15 nuclear bombs were hopped into the appropriate dimension, from Observation, to the mines on the planets being ravaged for their mineral resources.

The losses for the Tanmir were over four million workers, builders and military on the ships. They lost over thirteen million slaves at the mines. The nuclear bomb that went off on the home planet took another 800,000. The Tanmir now had no more capability of dimension hopping and no spaceships capable of light speed, just a few light shuttlecraft.

Now that the major items were gone, the Owlamites busied themselves with the task of stealing all of the shuttlecraft, capable of space flight, from the Tanmir.

Chyning gave an order, after the bombs went off, to get to the home planet and steal anything of value. For the next eight days, the Tanmir saw just about all of their wealth vanish into thin air and there was nothing they could do about it. The Tanmir were now tamed (and broke, seeing as how many Owlamites ransacked all wealth they could find).

The remnants of the Tanmir were scattered in 26 different dimensions and none of them had any capability of getting back to Home dimension. The planets that had been conquered by the

Tanmir were now taken back by the local inhabitants and soon, the only Tanmir left in Home dimension were the ones on their home planet with no military backing from anywhere. The Tanmir Extra-Dimensional, Galactic Empire did not exist any longer.

There was a contingency of Owlamites that went to the Tanmir home planet and made sure that any information they had on building ships capable of space travel was erased from any library or school of higher learning. Any physicists and engineers involved in space travel were disposed of as well. The Tanmir would now have to start their space program from the beginning… without any of the most brilliant minds available or any of the written word concerning their technology.

Bonarain read the reports about all of the destruction and ransacking. She shook her head and looked up. "Do you think they'll try it again?"

Soolchakan shook his head. "I hope not. Hopefully they learned a valuable lesson from this and…" He shook his head. "I just hope they learned."

Chyning snickered. "They don't have enough resources on their planet anymore. We got just about everything they could use to build spaceships. If they ever do build another one…they'll have to figure out how to make it out of wood and ceramics. Their mines containing any metals are almost tapped out planet wide."

Kiyalee leaned back as she patted her expanding abdomen. "Is this going to be a race of people that we allow them to… survive?"

Soolchakan nodded. "As long as they don't try anything against us again, we'll leave them alone. Genocide is disgusting."

Bonarain had a strange look on her face. "You said that you'd take advice from any man or woman who had something intelligent to say…when did you ever take advice from Chyning?"

Chyning was now giving Bonarain the evil eye.

"I don't remember ever taking any advice from Chyning," he said lackadaisically. "I said that it had to be something worthwhile, intelligent and appropriate."

Chyning was now giving both of them the evil eye while Kiyalee was quietly giggling.

The year 5522 saw the Owlam population go over 11,600. Among those new children, Bonarain gave birth to twin girls: Yarmisi and Yarmasi. Kiyalee had another daughter named Binleena. Chyning had a new son named Esuzgor. There were now 26 children sired by Soolchakan. Bonarain had seven children, Kiyalee had ten and Chyning had nine.

Late in the year 5529, Cimtroy and Gibatay of the Nineteenth announced the birth of their daughter Banatsa. At the birth of Banatsa of the Twentieth, the Owlamite population was officially at 12,000.

In the year 5542, Soolchakan was reading a book that he

could not remember reading before. It was in the memory banks of his computer, however, it had been so long since he read it that he could remember nothing of the plot as he read it. Bonarain walked into his bedroom with a rather deadpan look on her face. He raised his eyebrows in anticipation of her saying something. Instead she ran a stripe of her neck mucus across his forehead. She sighed as she stood there waiting for him to respond. He stood up glaring at her. He striped her forehead with his neck mucus. She grunted as if in surprise. She walked over to his bed, dropped her robe and crawled in the bed to await as he undressed.

In the middle of the year 5543, Bonarain gave birth to a boy she named Whegron.

Not long after Bonarain gave birth, Kiyalee got the itch again. She gave Soolchakan the same amount of "no warning" as Bonarain. Early in 5544, Kiyalee gave birth to a boy she named Emponim.

Soolchakan started wondering if Chyning was going to get in on this business as well. They now had several young (as Owlamites go) children and a couple of babies. Finally in early 5546, Chyning decided to be a mother again. Near the end of 5546, she gave birth to twin girls: Milatha and Malatha. At the birth of Malatha, the population of the Owlamites was now 12,635.

Now Bonarain had eight children, with five of them being ages 70 and under, Kiyalee had eleven children, four of which were under 70 years old and Chyning had eleven children as well, with five of them being under the age of 70. Soolchakan was very glad to see all of these children, he was also very grateful for a place to escape to in order to have a little peace and quiet. Fourteen young children (four of which were newborn or toddlers) was very distracting.

Very early in the year 5558, Quonnd and Hammpeti of the Eighteenth had a new son they named Remkozik of the Nineteenth. Remkozik became number 13,000 in the Owlam population. Soolchakan was jubilant about the numbers continuing to go up. He was also very happy over the fact that there did not seem to be any new enemies showing up, either on the planet or from outer space.

Very quickly, in the middle of the year 5561, Foban and Teefiy of the Ninth announced the birth of their son, Xyquonik of the Tenth. Xyquonik became number 14,000 in the Owlam population.

A small population explosion seemed to be going on. Early in the year 5563, Whishgol and Vajeda of the Eighteenth announced the birth of their daughter Kiykaya. She was number 15,000 in their census count. Soolchakan hoped that there would be no more of the Teltermak machines or surprise attacks from outer space. Bringing back the herd that was developing would be a very formidable task.

Early in the year 5568, Bonarain decided that she needed another child. Soolchakan was wondering if she had some kind of desire to catch up with Kiyalee and Chyning, as far as how many children she birthed. Near the end of the last days of 5568, she gave birth to a daughter that was named Reedeka of the Second. Shortly after that, Kiyalee got the urge. In the first days of 5570, she gave birth to a daughter, Whelatha of the Second. Soolchakan was wondering if Chyning would, again, follow this trend – she did. In 5571, Chyning got the maternal instinct going. She then gave birth, early in 5572, to a boy she named Yonz. This came to nine children by Bonarain and twelve by both Kiyalee and Chyning. Soolchakan could not help but to wonder what the population would have been if they had known about that slimy stuff dripping down their backs, twelve or thirteen thousand years ago. Things would have been very different if...

There was a bit of a slowing in the population explosion. It was not until the later part of 5572 that Amat and Daspesa of the Ninth announced the birth of their daughter Eezooya of the Tenth. She brought the total to 16,000 living Owlamites.

The hallways of the first four levels in the gorge were constantly a playground for the children. They could be heard running and making all kinds of noise at any time of the day or night. The adult Owlamites did not need that much sleep and neither did the children. None of the adults had any complaints about the noise. The sounds of children laughing, shouting and playing was much more preferable than any sound of war...with either worlders or outworlders.

In the last month of 5572, Troygoff and Einasa of the Ninth, moved into the last vacant apartment on the fourth level. Soolchakan could not help beaming with pride. For the first time in several millennium, four levels were full and the fifth was now going to be populated. Arbrem and Senakee of the Twelfth became the first family to claim an apartment on the fifth level.

Soolchakan was smiling even more as another high point was reached. Late in the year 5574, Plezim and Hemezena of the Ninth announced the birth of their son Toolokon of the Tenth. Toolokon brought the population to exactly 17,000 Owlamites. All of these numbers were being accomplished while the lookouts all over the planet and the ones looking out into outer space were seeing no new dangers to any of the Owlamites.

Another landmark moment occurred in early 5575. Pronthor and Beshaba of the Twenty-Second announced the birth of their son Xachool of the Twenty-Third. Xachool was the very first member of the twenty-third generation. Soolchakan wondered, again, how many more generations he would see during his lifetime. Bonarain and Kiyalee were also pleased with this moment. Chyning could only sulk over how old she was. None of them felt old or looked old. They still looked like any Heyyah in their 30's…except for their gargantuan ears, which were still growing.

In early 5586, Bonarain had been bitten by the motherhood bug again. She gave birth to another daughter that she named Xibia. Now Soolchakan was the father of thirty-four children. He was very glad that the women had been waiting several years in between each child. That way, their home was not completely overrun with toddlers and infants…and hundreds of dirty diapers.

Still during a long era of peace, another landmark came about. In 5588, Noromyt and Sixkana of the Sixteenth became the parents of a baby girl they named Mahandi. Mahandi of the Eighteenth brought the number of Owlamites to 18,000.

In 5589, Kiyalee gave birth to her thirteenth child. Romtoana of the Second was the tenth daughter of Kiyalee and the thirty-fifth child of Soolchakan.

The landmark of 19,000 living Owlamites was reached in early 5599. Uyondak and Rontana of the Seventeenth became the parents of Sendani of the Eighteenth. Even though it was another wonderful step, Soolchakan still remembered that they were still not up to what the population had been just after the firestorm. Still…it was nice that they were able to reach this number during a lasting peace.

In the middle of 5599 ATUT, Bonarain gave birth to triplets. Two girls and one boy. The girls were Nabtami and Nabtemi. The boy was Nabovon. Soolchakan was wondering, again, if Bonarain was trying to catch up with Kiyalee and Chyning. Both of them had thirteen children and with the triplets, now, Bonarain had thirteen children as well. He decided to leave that issue alone because he had left it up to the women as to whether or not they wanted to procreate. He was still curious – was it possible for Bonarain to manipulate her ovulation in order to come up with birth multiples instead of just one? She had been able to come up with some extraordinary things in the past. She just might be capable of doing something just like that.

Soolchakan was watching with a big smile on his face. They were in their home on the twelfth level in the gorge, watching over all of their unmarried children (of which there were 17 at this time). The two youngest daughters of Kiyalee and Chyning were very interested in watching as Bonarain changed the diapers of her triplets.

Then the klaxon went off.

Kinbood of the Seventeenth sent out a mental call to all Owlamites. **"Some unknown vessel has just come into orbit around Denhahbon!"**

Bonarain suddenly had a look of fear and desperation on her face. She scooped up all three of her triplet babies and hugged them to her chest while looking at Soolchakan in terror.

Soolchakan growled to himself. He knew that the three women would not be going out there to investigate. Bonarain had Xibia who was thirteen years old plus the triplets. Kiyalee had 11-year-old Romtoana. Chyning had 8-year-old Varlana. He made a mental call to Bikaropin to be the primary assistant in the investigation. He Jumped to the Chok ship in #45.

Soolchakan looked around the hangar as other Owlamites Jumped in and started donning their spacesuits. He sighed as he grabbed his suit and started putting it on. After getting dressed and testing for leaks he walked over and climbed into the seat. He scanned the hangar again. There were four more who had finished the suit tests and were climbing in their fighters.

He waited until there was no more activity outside of the fighters and all were looking at him. **"Is everyone ready,"** sent Soolchakan?

All of them responded affirmatively.

"Start your engines, hop to Spy and Jump to

Denhahbon."

The hisses of all of the engines firing up was heard. Soolchakan checked his instruments, closed the canopy and hopped to Spy. He then Jumped to an orbital location near Denhahbon. All the other fighters started appearing in the planned mass formation.

Then Soolchakan noticed that the fighters used by Kiyalee and Chyning were in the formation.

"**Kiyalee! Chyning! Are you here to…what're you here for**?"

"**I'm here to do my job**," sent Kiyalee. "**I'm not getting left out of this. I'm here to make sure that my children are safe. If I have to come out here and assist in order to get the job done…here I am. So don't complain.**"

"**You're not getting at any of the goodies without me**," sent Chyning. "**I don't like leftovers! I want first grab at something…anything. I don't care what it is!**"

"**What about your youngest children? Where are they**?" Soolchakan could not believe that they would leave them with Bonarain. The triplets were a big enough problem without two more very young children.

"**Mahanee has them**," sent Kiyalee with a giggle. "**You know she loves being around children…any children… especially small children…and babies.**"

Soolchakan shrugged. He still could not argue with that. Mahanee was always there if needed to take care of any and all children. **"All right people! Let's find this ship and find out about the…inhabitants of the thing."**

They broke formation and started looking for the ship orbiting Denhahbon. Soolchakan took three orbits himself and found nothing. Everybody else was reporting the same thing.

Kiyalee was the first to vent her anger. **"Hey, Kinbood! I thought you said that there was something out here orbiting Denhahbon. Where is the *chokwad* thing?"**

Kinbood responded. **"I've been trying to tell you, but everyone was chattering about what they were not finding. That ship broke orbit before you got there. It dropped some kind of mechanism on the planet before it left. I think…from what I saw of the direction it was going when it left…that ship is headed for Bri."**

Soolchakan snarled to himself. **"Kazil and Falchon, take some low laps around Denhahbon and look for whatever this mechanism is. Once you find it do with it as you will…better yet, keep track of it in case we want to give them a mystery by putting it back on their ship. That way, if it is something that can send back a signal to them…or anyone else, it'll be on their ship and we won't have to worry about it…if we have to destroy them. The rest of us…Jump to Bri."**

11

They had to wait a while before the alien ship came into view. During the wait several of them had to Jump back to #45 and the Chok ship in order to replenish their oxygen, or get something to eat…or a latrine break. Once the ship was spotted, all of them were called back orbiting Bri.

The ship was a very large saucer shape with four cylindrical appendages hooked to opposite edges of the saucer - two cylinders above and two below. Several random spots of light could be seen on all areas of the main saucer portion. None of the cylinders had these spots of light.

Soolchakan took a deep breath. **"Okay, my children. Let's get in there and find out who these aliens are."**

Soolchakan headed for…what appeared to be the main bridge of the ship with Bikaropin by his side. Kiyalee was a little lost as to where the engines would be, however, she was not afraid to search and ask others if they could identify a main engine room. Chyning headed for the central part of the ship with nothing but pure greed in her eyes and heart. Each new species had treasures and she wanted to get them.

The first place they went turned out to be some recreational area. They then tried the exact center of the top side of the ship and that was where they found the main bridge.

"**They look very similar to Heyyah**," sent Bikaropin.

"**Most of them**," sent Kiyalee. "**I'm seeing at least five different species of beings here in the main engine room.**"

"**I found a dining room**," sent Chyning. "**I count at least fifteen different species.**"

Soolchakan was a little worried. "**Do any of them appear to be slaves?**"

"**Nope**," sent Kiyalee. "**They're all wearing the same uniforms and they all seem to be getting along just fine. Some of the uniforms are different because of the anatomical design of some of these people, but...for the most part, they look the same.**"

"**I'm in some kind of gymnasium**," sent Alero. "**I saw two different species in a fight but...it looks like they're in some kind of sanctioned match. The referee appears to be some kind of different species to the two combatants and...uh...the fight is over and... they're smiling and shaking hands and...it doesn't look like they're real enemies...just competitors in some pugilistic sport.**"

"**I'm in...I guess that this is the private room of one of the crew**," sent Garedo. "**The individual in this room fell asleep at a console that's still running. I can**

look a few things up...once I get the language."

Soolchakan was puzzled at what he was seeing. Was it possible that this was a multi-species ship where all of these different races were actually cooperating with each other – on a friendly basis? "**Okay, let's start reading some minds, get some languages and...figure these people out. If they are friendly types and not trying to conquer us...we may have someone we can actually trust.**"

Chyning was miffed. "**Does that mean that I can't swipe these candlesticks?**"

Soolchakan grunted in disgust at her question. "**If they *are* a friendly type then we steal nothing from them.**"

Kazil broke in. "**What do we do with this machine that we picked up from Denhahbon?**"

Soolchakan chuckled. "**Again – if they are friendly, we give the thing back to them...unbroken, unblemished and untarnished.**"

Senbower broke in. "**I'm listening to all kinds of conversations in this...recreational area. Everyone seems to be friendly with everyone else. The conversations are about home, friends...some of them are talking some technical stuff. I don't think that there are any slaves on board this ship. These people all seem to get along with each other...regardless of species.**"

Over five thousand Owlamites were all reading minds and picking up several new languages. Everything they learned about this new ship told them that this was a scientific exploration vessel from some kind of coalition of planets and races. They had all kinds of rules and regulations about not interfering with any inhabited planet – unless they were already technologically advanced. Then they would attempt a peaceful meeting to add to their partnership.

Soolchakan was now euphorically dumbfounded. Is it possible that there could be peace? Is it possible that they could get along with this collective without having to commit genocide... again? Hopefully yes. He wanted to be absolutely sure about this finding. Even more Owlamites were put on board to read through their computers and read their minds as well. He had tears of joy in his eyes in the hope that this was a peaceful mission of exploration and not conquering.

The thought of "zero" in the thieving department – Chyning was visibly upset. She was, however, rather intrigued about this collection of different species, all living and working together in harmony.

After several days of observation, once the ship was in orbit around Hardooth, Soolchakan listened in on one of the meetings that these people had concerning their findings so far. The Commander of the ship gave strict and specific orders to his people. If they wanted to find out about all of the different races on Hardooth, they had to do so without harming anyone. It appeared even more that this was a friendly spaceship. They were trying to gather data about the planet, not for conquering, just for learning and studying any sciences appropriate to the planet.

Bonarain was equally mystified by this new bunch that had invaded the star system. She went on a mission of her own to pick the brains of these people and see if there was any form of hidden agenda. She could find none.

Kiyalee could not find any special differences in the light speed engines. The technology was the same. Like all others, there was a slight difference in exterior design. She was going around the ship reading minds in an attempt at gleaning any information concerning new and advanced technology.

Chyning was still irritated that she could not steal anything. She has seen some very nice things on the ship in private rooms, however, she was not allowed to filch any of them. It was very frustrating – for her. Some of them had some really nice looking goodies…some of which, she had no idea what the things were.

Soolchakan was wandering around in some lower section of the ship. He saw several of the crewmembers walking around carrying some noisy little machine of some kind. They would point one end of the machine at…something. They would press some buttons on the machine and then stare at a tiny little readout on the machine. He wanted to see one of them up close, however, whenever someone put the machine down, they would turn it off. He was looking for one moment when someone did not turn it off. He had been reading minds of the personnel who were working with these things and had a rather good idea what it was and what it was used for, but again, no one would leave it running when they set it down.

He finally got tired of waiting. He came across two people going in opposite directions in a narrow corridor. Both were using their noisy machines to look at different things in the area. One of the pair was female and she was thinking about how tired she was. He took that moment to initiate a thought in her mind that she was more fatigued than she actually was. She needed to stop and stretch some tired muscles. She placed the box in front of a console and started stretching. At that moment, Soolchakan reached through several favorite dimensions, grabbed the device and brought it back. He looked it over as quickly as he could. He did not know which button to push to turn it off or on or make it do any of the functions that it was designed for. He was even more baffled as to how they were getting any information from these silly little things. He knew that it would take more than just this little cursory glance to understand this strange box. Maybe Kiyalee could study it closer and get some answers.

The woman had stopped stretching and was now accusing her colleague of stealing her box. She thought that he had run off with her scanner. Soolchakan muttered a quick curse and put the scanner back where he grabbed it from. He then decided to see what was going to happen between the two people. The accusation was brief when the male pointed back at the scanner she had been using. She had a surprised look on her face as she came back to retrieve the scanner.

After a few looks of confusion, the woman had a bit of a stunned look on her face as she grimaced. She did something else with the scanner and then had a look of horror on her face. She called her colleague back to assist her with…what?

He came back looking rather puzzled about her demeanor. After a brief conversation, the man did something with her scanner and then called that man in charge, Captain Milch, requesting that the Captain come to this location to see the mystery these two found.

Soolchakan wondered if he had just stepped into something that he could not get out of. Best thing to do – sit here, wait for them to investigate and then go from there.

Zirsha of the Ninth had been assigned to follow this specific woman. Hajan of the Eighth was following the man. They were rather interested as to what the results of the examination by Soolchakan were going to be. They were also very glad that they had not been the ones who started this extracurricular investigation.

"We'll just wait and see what they all say," said Soolchakan with a shrug.

Zirsha giggled. She looked at the console that the scanner had been hooked up to. "I'm glad that it was you that did that and not me. You'd probably be upset with me."

Soolchakan shook his head. "One way or another, we're going to have to have a conversation with these people… eventually. Especially if they are peaceful."

Hajan nodded. "Find out if all of the stuff in their logs is real or a colossal cover-up. Are they really as benevolent as they are showing themselves to be?"

Soolchakan just grunted and shrugged.

Milch showed up with someone named Boris. Another man named Gomez came in as well. All three of these ship personnel had an Owlamite following them, so it was getting rather crowded in that small corridor. The newcomers had a conversation and Gomez re-hooked the scanner up to the console. They had a brief conversation about different dimensions and alien beings and DNA.

Soolchakan scoffed. He had not bled or spat on the machine. He just touched it. How could they possibly come up with any form of a DNA specimen from him? The very thought of it was complete nonsense. Then the Captain came up with some idea on how they could find the DNA. Now Soolchakan was even more bewildered. He decided that he was going to have to watch that process very closely. DNA from…what…a fingerprint? A smudge? The slightest touch? Ridiculous! Preposterous! Impossible…I think…I hope.

They did find DNA and then they had a meeting in the main conference room. Soolchakan listened to another briefing where they discussed the DNA evidence that had been discovered.

Bonarain was at this meeting while Mahanee was taking care of the triplets. "What'd you do? Did you…spit on that thing? Did you bleed on it?"

Soolchakan just shook his head in desperation. "I just… *touched* it…just for a few heartbeats. I didn't…rub on it, I didn't spit on it and I didn't bleed on it. I just looked at it. I only touched it lightly with my right hand."

Kiyalee chuckled nervously. "They've got some fantastic technology. They got your DNA just from a slight touch. That is...incredible."

Chyning had her nose even further out of joint. "Did he just say that everyone was supposed to inventory...even their personal things?"

Soolchakan looked at her horrified. "You didn't steal anything did you?"

"NO, I DIDN'T STEAL ANYTHING," she shot back angrily! She sat there with her lips clenched tight. She looked back at Soolchakan. "Some of them have some nice goodies but, if they're as benevolent as they're appearing to be...I can't swipe any of them at all." She looked off to the side while pouting. "I touched some things and...I wonder if they might find my DNA on some of that stuff...the same way they found yours."

"We may even have to make friends with them," said Bonarain. "We *absolutely* want to keep everything friendly."

Chyning smiled at Soolchakan. "Maybe I could grab something...just to show them what we're capable of?" She saw Soolchakan, Bonarain and Kiyalee all glaring at her. She crossed her arms across her chest and continued her sulking.

Bonarain turned to Soolchakan. "What was that woman talking about when she said that - a crawler - was back in the storage compartment?"

He shrugged. "Some mechanism that they dropped on Denhahbon. I wasn't sure about them at the time, so I told Kazil

and Falchon to…go find it and…do what they wanted with it."
He snickered. "Putting it back where it belongs…I told them to
do that until we figured out whether these people are worth our
time…or not."

Bonarain gave Soolchakan a dirty look. "You *are* going to
contact these people aren't you?"

Soolchakan nodded as he spooned another big lump from
the kwatha into his mouth. **"These people are fascinating."**
He sent his thoughts as he chewed on the lump. **"The one in
charge gave specific orders that if they go down to the
planet to gather DNA from the citizenry, any citizenry,
there were to be zero casualties and especially zero
fatalities."**

Kiyalee slurped loudly from her mug of kwatha. **"What
about all of their entries in their ship and personal
logs? Have we found anything that says that they're
conquerors?"**

Soolchakan swallowed and shook his head. "Not a thing.
This crazy ship is just out to survey and…learn what they can
about any and all star systems that they come across. If they find
a planet that is inhabitable, but not inhabited – they colonize. If
it is inhabited - they observe. According to the history of some of
the planets that they observe…they will observe for…centuries.
They've been doing this for quite some time and have never
conquered anybody. They have been attacked a few times and
beaten the adversaries back but…they don't conquer."

"It still sounds too good to be true," muttered Chyning bitterly.

Bonarain sighed. "Then the only way to find out is to… contact them, put some direct questions to them or…listen to what they say while we're reading their minds."

"Reading their minds while looking for any fabrications," said Kiyalee.

Chyning looked up with an evil grin. "Any fabrications on their part and…those pretty candlesticks are *mine*." She gave him a side glance. "All ten of them." She looked off to the side. 'Along with a lot of other little pretties,' she thought.

Soolchakan just shook his head, rolled his eyes and grunted in disgust.

Soolchakan was in one of the cargo bays in the lower decks. He was looking around at all of the items stored here. Most of the things were above his capability to even make a guess as to what they were or what purpose they served. He just sighed and surrendered to the fact that he was still ignorant of a lot of their technology…or any technology.

He knew that there were motion detectors in each of the cargo bays. He had decided that he was going to make his presence known by wandering around in the bay and let them come to him. He was going to toy with them by walking through the wall into one of the adjacent bays. He hopped from Spy to Ghost dimension. He looked around. He neither heard any alarm nor saw any lights go crazy. He waved his arms and jumped up and down. Still nothing.

Bonarain Jumped in the bay in Ghost dimension. "I think that their sensors can't see anything in Ghost. The machines probably think that you're some kind of...shadow."

He grunted. "So what do we do?"

She snickered, hopped to Home dimension, kicked over a large plastic barrel and then hopped to Spy. As soon as she kicked the barrel, a blaring klaxon went off. A mechanical voice started hollering a warning about an unknown intruder. Several beams of light started randomly going around the room.

He shrugged and hopped to Home. Now all of those strange moving beams aimed themselves directly at him. He hopped back to Ghost. The beams still followed him. 'Interesting,' he thought. 'Now that they know I'm not a shadow, they look at me.' He wandered around the bay for a few moments. He heard some shouting in the hallway outside the bay. He chuckled as he headed for the closest wall. He walked through the wall. He now found himself in, what appeared to be, a public latrine. He was very impressed by how clean it was. He frowned because he did not see any of those moving beams of light in this room. He continued in a straight line through the next wall. He found himself in another cargo bay. The roving beams were searching in this bay. He hopped to Home and all of the beams were suddenly not moving, they were all fixed on him. He heard more shouting in the hallway. He grinned and chuckled to himself. He ducked behind a stack of barrels and dropped down through the floor. Far less noise in here. The roving beams were in this bay as well. After several moments they fixed on him again. He snickered, hopped to Spy and Jumped to the main bridge so he could listen in on all of the pandemonium he had caused as it was coming in to the main bridge.

He was standing behind the big fancy revolving seat where that Captain Milch sat whenever he was in this room. Milch was in the seat, however, he was not wearing the customary outfit he had always been seen in. He looked around the bridge at all of the outworlders that were here. Behind each one was an Owlamite. All of the Owlamites were in Spy. They were reading the minds of the person they were assigned to watch. Every person on this crew was being scrutinized around the clock.

After a few moments of listening to them attempt to find the intruder. Soolchakan hopped back to Home dimension. He chuckled as he was unnoticed for several moments. Finally a man named Overton happened to look up towards the Captain's chair and notice a stranger standing there. Overton looked rather nauseous as he told the Captain that he had found the intruder. Milch was rather upset and shouted at Overton. Overton told Milch that the stranger was standing behind the Captain's chair. It suddenly became very quiet on the bridge as all of the outworld crew stopped talking and looked up at the stranger. Nothing could be heard other than some beeping noises from some of the consoles.

With a rather weak smile, Milch looked at Overton. "Is... are the Security personnel...aware of your...discovery?"

Overton cleared his throat again. "I…believe that they heard it…over the intercom. It *is* currently…an open line… throughout the entire ship."

Milch nodded and sniffed loudly. "Thank you." He stood up slowly. He reached down to straighten out his tunic. He felt the robe and his face flushed. He realized that he was wearing only his trousers slippers and robe. He closed the robe, tied it and slowly turned to face this mysterious intruder.

Soolchakan and Milch stood there giving each other the once over. Soolchakan did a little mind reading and found that Milch was pondering what he was going to say. He was trying to form a very careful, diplomatic statement.

Soolchakan decided to speak first. "You are not dressed the way that you have normally been attired…Captain Ronald Milch."

Milch gave a wan smile. "I…was getting ready to go to bed…when you made your…sudden and shocking appearance."

"Bed?" He looked thoughtful for a moment. "Oh! A bed! Yes, one of those things?"

Milch was momentarily taken aback. "That…is where one sleeps. Don't you…sleep?"

"Not…often enough that I would have a…bed…just sitting there…waiting to be…used." He was fighting to keep from smiling, or laughing out loud.

Chyning, still standing there in Spy, scoffed and rolled her eyes. "*H'oolyach*! Of course we have beds." She huffed. "You fabricating hypocrite."

Milch cleared his throat. "Don't you get tired and have to go to sleep in order to refresh yourself?"

"Sleep...sleep...only...after an occasion where I've really exerted myself. Again, that doesn't happen very often."

"Uh...when was the last time...you awoke from sleeping?"

"I...don't remember. It has been quite some time...since I needed to...sleep. It's been...at least ten months."

At that moment several of the Security personnel came running onto the bridge, panting, puffing and sweating from their run.

Soolchakan turned to them. "There's no reason for any form of force..." He faltered for a moment. **"Who was following this man and what is his name**?" After receiving the information he continued his sentence. "...Lieutenant Commander Ivan Emerson."

One of the other Security men spoke without thinking. "You...know *his* name?"

"I know your name too...Lieutenant Marcus Eli." As each person was coming in, the Owlamite assigned to them was telepathically sending their names to Soolchakan.

Milch was getting a little miffed. "How many other personnel do you know the names of?"

Soolchakan had to do a full roll call of all his spies. Each one gave the name and duty assignment of each one of the personnel on the main bridge. As soon as he finished he looked up at Milch. "Did I miss anyone?" He tried to not sound, or look, too facetious.

Milch cleared his throat. "You have us...at an extreme disadvantage, Sir. You seem to know all of us...and we don't have the slightest idea...who you are...or where you came from."

"I am Soolchakan, Drey Sssorg of the Owlam. That is who I am. I come from the planet that you are now orbiting...we call it...Hardooth. If I were to translate that, it would mean...Heart!" He smiled. "What you call - the small moon - we call: Niygool. What you call - the large moon - we call: Zhagool."

"Okay," said Milch cautiously. "You can answer the question about our immediate vicinity. How long...have you been watching...and studying us? I mean...you can't learn all of our names...in an instant."

Soolchakan looked around the bridge. "I've been with you...and studying you...ever since you dumped that contraption on Denhahbon."

Milch felt a little foolish. "Den...what?"

Soolchakan looked a little impatient. "Denhahbon! The planet that you have designated as NZ dash 3591 dash 14. I was also there, when you discovered the mining operations...on Bri. Bri is the planet that you call NZ dash 3591 dash 12."

"So...if you have been with us...all of that time...why did we not see you...until now?"

"Because I didn't let you see me."

"Really? Uh…how do you do…that?"

Soolchakan hopped to Spy, took one step to his left and hopped back to Home. "By willing myself to go through the different dimensions. There are two of them…where I can walk among you…aliens…or anyone else without being seen. I can see you, I can hear you, and I can watch your every move. *You* have no idea that I am there. It is quite convenient…for observing you and determining whether or not you are…hostile to us." He smiled.

Milch felt a few beads of sweat trickle down his spine. "And…have you…determined…whether or not…we are… hostile?"

Soolchakan smiled. "If I thought that you had hostile intentions toward my home planet…we wouldn't be talking. You'd be wondering: Why is this ship flying, totally out of control, at over 4,000 kph, directly toward one of the gas giants?"

Milch's eyebrows went up. "You…would not crash us… on the small moon?"

Soolchakan grunted. "Niygool has been littered with too much debris. We now hide the wreckage on either Ragath or Rogoth."

Milch smiled helplessly. "And those…are…?"

He sighed. "Ragath is what you call: NZ dash 3591 dash 8. Rogoth is what you call: NZ dash 3591 dash 7. We also call them the running twins. Ragath is the runner, Rogoth is forever chasing Ragath across the night sky."

"So...now you hide the crash sites...inside two gas giants?"

"Oh yes, there's *so* much more room there. I can send it there, they can't send out a distress call, they don't know what's happening and any corpses are...stuck in the gas...forever."

Milch now looked at the intruder with a questioning frown on his face.

Soolchakan noticed this and with a smile asked: "Is there something wrong?"

Milch grunted a little. He was trying to think of the best way to word his question. "From what we've observed...of the planet - *Heart*...there is very little...sophisticated technology - or more correctly - practically none. For someone who comes from a planet like that...you have an amazing knowledge... of astronomy...and it seems that you know...quite a few things about the technological workings of...a spacecraft."

"Our planet...was not always like that."

"You mean...there was technology...and you... digressed...back to what it is...now?" Milch was very confused.

Soolchakan stroked his beard. He looked up at Milch and smiled. "Do you have time...for a *long...long...long* story...of our history?"

Milch put a big smile on his face. "Absolutely! That's why we're here. We are here to learn about...everything...that we can regarding this planet and star system. We came here to learn...maybe to even improve ourselves by observing you."

Soolchakan chuckled. "Aren't you wanting to…bed…for a while before hearing…any of my history?"

Milch smiled back. "I am way too excited, right now, to be able to go to…*sleep.* I would love to hear…something… that explains your knowledge of…astronomy, engineering, spacecraft…and whatever other things that seem just…*way* too far ahead of the technology we see down there on the planet. I also am curious about why you're talking to us and not killing us." He cleared his throat. "I'm very glad that we're talking and not being killed."

"Shall we go and sit down in your conference room and discuss it, for a while?"

"Oh, by all means, yes. I'd love to have a long, long, long chat…with you."

Shalam had been the one assigned to Milch. Shalam shook his head as they headed to the conference room. **"Why didn't you tell us that you were going to do this before? It might have saved us from a few headaches about the plans to kill all of these…Earthlings…and all of their allies."**

Soolchakan chuckled. **"So far we haven't seen a reason to kill them. If they are just explorers and if they are the type who would invite us to join them instead of doing any conquering, they're worth listening to. Besides, that'll give us more time to listen to their minds and see if there is any…fabrication."**

Shalam sniffed. **"Good point."** He followed Milch into the conference room and took his place behind the tall man.

12

Soolchakan contemplated for a few moments. "**You called them Earthlings? Is that what they all call themselves?**"

Shalam came back. "**Most of the crew are from one planet called Earth. There are at least fifty other species on this ship. All of them are here voluntarily. No one seems to be any kind of slave or...someone in any kind of involuntary servitude. They all wear basically the same uniforms, with a few modifications for physical differences, and seem to be getting along...quite well. The only other difference in uniforms is some kind of differentiation concerning their specific job. They do have a military rank structure and no one seems to be upset with it.**"

"**Interesting.**" Soolchakan smiled. "**Let's hear what they have to say. This might actually turn out to be something good.**" He looked around rather confused. "**Does anyone see any species that we've come across...and battled with...anywhere on this ship?**" He waited for any answer. No one recognized any of the different races represented on the ship.

Milch sat down at the end of the conference table. "Computer, annotate the date and time. This is Captain Ronald Milch. We're having a first contact meeting with one of the inhabitants of NZ-3591-4. These people call the planet 'Hardooth' or translated into our language - 'Heart'. While, technologically, the inhabitants of this planet appear to be in the time frame of the Earth Renaissance, the individual, who has identified himself as Soolchakan, seems to be very familiar with advanced sophisticated technology. He is also very capable of coming and going...just about anywhere he pleases...without the aid of any technology. We're going to have a nice long conversation with this person and find out a few things about him and the history of the planet that we are currently orbiting. We will start with the roll call of personnel in the room...starting with our guest." He turned to Soolchakan and smiled.

"I am Soolchakan, Drey Sssorg of the Owlam."

"Commander Alejandro Gomez, Chief Science Officer."

"Lieutenant Manuel Montalvo, Anthropology."

"Lieutenant Joyce Upton, Zoology."

"Lieutenant Commander Ivan Emerson, Chief of Security."

"Lieutenant Richard Avery, Security."

"Lieutenant Marcus Eli, Security."

"Lieutenant Mark Angelo, Security."

"Lieutenant Robert Schmitz, Forensic Pathology."

"Lieutenant Commander Samuel Jones, Physics."

"Lieutenant Paul Smith, Astrophysics."

"Commander Henry Lewis, Doctor, Chief of the Medical section."

"Commander Hiroko Kasaki, Executive Officer."

"Yeoman Iolani Aua."

The first question asked by one of the crew was about the planets in the star system. Soolchakan gave the names of each planet. The next question was about some silly thing they called 'evolved'.

Soolchakan sat there rather confused. "**Does anybody know what she's talking about? What is...evolved**?"

Everyone came back with negative responses.

Soolchakan looked a little baffled. He slowly turned his head towards the woman who asked the question. "E...evolved? What is evolved?"

Now Upton looked a little baffled. "Evolution! You know, how the higher life forms, over several million years and several million generations, evolved from lower life forms, into the beings that we are today."

He looked a little sick. "Is this...an attempt...at humor? What makes you think that...*your* ancestors were...what did you say...lower life forms?"

"Are you trying to tell me...that, as you called yourself - an Owlam? You and your kind...just appeared on the scene? Did all of the other races, on your planet, just appear out of nowhere?

I'm sorry, Sir, but you had to come from somewhere. You can't just pffft from out of nothing...and there you are...a fully grown Owlam...with this 25% male and 75% female. Your ancestors had to come from somewhere...or something."

Soolchakan stared at her totally bewildered. "You're serious?" He looked around at the other faces. "You people...are serious...about this...evolved?"

Upton looked a little more upset. "Whatever you are, your ancestors had to be just like you...for several generations. They had to come from somewhere or something. Are you going to try to say that your people, the Owlam, have always been Owlam, ever since time began?"

"Are you saying that your people...the human beings... were...*not*?"

Upton shrugged. "All creatures, great and small, evolved from some lower form, at some time in the past - that is evolution."

Wenoto of the Thirteenth sent a message: "**This woman is serious! She actually believes in this...silly...evolved**."

Soolchakan raised his eyebrows, closed his eyes and shook his head. He sighed. He opened his eyes. "When I was born...I was born into the race of the *Heyyah*." He looked at Upton. "This is the race that is the most prevalent on the planet. I am no longer a member of the race of Heyyah, because of a weapon. This weapon...changed me...and everyone else of my...race...when it went off. I don't know what the original builder of this weapon called it, but I...we call it...a firestorm weapon or genetic bomb. When it went off, it changed...me and my Owlam colleagues. It made…many new species…all over the planet."

Milch shook his head. "We're gonna need a *lot* more information on that particular incident. It sounds incredible."

"Yes…," said Soolchakan staring down at the table. "…I'm not surprised…that you'd want to hear that…time of our history. Before those…genetic bombs…went off…we were all one race - one species - the Heyyah." He looked around the table at all of the faces. He knew he had their complete attention. "Before I start telling you about what happened, maybe I should introduce you… to my wives. They'll confirm what I'm saying."

Milch smiled. "Oh, by all means, let us meet them. How can we get them aboard the ship?"

Soolchakan smiled. He tilted his head back and closed his eyes. Bonarain Jumped to the conference room. As soon as she appeared, the intruder alarm went off.

Milch ordered the intruder alarm to be turned off.

Chyning appeared next. Again the intruder alarm went off

Again, Milch ordered the intruder alarm to be turned off.

Kiyalee now Jumped to the conference room. Again the intruder alarm went off.

Again, Milch ordered the intruder alarm to be turned off.

Bonarain was rather upset about this call for her to appear here. She had three newborns to take care of and she did not like being here instead of there. She made sure that she could not be understood by the humans in the room by using a language that only the Owlamites knew.

Soolchakan glared at her and she stopped talking. He closed his eyes and sat there very still. All three women jerked their heads and stood motionless with their eyes closed. "**We're going to talk to them together. We're going to do this**." After about thirty seconds, all four opened their eyes.

Emerson leaned over to Milch. "I believe that they're communicating telepathically. We won't be able to find out anything from that."

Milch looked at Emerson. "We just found out that they can communicate telepathically. That *is* something."

Bonarain looked around somewhat disgusted. "May we have a place to sit?"

"Oh…yes," said Milch as he stood up.

Milch signaled to Angelo who quickly produced some chairs for the three women. He pulled them up to the table trying to smile and be as polite as possible. The three women sat down, glaring around the room at their hosts.

Soolchakan stood up. "Let me introduce my wives. The one in blue, is Bonarain. The one in yellow is Kiyalee and the one in green is Chyning." Each one of the women bowed their head slightly as she was introduced. He looked down at the three women smiling. "Be sweet…or else!" All three snarled back. He sat down. "I don't know if the words translated or not… if they didn't, let me do some translation for you. My name is Soolchakan. In our language, that means: Scholar. Bonarain, her name translated is: Beneficial. Kiyalee is Stormy and Chyning is Cunning. I notice that all of you have…more than one name. After looking at some of your history, I understand why. We don't do this practice…any more…or at least not at this time. We used to…but…it became irrelevant. I used to be known as: Scholar, son of Treecutter and Nice. Now…Scholar is enough."

Montalvo frowned. "Why did you drop it?"

"Because no one…of this day and age, has any clue who Treecutter and Nice were."

"They're still your parents."

"Yes, but they were Heyyah. Now, I am not."

Montalvo looked around at the other people at the table. "This conversation…is getting a little strange. You say that you were born into one species…and now are another species - how could this…possibly happen?"

The four Owlam all looked a little saddened and somewhat disgusted.

Bonarain looked at Soolchakan. "Should we each tell our own rendition of what happened, or are you going to tell it all yourself?"

"I'll tell it," he said despondently. "It's something that we haven't thought about…in a very long time." He looked at Bonarain and scoffed. "Maybe if we tell them what happened to us…they'll give up this ridiculous ideology of…evolved."

Milch cleared his throat. "You have our undivided

attention."

Soolchakan described the fragmented governmental system that was all over Hardooth. He described how they warred against each other and accomplished nothing positive for several centuries. He described the sophisticated weaponry and defensive systems. "Anyway, let's get to that fateful day…so long ago. That day when we ceased to be Heyyah and became…Owlam Elf…we are called Owlam Elf because that's where our race…began. The Axswain Elf came from the city of Axswain, the Kalash Elf from the city of Kalash, the Galsino Elf from the city of Galsino…and so on."

"Excuse me," said Montalvo. "You use this word "elf" as if it means something. We use that word as well, but, maybe it means something different…in our respective tongues. What exactly does…elf…mean in your language?"

Soolchakan looked puzzled. He looked up contemplating for a few moments. "It means…something that has mutated: Any animal, organism, cell, or gene that has mutated. Undergoing or resulting from genetic mutation. Why, what does the word mean to you?"

Montalvo pulled out his pad and made an entry. "According to our definition, of the exact same word, it means: Small supernatural mischief-maker: in folklore, a small lively imaginary being resembling a human with pointed ears, often considered to have a mischievous nature and magical powers."

Soolchakan looked a little perturbed. "Imaginary?"

Bonarain looked at Chyning in a patronizing manner.

"Mischievous?" She cleared her throat and shook her head.

Kiyalee just sat there giggling.

Chyning looked up at the ceiling, sucked her lips in and blushed.

The crew of the ship sat there wondering for a few moments why the reactions by the three women. Apparently it had something to do with the history of those women, however, diplomacy dictated they should not ask...yet.

"Yes," said Montalvo. "The word is pronounced the same, in both of our languages, but, the definition is *so* different. Mutation in your language, and a mythical sprite in ours."

"The word *elf* also is the number eleven in one of our Earth languages," added Milch.

Soolchakan cleared his throat. "We may have to do some other comparisons...later on."

Montalvo nodded with a smile. "Yes, I certainly hope we will."

Soolchakan started the oration of that particular evening at the wall watch station. He did not give any indication of his drunkenness or soiling his linen...or any of the mistakes made by the women. He explained how there would normally be at least ten personnel on duty, however, because of the fact that Command Central was expecting some kind of attack from the north, this watch station, facing west, would be on minimal crew for the night. He embellished somewhat in telling how he and the three women all came in and prepared for their duties without any problems.

Kiyalee gave Soolchakan a sideways glance. **"Why don't you pile it on deep? You make it sound like we're perfect."**

Chyning grunted. **"Do you want us to tell them how much you fouled things up?"**

Bonarain glared at both of them. **"Hush! We all made a lot of silly mistakes. They don't need to know any or all of that."**

Soolchakan told of how the power just shut down completely and then the blinding flash of light that occurred.

Milch broke in. "That sounds like an electromagnetic pulse that precedes a nuclear explosion."

Shalam started sending. **"I don't know what a nuclear explosion is but he seems pretty sure of himself."**

Milch went on to talk about alpha and beta particles – which left all of the Owlamites even more confused. The Captain told them a little more of his knowledge of a nuclear explosion.

Shalam sent another message. **"According to what he's thinking, his race used that kind of weapon in a war...a war where different people of his planet were warring against each other."**

Milch had his computer bring up some video from the archives. "Show the video," he said solemnly.

Soolchakan stared at the monitor with sagging shoulders

and jaw.

Bonarain looked away and sniffled.

Kiyalee stared with her jaws still clenched tight.

Chyning looked as if she wanted to be somewhere else.

Gomez crossed his arms and grunted in disgust. "You liar! What makes you think that I should believe that...*story*?"

All three women looked up with anger and hatred in their eyes. They were ready to stand up and do...who knows what.

Soolchakan closed his eyes and bowed his head slightly. **"Hold on! We'll teach this *bimyock* a lesson without killing him...or anyone else**."

All three women suddenly looked at him and then sat back down. Their gazes of sheer hatred went back to Gomez.

Soolchakan leaned forward a little. "What makes you think that I'm fabricating this incident?"

Gomez scoffed. "You said that four hundred fifty-five minor cities and one hundred twenty-six major cities were all hit by...nuclear bombs."

"Yes! That's what happened. Why're you calling ME A LIAR?"

Gomez snickered as he shook his head. "Five hundred eighty-one nuclear bombs, all going off, within a very short time frame, inside the planet's atmosphere...all over the globe...the massive gamma rays would be devastating to the entire ecology of the planet. Every form of life...plant, fish, mammal, avian, mollusk, reptile...insect...and microorganism...all of them would suffer for years, if not centuries...*if* they survived. The weather patterns would be disrupted. Plus, we'd be able to measure that kind of residual radiation - which *would* be around for a bare minimum of seventy-five years - on our sensors...*nada*! We would *see* the devastation that it would do to all of the living creatures on the planet, for at least three hundred years...again *nada*!"

Soolchakan cocked his head to the side. "Three... hundred...years. Is that all? Just three hundred years?" He snickered.

Peldom had been the one tasked to follow Gomez. **"This guy is the number one science *bimyock* on the ship. He seems very sure of what he's saying. Maybe we should find out more from him about all of this alpha and beta particles or that gamma ray stuff**."

Gomez was momentarily confused and slowed by the reaction. "Yes. At least three hundred years. I see no sign of any form of devastation, the likes of which you're describing. I see an ecology that's not suffering from any form of that kind of radioactive cataclysm. I find no high residual radiation."

Soolchakan snickered again. "Three hundred years!" He leaned forward with a somewhat sinister look on his face. "How *old* do you think I am?" He quickly held up his right hand to stop Gomez. "Before you answer that question, I want you to think of something - don't measure my age, by the way *you* age...measure it by the way *I as an Owlam* age...if you have any clue as to how I age. I'll give you a clue…each orbit of our planet around the star, Holgotho, equates to one year. Now…how old am I?"

Gomez did not look quite so cocky. He thought of how they had come across several different species who aged very slowly and lived a lot longer than any human could imagine. The way that Soolchakan had presented the question made Gomez worry a little. He needed to stall a little. "Can you give me any other clues?"

Soolchakan smiled. He looked at the three Owlam women. "Chyning, my third wife…she's the youngest of the four of us." He glared back at Gomez with an even more sinister look.

Gomez decided to give up. "I…don't have a clue…how old you…are, or how old Chyning is. You don't look…very old."

Soolchakan leaned back in his chair. "I was born in the eighth year of the tenure while Shongorath was in command of the City-State of Owlam. He was in command for five more years, after my birth." He looked at Bonarain.

Bonarain leaned forward. "After Shongorath stepped down from command, it was Olbiy who took command. I was born in the seventh year of the administration of Olbiy."

Kiyalee leaned forward. "I was born in the eleventh year of the administration of Olbiy."

Chyning cleared her throat and just sat there looking smug. "I was born in the twelfth year of the administration of Olbiy."

Soolchakan chuckled. "Olbiy stepped down from command after fifteen years. Then there was Nontoor - who took command and his administration lasted for sixteen years. I joined the military, just as Nontoor took over. I was twenty years old."

Bonarain broke in. "I joined the military in the twelfth year of Nontoor's administration. I was twenty at that time."

"I was thirty-two when she joined," said Soolchakan.

Kiyalee now took her turn. "Nontoor stepped down just before I joined the military. Joonatha became the Supreme Officer when I joined. I was twenty."

"I was now thirty-six," said Soolchakan.

"I was now twenty-four," said Bonarain.

"I joined the military, when I turned twenty," said Chyning. "It was just about one year after Kiyalee came in. Joonatha was just about to start her second year as the Supreme Officer. She was diagnosed with a very rare disease called: The Red Death. She died and Nagasoom became the Supreme Officer."

Soolchakan gave Gomez another condescending glare. "It was about three months after Nagasoom took over that...the bombs...those...weapons of mass destruction...hit. You said that the cataclysmic devastation would be evident...for three hundred years...after the bombs hit. You see no devastation. You find no...residual radiation. Now...how old do you think I, and my wives, are...seeing as how there is *no* residual radiation present and that stuff would be around for at least 300 years?"

Gomez licked his lips. "From what you're saying...you have to be at least...three hundred and thirty-seven years old...or more."

All four Owlams got a good giggle out of his response.

Gomez felt his dander rising. "What...too much?"

Soolchakan turned to Chyning. "You like keeping track of that. Why don't you tell him? I don't think that he'll *ever* come close to guessing the correct answer."

Chyning leaned forward looking really smug. "We have two time factors. One is the 'Unknown Times'. Everything that happened in the...'UT', was not and has not been recorded... accurately, by any historian, of this day and age. The next one is called: ATUT, After the Unknown Times. That's when the historians started recording what was going on where...and when...and to whom it happened. They keep that information in special libraries all over the planet. Anyway, the current year...is now 5599 ATUT. The four of us...we were born...during the... UT."

Gomez had been attempting to show his best poker face, with his arms folded high across his chest. Now he sat there stunned. His arms dropped to his sides and he sat there staring in shock.

Chyning's smile got bigger. "I was born in the year...-9027...UT. 9027 plus 5599...equals 14,626. *That*...is *my* age."

"I am 14,627 years old," said Kiyalee merrily.

"I am 14,631 years old," said Bonarain flatly.

"That makes me...14,643 years old," said Soolchakan. "I was a mere...37 when that horrible...*incident*...took place. You people said that the first crash, of those spaceships, on Niygool, took place approximately 13,500 years ago? It was *exactly* 13,414 years ago. I was there. I was one of the ones who brought it down on Niygool...at over 4,000 kph. I was involved in *all* of the crashes on Niygool." He put his elbows on the table. "Is fourteen...*millennium*...long enough for the...ecology to come back...from a...gamma ray cataclysm?" He gave Gomez an innocent smile.

Gomez swallowed hard. He felt his face flush. He looked around the table at some of the other people. They all seemed to be waiting for his response. "I...apologize...for my...inappropriate remark. It is...very rare that we come across a...race that...lives anywhere near as long...as you...do."

Soolchakan stared up at the ceiling and started his oration again. "When we were Heyyah, our lives would have been just as brief as yours. Since that genetic bomb...or weapon of mass destruction...went off, we don't seem to be aging at all. We just keep going on. No Owlam has ever died from...old age. Murder, war wounds, or suicide...those are the only ways that any of us Owlam have...died...in the last 14,000 years."

Milch cleared his throat. "How...did you...survive the initial blast? I mean, when a nuclear bomb goes off...it covers a massive area. It should take out an entire city."

Bonarain looked at him sadly. "The perimeter of those... horrid firestorms...didn't reach the outer wall...of Owlam. It completely...burned everything...and everyone...in the inner part of the city. The outer farming and livestock areas...were not really touched...by the blast or the firestorms. All of the people who were...outside the firestorm blast perimeter were changed...genetically. Anyone who was on duty at the perimeter watch bunkers and in the homes in the crop and livestock areas survived...but changed."

Upton looked at her in shock. "Changed...to...Owlam Elf?"

The look that the four Owlams gave Upton answered her question.

Montalvo leaned forward. He wanted to change the angry attitudes that he was seeing on the faces of the four guests. "I heard you say that the outer...farming and livestock areas were unaffected...by the firestorms. Are you saying that the area, inside the walls, had crops and livestock...farms and ranches?"

"Yes," said Bonarain. "It was necessary. If someone came along and took over any farmlands or ranches that were outside the wall...you lost them. We had to have some form of food sources inside the walls, just in case there was a siege."

Montalvo's jaw dropped. "You're telling me that the walled in area was...that big?"

"Yes." Bonarain smiled. "The Trams that were on the rail, going around the inside of the perimeter wall...if you got on one at...oh say, station one, at sunup...and you rode in that same Tram all the way back around to station one...it would be well past sundown before you got back to station one. There were two hundred sixty Tram cars on that rail and they were never close to each other at any time."

"That's quite an area," said Milch. "Were all of the major City-States that big?"

Soolchakan shrugged. "In most cases…yes."

Gomez spoke up, trying to get back 'in the good' with the Owlams. "So…anybody who was in Owlam…who was outside of the area of the destructive firestorms, ended up being changed genetically…to what you are…today. How many of you were there?"

Bonarain looked at Soolchakan. **"We're supposed to lie about this aren't we**?"

"Never let anyone know the full truth," sent Soolchakan.

"There were 7,016 survivors," said Bonarain. "5,262 women and 1,754 men. And yes…we *did* just pffft out of nowhere…as Owlams."

Milch looked a little skeptical. "How soon were you able to establish any form of hierarchy? I mean…if your main command center suffered a direct hit from the bomb, and was incinerated… who was in charge?"

Soolchakan smiled. "It was immediate. Our Supreme Officer, Nagasoom wanted to do a visual inspection of the perimeter watch bunkers himself. Instead of being at Central Headquarters, in the middle of the city, he was in one of the bunkers…facing north…towards the city of Axswain, along with all of his Staff, when the bomb hit. As soon as the power came back on…he let it be known that he was still alive…as soon as all of the panic chatter ceased." He shook his head. "He became the very first Drey Sssorg."

Now they had to explain their entire rank structure to these outworlders. Soolchakan was wondering if he was giving up too much information to these people. Not that it really mattered. If these people were actually obfuscating, then he and his children would be able to read it in their minds. So far, no one was giving any indication that they were hiding a conquering horde, just beyond Denhahbon.

Next, the oration was about some of the first Drey Sssorg and what happened to them. Soolchakan told several false renditions of what actually happened. The three women sat there without any smirks or smiles. They went along with his inventions.

Bonarain interrupted mentally. **"Should we tell them that we're completely immune to any of that...gamma ray stuff**?"

Soolchakan cleared his throat to get in his thoughts. **"No. We can keep a few things from them...if not a lot of facts**."

The three women sat there quietly smiling, again.

"I am the fiftieth Drey Sssorg," said Soolchakan. "During the administration of each of the other forty-nine Drey Sssorg... other Owlams died. Today...there are only the four of us...from the original 7,016 who survived that initial blast. We do have children...but no colleagues. So, we're doing everything we can to assure that they are not murdered, slaughtered or...abused in any way. We've made a few mistakes along the way, however, we have also discovered a few...wonderful things about ourselves and what we can do." He leaned forward. "We will protect our family. We will protect them...without any concern for anyone else. Try to hurt any of our family...and we will fight you in the only way we know how to fight our enemies...genocide."

"Others tried to fight us," said Bonarain. "They are now... extinct. The Axswain, the Cacktash, the Sodle, the Teltermak, the Gabeesh-Or, the Maka-Or, the Rakab-Rosh, the Zee-Altha, the Bising, the Twakon, the Noga-Or, the Parash-Zanab, the Neksheth-Or, the Towlayaw-Or, the Yagalom-Ayin, the Beetsik, the Perfor...and the Heyyah of the City-State of Algothon."

"I didn't hear anything about those Galsino or Kalash," said Emerson. "You've mentioned them several times as far as geographically close enemies...but you didn't say anything about wiping them out."

Soolchakan gave him a sinister smile. "They stopped attacking us...before we started the ultimate campaign of destruction against all enemies. If they ever start it up again, we will *not* hesitate to rid ourselves of those pestilences...forever. The Kalash, they seem to be like us, though. They're more interested in just, live and let live, find out what we are and leave all the others alone...while we're discovering ourselves. The Galsino... they could be a problem...someday. We will take care of any problem that comes along...when it comes."

"Including those from outer space," said Milch flatly.

"Yes," said Soolchakan with a smile.

"Going back to that one thing you referred to," said

Montalvo. "…this thing about how you could make someone do something…by just thinking about it and they would unconsciously do it. According to what I heard, you could make someone commit suicide. How do you control your temper…that well?"

Soolchakan took in a deep breath and let it out slowly. "Believe it or not, I am in contact with all of the other forty-nine Drey Sssorg. They have all said that they don't want to come back…if we had a way of bringing them back…but they do help advise me…on many things. I know that's difficult for a lot of others to believe and I can't really prove it. You'll just have to take my word for it. They do help with controlling my temper… even the ones that committed suicide themselves."

Kiyalee mentally scoffed. **"You're in mental contact with all of the other Drey Sssorg? That sounds like a load of *h'oolyach*!"**

Soolchakan inhaled deeply as if in thought before speaking out loud again. **"Then let me hear you prove it wrong."**

Kiyalee sat there looking and feeling a little confused. She decided to shut up for a while.

Bonarain frowned. **"Only one of them committed suicide. You make it sound as if there were several."**

Soolchakan cleared his throat again. **"They don't know that."**

The next part of the oration included how the Drey Sssorg Till had educated all of them regarding outer space. He was the one who had them search the skies for any form of life out there.

When it did come, as invaders, they were all dispatched in a genocidal manner.

The question was asked as to how the Owlamites could possibly take over a ship that they knew virtually nothing about, technologically.

Bonarain let loose with an evil laugh. "We took over. We started stealing just about anything and everything that we thought we could use. They were absolutely mystified as to how all of their systems were going crazy and all of their equipment was disappearing…then they were no longer in control of the ship… and we flew it on a suicide flight…directly into Niygool." She chuckled again. "Boom," she said quietly. "It was somewhat satisfying to see the look of horror and fear on their faces. Fearless conquerors who were losing control of their bowels…as the ship got closer and closer to the moon. Moments before impact, we all went back to Hoyani Kel…and departed the ship."

Milch tried to ask something and had to stop and clear his throat first. "Uh…where…did…these people come from? Who were they?"

Soolchakan laughed and shook his head. "Who cares? They came here to search out an inhabited planet that they could conquer. They found an inhabited planet and started mapping it. We took over and got rid of them…before they could do any more damage than they had already done."

Montalvo was a little curious. "What about others of their race? Did others come…at a later date…and try searching this system…again?"

Soolchakan shrugged. "Who knows? We've never taken an inventory of the would-be-attackers, to see if any of them were second timers...or third timers. Anyone who comes here as a conqueror, gets to visit one of our other planets...the wrong way."

Again Emerson came in. "All of those different species... coming from all kinds of different places...how were you able to figure out all of the different...technological systems...without any foreknowledge of that or any system like it?"

Soolchakan smiled. "Learn the entity, learn the language, learn the systems...take over...simple."

"But...just the four of you..." Emerson stammered. "How?"

Soolchakan looked up and closed his eyes. "Bikaropin... Shalam...I need you to show yourselves."

Two new Owlam men were now standing in the conference room. Again the intruder alarm went off.

Milch ordered the intruder alarm to be turned off completely...until further notice.

With a big smile on his face, Soolchakan addressed the two newcomers. "Do you think that you'd have any problems, taking control of and flying this ship?"

"Not a problem," said one.

"Very easy," said the other.

"Thank you," said Soolchakan.

The two newcomers disappeared.

"There's a lot more than four of us," he said with a big smile.

Milch let a small growl come out of his throat. "Just…how many of you…are on board?" He cleared his throat nervously.

Soolchakan chuckled. "Let's go back out on your bridge."

Soolchakan, Milch and Emerson all walked out to the bridge.

Again Soolchakan chuckled.   "My children…show yourselves."

Immediately the population on the bridge, more than doubled. There was at least one Owlamite standing near every crew member on the bridge. Some of the female Owlamites had small children with them. All of the crew members were staring at all of the new comers with stunned silence.

Soolchakan looked at Milch with a smug smile. "You can tell Boris that you found the source of all that excess carbon dioxide."

Milch gave Soolchakan a weak smile, turned his head away and groaned.

Soolchakan looked back out over the bridge. "You may go back to your chores, my children."

All of the Owlamites disappeared. All of the crew members were looking around - some with apprehension, some with fear, some with disgust, some with gloom - all with some form of trepidation.

Again Soolchakan looked back at Milch. "You have absolutely no secrets from us. The fact that we have not found any…conquering ways in your logs…is the only reason that you people are still alive. You came here to watch us, and during that operation, we are watching you. I believe that you have a legal term…what is it…oh yes, *Quid Pro Quo*."

"Yes, we do," said Milch nodding with a helpless smile. "Yes, we certainly do."

Once they were back and seated, Montalvo spoke up: "You say that the four of you…are over 14,000 years old. If you are that old…the population of your race should be…in the multi-millions…but I don't find any of you…anywhere on the surface."

"We hide rather well," said Soolchakan. "We don't want to be found. All of the conquerors…be they local or from somewhere else, have been fooled by the fact that we hide. We also hide because we have been hunted. In each case, once we figured out who the hunter is…we destroy them, without hesitation. Whether or not it's an individual or an empire…we destroy them."

"I can understand that, however, your numbers…how do you hide that many people so completely?"

"I've told you why we hide. How and where is none of your business. I will tell you that our…*numbers*…are not as high as you may think. Because of our longevity, we don't practice procreation…very much."

"How do you stop them? I mean, young people of almost

every race that we have encountered…they start maturing and their hormones go wild and they want to experiment…with sexual encounters."

"I don't allow them to…experiment."

"How do you stop them?"

"By the power of Drey Sssorg!"

"That…power…that power is that strong?" Montalvo looked flabbergasted.

"All Owlam obey the power. Whether they like it or not - they obey!"

"What's the earliest age that…you allow them to…wed and procreate?"

"None of them are allowed to mate until they reach a minimum age of 95 years old."

"You're telling me that this Drey Sssorg power…can keep their raging hormones under control…for 95 years?"

"Their hormones don't start getting…in a rage…until they're at least 65 years old. We age very slowly…even as children. We also require an outside stimulation, before any hormones can start raging."

Gomez started snickering. "No youth needs any outside source to get interested, sexually, in the other adolescents around them." He shook his head with a sneer on his face. "Plus, you're telling me that they're not interested, in any way, shape or form, until they're 65 years old, that's pure nonsense. They *all* start getting interested after they hit twelve years old."

Soolchakan scowled at Gomez. "Maybe among your species, but *not* with mine."

"What," scoffed Gomez? "Is it because you tell them not to? Is that Drey Sssorg that powerful?"

Soolchakan sat there with his eyes shut for a few moments. **"Mahanee, I need you in this conference room on the spaceship. Bring your three youngest children with you when you come**."

Mahanee grunted in disgust. She was already on the ship looking over a few things in the computer. **"You'll have to wait a bit. I'm on the ship. I have to go back and get my girls. I'll be there as quick as I can**." She Jumped back to the gorge, gathered her three youngest, hopped to Spy and Jumped to the conference room. **"Do I make some grand entrance or do you want me to just show up**?"

"Just appear with the girls."

Bonarain looked a little upset. **"I thought Mahanee was watching the triplets. If she isn't...who is**?"

Mahanee came back with a response. **"Hisang**."

Bonarain looked a little less upset now.

Suddenly a female Owlam with three younger girls appeared in the room. "What's going on? Why did you want me...and these specific three of my children?"

Soolchakan calmly looked at the ceiling. "Please introduce

yourself…and your three children."

She grunted in exasperation. "I am Mahanee of the Fourth." She placed her hand on the head of the tallest girl. "This one is Anahaya of the Fifth." She placed her hand on the head of the middle one. "This one is Yanvani of the Fifth." She placed her hand on the head of the smallest. "This one is Xahayi of the Fifth." She placed her fists on her hips. "Now, what's going on?"

Soolchakan snickered. "They don't believe us…about certain things."

"What things?"

Soolchakan closed his eyes. **"They don't believe that we age slowly. They are of the opinion that we age at the same rate they do. We have to convince them that your children are not all toddlers. I believe that the eldest of the three is older than any of the Earthlings in this room**."

Mahanee stood there staring at him. Her expression changed several times as he was updating her, telepathically. She had a condescending look on her face as she glanced around the room at each one of the crewmembers of the ship. She scoffed. She looked up at the ceiling and started scratching her chin. "Oh really," she said in a disdainful manner.

"Yes," said Soolchakan flatly. He turned his gaze to Gomez. "Okay Mister Know-it-all, take a look at the three girls and tell me how old you think each one is."

Gomez looked at Soolchakan and shook his head in disgust.

He turned to the three girls. "The youngest one...I'd say that she's just past the toddler age. She's probably four years old...at best."

All three girls fought hard to keep from laughing out loud.

Gomez looked a little confused, however, tried to keep his composure and go on with the guessing. "The middle one...she looks to be about...oh say seven or eight...nine at the most."

All three girls were now having an even more difficult time at attempting to not laugh out loud.

Gomez figured that this was some trick so he kept on. "The oldest one is...probably twelve or thirteen, fourteen at most."

The two youngest now did laugh out loud. The oldest turned aside, and giggled with her hand over her mouth.

"They don't agree with you," said Soolchakan flatly. "Again you've made the mistake of thinking in terms of how *your* species ages." He looked at the three girls and smiled. "Xahayi, how old are you, my dear?"

Xahayi clasped her hands in front of her, puffed her chest out and proudly exclaimed: "I'm fifteen years old."

All of the ship's crewmembers gawked in shock at this revelation.

Soolchakan chuckled slightly. "What is your interest in boys...at this time?"

Xahayi looked a little confused. Her arms dropped to her sides. "Uhm...as far...as...what?"

"A mate," said Soolchakan flatly.

Her shoulders and lower jaw sagged. "I...I...I'm only... fifteen! A mate? That won't...that's not...at least eighty years from now! I'm only fifteen...I won't..." she looked at her older sisters a little confused. She turned back to Soolchakan. "Why?"

"We have someone here who does not believe certain things about our race."

Her brow furrowed. "Like what?"

"We'll explain it to you later, my child." Soolchakan now turned to the middle one. "Yanvani, how old are you?"

With a big grin on her face, she said: "I'm thirty-eight years old."

It did not seem possible, however, Gomez now had his eyes and mouth open even wider.

"What do you think about boys...as far as mating?"

She giggled and shook her head. "That don't happen...not at my age...not for another..." She looked up thinking. "...fifty-seven years...at least."

"Thank you," said Soolchakan with a smile. Now he turned to the oldest who had her lips clenched tight in a grin. "Anahaya, he said that you look about fourteen...what is your age, my child?"

She snorted through her nose, attempting to stifle a laugh. She stood tall and sniffed. "I'm sixty-three years old."

Gomez leaned his head back with his eyes closed and just shook his head, still slack-jawed.

"What have you thought about, so far, with boys and mating?"

She stood there with her mouth wide open. She threw her arms out. "I...I'm not ready...my body...not ready. I need to mature...physically and mentally...before I think anything about...mating and...having a baby! Taking care of a baby... and...being with a mate."

"Thank you," said Soolchakan. He turned to Gomez. "Hey! Mister brilliance! How old do you think their mother is?"

Gomez looked as if he was nauseous. He took in and let out a deep breath. He shrugged. "I...dunno." He took a look at her. He looked back at Soolchakan. "1,000? 2,000? I dunno."

Mahanee stood there with her fists on her hips and a smug look on her face. "My oldest daughter - Hisang - was born in the year 599 ATUT. *She* is now 5000 years old."

Gomez looked off dejectedly. "Of course she is," he said gloomily. "Why not?" He sighed and hung his head.

The zoologist, Upton, decided to try to get some of the tenseness out of the room. "Uh, excuse me, but...I'm noticing something about your ears."

Soolchakan gave her a smug look. "Yes?"

"Well...your ears...the four of you...who call yourself the first generation...your ears are...so much larger than any of the other…Owlams that have come into the room. Is there a reason for this?"

Kiyalee chuckled. "Our ears never stop growing. They grow *very* slowly, however, they do grow. The larger the ears, the older the Owlamite."

"Oh, I see," said Upton. "Would it be…possible to see a… newborn? That'd give us a real good example of this…growth." She sat there with a weak smile.

Bonarain sucked in a deep breath, glared at Upton and then at Soolchakan. Her eyes darted back and forth from Upton to Soolchakan, while her breathing was coming in and out quickly through clenched teeth. She could not even think right now.

Soolchakan stared at Bonarain with no emotion on his face at all. "Like any mother, my dear wife Bonarain is very protective of her children. Especially the newest ones."

Bonarain's expression got even angrier. "You're not…"

"Yes I am," said Soolchakan firmly. "They just want to see the ears. If these people, even attempt, any harm to your babies… our babies…I give you permission to wreak *havoc* aboard this ship."

Milch put his hands up in a form of surrender. "No one is even going to think about harming any babies! Absolutely no one on this ship wants to harm babies…not at all. Your children are safe here on this ship. If anyone tries to…or even looks as if they're going to harm your babies, I will wreak havoc on that, or those, persons…myself…without hesitation."

Bonarain still glared at Soolchakan. Her fists and her teeth were clenched tightly. She closed her eyes for a moment. Three female Owlams appeared, each holding a small sleeping baby in their arms.

Soolchakan spoke quietly. "I would like to introduce you to three of our newest additions to our...extended family. Two girls, Nabtami and Nabtemi, and the boy Nabovon."

"They're beautiful," said Kasaki.

"Oh, they're so cute," said Aua. "How old are they?"

"Yes," said Upton, "I can see the difference in the ears. Rounded tops, very narrow at the base and much smaller lobes. So...later in life all that grows out?"

"Yes," said Bonarain through clenched teeth, looking around for any threat at all. "Like all Olwams, their ears will get larger...and they're exactly fifty-five *days* old." Her angered gaze went to Doctor Lewis. "What are you doing?"

Lewis cleared his throat. "I...uh...it's my duty...to do a quick...scan, uh...medical scan on anyone new arriving on the ship. It doesn't hurt them, it just...looks for any...sickness in them, or possibly a...parasite on them. I assure you, they are *not* being harmed."

"Stop scanning," snarled Bonarain in a threatening manner through clenched teeth!

Lewis shut the scanner off and put it away. He gave her a bit of a guilty smile as he did so. "My apologies, dear lady. I absolutely meant no harm of any sort. I'm a medical doctor and one of my sacred vows is: First of all - do no harm. Uh, whose... babies...are they?"

"I live by no such vow," said Bonarain menacingly. "I kill anything that I think is going to harm my babies...and they're all three mine!"

Kasaki looked at Bonarain with admiration. "Triplets?"

Bonarain glared back at Soolchakan. "All right! They've seen them! Can I send them back now?"

Soolchakan gave her an understanding smile, closed his eyes and nodded assent. The three newcomers, with babies, vanished.

Milch yawned involuntarily.

Soolchakan noticed the yawn. "Why don't you go to your bed? Get some rest. We'll continue this discussion later, after you're...bedtime."

"Thank you," said Milch through blurry eyes. "I appreciate that. While this is all incredibly interesting, I must admit that I am very tired."

Soolchakan sent a mental message. "**Everyone hop to Spy. Let them think we've gone home**."

All of the Owlams in the room vanished.

Milch yawned again. "We all have a little something to contemplate - from this first encounter. Go contemplate, while I go get some sleep. Everyone, *except Gomez,* is dismissed."

The other people filed out of the room. Gomez sat there staring off into space. Finally it was just the two of them.

"You're an idiot," growled Milch!

Gomez looked at Milch with surprise and anger on his face. "I'll have you know that my IQ is…"

Milch leaned towards Gomez and yelled as loud as he could. "SHATTUP!" He sat back in his chair glaring at the surprised face of Gomez. "IQ is meaningless. You have all kinds of book sense, but you have absolutely no *common* sense. What kind of stupidity was that, calling someone who could, without us even knowing it, take over this ship and slam us into a…grave where no one could find us or even trace us in a gas giant?"

"From the information he had given us and the readings that we had, he was not telling the truth…I got the truth out of him!"

"There are more tactful and diplomatic ways of saying it!"

Gomez was getting angry as well. "Like what?!"

Milch held his arms out in thinking. "Oh, something like: Excuse me, but the readings that we're getting tell us that this mass detonation of all those nuclear bombs…had to have happened a long time ago - how long ago *did* this battle take place?" He leaned forward. "And you say it in a nice manner. You DON'T *ACCUSE*!"

Gomez got even angrier. "What's your problem?! I got the truth out of him…don't you like the truth? Don't you…?"

Milch stood up and leaned towards Gomez with his fists on the table. "QUIET!! I don't want to hear another word out of you! This has just become a one-way conversation. You keep your big mouth shut and listen! Everything that you're doing and saying is offensive with no justification for attacking those people needlessly. From now on, while we are dealing with these Owlams, you will keep your mouth SHUT! If you have a question, you submit it to me or someone, with a little more diplomatic capability, in writing." He sat back down. "You have almost as much tact as...as a rabid wolf! When we are dealing with a species like this...who have all kinds of...strange and unknown capabilities...tact and diplomacy, these are very necessary. You are a wonderful and very intelligent scientist. That's why you're in the position that you're in. You're a good scientist, but, as a diplomat, you *stink*...out loud. Stick to your science and leave the diplomatic discussions, with foreign species, to those who can talk to them without sending them into some vengeful rage."

Gomez sat there with his teeth clenched. "You mean... kissing their collective butts?"

Milch leaned forward and tried to look as sinister as possible. He spoke through clenched teeth. "If that's what it takes to get this ship and this entire crew out of this system, alive and intact... YES! You will be on your knees and you will enthusiastically be placing big wet, sloppy ones, fanatically, to whichever part of their anatomy they want kissed...however many times they want it kissed! Is that clear?"

Gomez glared back. "Yes, Sir," he growled through clenched teeth.

Milch leaned forward a little, looking even more sinister. "Dismissed," he whispered angrily.

Gomez got up and stomped out, not moving his arms, with his fists clenched tightly at his sides.

Chyning shook her head. "Kiss our buttocks? That sounds nasty and unsanitary."

Bonarain shrugged. "I think that it's some kind of acquiescence."

"It still sounds nasty," said Chyning.

A man came back in the room. "Uh...Captain...excuse me?"

Milch looked up a little surprised. He calmed himself before responding. "Doctor Lewis. What did you need?"

"I was wanting to tell you something, while it's still fresh in my mind. Something about...these Owlams."

"You want to tell me something...extraordinary...about a species that has shown themselves to be very extraordinary... already?"

Lewis chuckled. "Yes. It is..." he cleared his throat with a bit of a sour look on his face. "...an anomaly."

Milch groaned. "That word has been used *way* too much, lately."

Lewis chuckled again. "Amen! What I have is that... Soolchakan was...*is* the entity who borrowed that scanner. The

DNA is identical. He and the three women that were here…all four…did go through some kind of incredible metamorphosis. How they survived is beyond me, but, they did. The others that showed up…are something altogether different."

Milch frowned. "How so?"

"They are definitely Owlam, I have to admit that. The difference is that…whatever happened to the originals…" He waved his hands around as if he were attempting to come up with the correct phrase. "…they were able to somehow…repair… the damage. The later generations show…no sign of this genetic damage that the originals went through. Somehow…in one generation, they fixed…*everything*!"

"How can you say something like that?"

"Those three babies. Bonarain, I believe her name is, said that she was the one who was the mother of those triplets."

"Yes."

"They're…perfect!"

Milch blinked his tired eyes. "What do you mean? Newborns that are healthy, that's really nothing very new."

Lewis looked up with his eyes closed, trying to think. "Healthy! Yes, healthy." He opened his eyes. "The problem is, healthy is one thing - *perfect* is something altogether different. Perfect babies from…what I could only say…they came out of parents that are…nothing but mutated…genetic…*garbage*. What I mean is that…while some of the children that I have helped deliver, they've been healthy, but, somewhere in their body, there is…one or two…non-perfect things. There's a bone that is slightly disfigured. There's a sinew or tendon or muscle or vein or artery…some part of the body…somewhere that's…*not*…perfect. It can be possibly too long or too short or twisted or too skinny or too fat…or some…imperfection. Those babies…those triplets… don't have that problem. Not one of the three…or none of the other Owlams that showed up have any imperfections either. Some of them have scars…but that could be expected, of just about anyone over the age of two…amongst *any* race. That has nothing to do with the fact that they have figured out a way to bear children… that are one hundred percent *totally* perfect. No flaws at all. I mean…if a couple were to come to me and they were talking about infertility, but wanting to procreate…and I checked them out and found that they were as flawed as…those four Owlams…I would discourage any form of procreation at all…even cloning. In my professional opinion, any…offspring would be…nothing but an amorphous mass that…would have no chance of survival…or any possibility of a normal life." He shrugged. "But *their* children… they show no signs of any of the mutated mess that their parents are and…I have no rational explanation for that conundrum at all."

Milch stared at Lewis through bleary eyes. "I'm so tired that I can hardly stand up and you had to hit me with something like that…now. Excuse me, but, I'm going to bed right now. Redo your information. Look it over again. Remind me of that…rather odd and interesting information…later! Good night, Doctor."

Lewis backed out of the doorway smiling. "Good night, Captain."

Soolchakan turned his gaze slowly to Bonarain with wide-eyed awe on his face. "Did you just hear what he said?"

Bonarain shrugged. "So?"

Kiyalee scoffed. "What of it?"

Chyning just frowned.

Soolchakan shook his head and sighed. "What he said… was that…when you tell me that you repaired your children while they were still in the womb, it wasn't just some lengthening of a bone or tendon." He placed his hand on her shoulder. "You repaired them…all the way down to the molecular level. You didn't just repair them – you completely redid everything…from head to toe."

Bonarain was now staring in shock at nothing.

Kiyalee and Chyning were both staring in shock at Bonarain.

"I…did…didn't…I," stammered Bonarain. She swallowed hard. She looked at Soolchakan and then turned her gaze to the other two women. "I…did…make them…all perfect. I made them…perfect and…I taught you two…how to make them perfect as well."

Kiyalee tried to say something but could not. She cleared her throat loudly twice. Finally she got it out. "Thank you for… helping me make my babies…*perfect*."

Chyning was still dumbstruck. She just nodded with her mouth hanging open.

Soolchakan snickered as he shook his head. "They said

that they had some things to contemplate. We've got something to contemplate as well."

Bonarain nodded slightly. "We made our...second generation so perfect that...we see no...mutations...or deformations...even to the twenty-third generation."

"I think that you need to keep on teaching this...wonderful thing...to all the women," said Kiyalee. "Just to make sure that... there never are any...deformities."

Bonarain just nodded.

"Let's go back to the gorge and contemplate over a nice hot mug of kwatha," said Chyning. "I'm getting hungry."

No one argued with that thought. They all Jumped.

13

The first quartet was sitting in the conference room on the outworld spaceship in Spy. They were waiting for all of the Earthlings, or whatever species happened to enter the room, to come in for the next meeting.

The first one to come in was the one named Montalvo (along with Rom of the Eighth). The one named Upton came in next (along with Wenoto of the Thirteenth). The tall man Milch came in (with Shalam of the Second), followed rather soon by that mouthy Gomez (with Peldom of the Third).

Peldom smiled at Soolchakan. "He's got some questions that he wants to ask, but, that Milch told him that he couldn't talk to us directly. He's going to write them down for somebody else to ask."

Soolchakan chuckled at the consternation of Gomez.

Chyning gave Soolchakan a nasty look. "Can I steal something from that Gomez?"

Soolchakan just glared at Chyning. She grunted and leaned back in her chair sulking - again.

Doctor Lewis (with Odan of the Third), the Physicist

Jones (with Ohar of the Eleventh) and Astrophysicist Smith (with Lasolker of the Ninth) came walking in, each with a cup of some aromatic brew in their hands.

"I wonder what that stuff is that they're drinking," said Kiyalee.

"They call it coffee," said Odan.

"They have all kinds of strange ways of drinking it," said Lasolker. "Some put white powders in it, others add different colored liquids to it. Some add different smelling liquids...as well as different flavored liquids."

Bonarain shrugged. "Some kind of liquid refreshment where...each one can flavor it to their own taste...I guess."

Lasolker nodded and shrugged. "I guess."

Yeoman Aua came in (with Inmoa of the Thirteenth). She got a different orange colored drink from the food dispenser and drank it down quickly.

Inmoa watched Aua guzzle her drink. "This stuff isn't hot like that coffee. They call it orange juice."

Kiyalee scoffed. "How mundane. An orange liquid named orange juice. Not very creative with that one, are they."

The three security personnel came in, Emerson, Avery and Eli, and took their stations (along with Sonshuk of the Seventeenth, Broltish of the Ninth and Worpono of the Seventh).

Sonshuk looked around. "Getting a little crowded in here, isn't it?"

Emerson walked up to Milch. "When do you think our…"

At that moment, Soolchakan, Bonarain, Kiyalee and Chyning all appeared in their seats.

Emerson's expression turned to one of aggravation. "…guests will arrive," he muttered? He cleared his throat and looked up at the ceiling.

Milch answered with a wan smile, a shrug and a mild chuckle. "How about now?"

"We never really left," said Soolchakan smugly. "Bonarain was the only one who left the ship…a couple of times…to take care of her very young triplets."

The pathologist, Schmitz, came rushing into the room (along with Ubok of the Fifth). He looked around with a bit of a guilty look on his face. "Sorry, I'm a little late…I was doing…" He cut himself off shook his head and took his seat.

Soolchakan turned to Milch. "All right! What needs to be covered today?"

A small light came on, directly in front of Milch. He looked down at his small monitor - Gomez had a question. Milch quickly read the question. He looked at Soolchakan with as friendly a face as he could muster. "We put a planet crawler on…the fourteenth planet. It suddenly showed up, back in the storage bay. We were wondering if you…were the one who put it back there."

Soolchakan smiled. "No, that was Kazil and Falchon. They were being a little mischievous. Normally, we would have thrown that thing into Serani Tan. They decided to put it back…

from whence it came…until we had a better look at you people and determined your exact policies…in regards to our home world."

"I was wondering," said Montalvo, "…you talk about some of the technology that you had…during your…wars of the past. A lot of advanced offensive and defensive technology. Now, we see none of that. What happened…if you don't mind my asking…to all of that technology? Why did you digress?"

Bonarain sent to the others. "**Oh, *h'oolyach*! What're we gonna tell them about that**?"

Soolchakan responded quickly. "**Just make up a bunch of lies and keep track of the lies we told them. Shalam… keep some notes!**"

Shalam was standing there giggling. "**Can do. I may need a lot of help from all of the others in the room, in order to keep all of the *h'oolyach* properly compartmentalized, but it'll get done.**"

Soolchakan lowered his head, closed his eyes and let his breath out slowly…in order to buy some time while they were sending telepathic messages. He tried to appear as solemn as possible. "We made up our minds, a long time ago, that nothing, *nothing*…like those…genetic bombs, would ever be manufactured again. We took all of that technology and either destroyed it…or hid it. We watch over our planet. If we find anyone who starts developing, or looking into the advancement of science…we stop them. There will never be another…what did you call it…nuclear bomb? *Not* on this planet."

"That's also why we stop any out-world intruder from

bringing that stuff here and changing our world," said Kiyalee flatly. "We saw what those things do. We don't want another… nuclear cataclysm."

"But…" Montalvo looked a little perturbed. "You are denying…all of those other people…any kind of advancement. How do you justify that?"

Chyning grunted in anger. "**Nosy *bimyock*! What difference does that make to you**?"

Soolchakan looked thoughtful for a moment. He wanted to admonish Chyning, but decided against it. "I once heard someone say: Everything happens for a reason. If *that* is true, then there was a reason that we - the Owlamites - have been selected, for a reason, to be what we are. We have, what most species would consider, an incredible longevity. We have powers where we can stop others on our planet from developing any new…nuclear devices. We also have a tremendous capability of protecting our planet from species whose technology is far beyond anything we ever had here…initially. Even after 14 millennium, we're still learning new things about ourselves. We are protectors and watchers. We have successfully stopped over 400 different out-world intrusions from claiming and enslaving our planet as part of their empire."

Kiyalee looked a little perturbed. "**Shalam, write that down quick! Over 400? Where'd you get that line of *h'oolyach* from**?"

"**Make it sound bigger and more heroic than what it really was**," sent Soolchakan. "**That way, they can't argue**

with the fact that we're protecting ourselves from a lot of enemies."

Montalvo was adamant. "You still deprive the others, of any advancement."

"We protect ourselves and we have the capability to do so. Some of those who've come up with *advancements*, have tried to use these things against us. It always seems to be the smartest, most inventive, most creative, most arrogant and ambitious who want to go after *us*…the Owlamites. A lot of them don't even know that we still exist. The ones who find out…who are ambitious beyond belief…we become one of, if not their first target, in an effort to obtain global domination. If somebody attacks us - we fight back - with everything we have. I have had to bury some of my children in the past. *That*…will *not* happen again if I have anything to say about it. Anyone who attacks my children…I kill! I kill without any thought to the survival of the enemy or their culture…or *their* children. If they feel that the only way that they can advance themselves or survive is to try to kill, or enslave, me…I kill them. Then, I and my children, are safer."

Montalvo looked down and grunted. He looked back at Soolchakan. "Like…who?"

"The Teltermak," said Kiyalee through clenched teeth. "We had a war with them…once. In defeating them, we were merciful in the aftermath, and allowed them to continue to exist. Centuries later…they came after us again. So, the last time, we handled them in a way that it won't happen again…" She smiled. "…genocide!"

Chyning added her opinion: "They were attacking and killing us, the Owlamites, to obtain certain of our internal organs for their appalling cuisine. They didn't ask, they didn't explain, they just killed some of us without any conscience. They carved out these *chosen* organs and left the body to rot. All for their disgusting dining pleasure."

Montalvo shook his head. "But...wasn't that the children of the ones that you defeated? I mean, why didn't you try to make a...merciful peace with them?"

Chyning was really getting upset. "**Change the subject, you *doovoft*! We've already told you why**."

Bonarain spoke in a scolding manner. "It wasn't *their* children! The Teltermak, like us have...uh...*had* a longevity that hadn't been established as to how long they actually live. While our hair hasn't turned gray, the Teltermaks, that we warred on the second time, were the same ones, only with graying hair. They didn't learn anything from their defeat in the first war...except how to be a lot sneakier."

Emerson let his curiosity get the best of him. "So, who were all of these people that you destroyed? Did they all commit the same outrage...against your race?"

Soolchakan looked thoughtful for a moment. "The Heyyah of Algothon were the first to go. They were the ones who invented that...*thing*! They also invented the rockets that carried the bombs to each of the cities. We found out that when they launched all of those rockets, they waited for a very windy day. That way, all of the smoke would be blown away...from them, towards the city of Shan-Ad." He chuckled. "A lot of the different Elf races said that that is why the Shan-Ad have such a nasty attitude...towards everybody - they were breathing all of the smoke from all of those launches *and* they got hit with one of the bombs as well."

Bonarain looked off to the side, doing everything she could to keep from slapping Soolchakan. **"Shalam, write that down! He's already gone way out of the sequence of events. It won't pay to come back and tell them something different later on."**

Montalvo finished making a few annotations on his pad. "Did all of the others make war on you?"

"Some, yes," said Soolchakan looking off into space angrily. "They came at us and tried to kill us or claim our guts or property...or they were mad at us because we had a skill that they didn't have...or they were just plain hateful as well as overly ambitious in attempting global domination."

"Some of them thought that *we* were the troublemakers and needed to be eliminated," said Bonarain with disdain. "They said that we were too dangerous and should not be allowed to live. Since they passed that judgment on us, without really knowing us, or any form of a trial...we took them out."

Montalvo sat there in shock. "You mean, someone just... came up to you, announced that they thought you were a danger and started...just killing?"

"No," said Soolchakan with a little disgust of his own. "They came to us and said that we should all line up, in a neat and orderly fashion and that they would be merciful in the way that they exterminated us...*if* we didn't agree to be their slaves."

Bonarain gave a loud grunt of repulsion. "One time, we thought that it was just one race of Elf. We found out as we were exterminating them, mercifully or not, that it was two different species. It was the Beetsik and the Towlayaw-Or. They looked similar. They both had skin that was a brilliant scarlet. That's why, at first, we thought they were one identical species. Then we found out the difference between the two races was height. The Beetsik were about...what do you call it - decimeters?"

"Yes," said Milch. "We usually talk about a person's height in decimeters."

Bonarain nodded. "So the Beetsik were about thirteen decimeters in height and the Towlayaw-Or averaged about seven decimeters."

Several jaws dropped in shock.

"*Seven...decimeters?*" Milch looked around visibly shaken. "That is someone...that would just come up...to just above my knee! Thirteen decimeters is somewhere just above my waistline. How could they be such a threat...to you?"

Kiyalee cleared her throat. "Short size doesn't necessarily mean weakness. The Towlayaw-Or were very short, but...each one was incredibly, physically strong, especially for their size. They also came in a very large group. There were not that many of us at that time. They came and *commanded* us to line up for slavery or extermination. They were very nasty, regarding the fact that they especially wanted us as sex slaves. No trial, no questions...no thought of our feelings whatsoever. Just line up and serve…or die!"

Chyning was confused. **"Hold on! We destroyed the Zee-Altha before we ever even knew the Beetsik existed**."

Bonarain responded. **"If he can go *chogo* out of sequence…so can I**."

Emerson could not hold back. "Were there any other judgmental jerks like that? It seems rather stupid to just walk in and order an entire civilization to just…surrender to slavery or be slaughtered."

Chyning snickered. **"If you can make up stories…so can I**." She smiled. "A few years later, the green-skinned Bising showed up. They claimed that the Beetsik and the Towlayaw-Or had every right to come in there to kill us and that we were totally unjustified in turning it back on them. That's when it was really confirmed that it *was* two completely different races. We told them that we had a right to live, just like they did and since we gave no one the right to pass judgment like that, over us, we had the right to fight back. They had unilaterally decided that we were wrong and didn't have the right to make any decisions they did not agree with. They were, now, going to enslave or slaughter us…so we unilaterally destroyed the Bising."

Bonarain scoffed. "Yes, the Bising. Next came the Rakab-Rosh, another green-skinned bunch. This bunch, though, had shiny skin. It seems that they had been friends of the Beetsik, the Towlayaw-Or *and* the Bising. Once again, another bunch who decided that they had the right to decide our fate and that we had no say in the matter. The main thing they hollered at us was: OBEY! They condemned us all to death, for destroying those others. They commanded us to all line up for execution. *They* were dispatched…in the same manner as the others."

Soolchakan called to Shalam. **"Are you getting all of this?"**

Shalam came back snickering. **"One way or another, we're getting all of your muddled and misdirected history…or should I say: Your mangled, revisionism mythology.**"

Milch felt a little troubled. "How…were you able to… completely get rid of all of them…without suffering too many casualties among yourselves?"

"Simple," said Soolchakan whimsically. "We went to Tanani Pay. We reached through Serani Tan to Tok. We grabbed them by the back of their belt and pulled them, from Tok to Serani Tan…and let go. They die in the void of space, in Serani Tan, and their splattered remains slowly float towards that one big star." He looked at Bonarain. **"I hope he's satisfied with that.**"

Bonarain just shook her head.

Montalvo was trying to take notes as the conversation went on. "I'm a little confused…about the names that you keep calling…these different dimensions. How did you come up with the names…for each one?"

The four Owlam looked at each other a little confused.

Soolchakan shook his head. "What…do you mean?"

"You call one of them, Serani Tan, another is Tanani Pay… how did you come up with these names?"

Bonarain looked at Montalvo as if he were an idiot. "They're numbers!" She frowned. **"Don't these *bimyocks* know what numbers are?"**

"Num…what? How could they be numbers?" Montalvo now looked thoroughly confused. "But…they're not… translating." He looked at Gomez. "Is there something wrong with our translator?"

Gomez looked at Milch. Milch nodded.

Gomez cleared his throat. "It's not the translator, where we're having a problem. The problem is with speech patterns and nouns. When they're saying the name of one of those dimensions, it comes through as a proper noun and the translator doesn't translate proper nouns." He sighed. "Give me a moment, I'll see what I can do…to remedy this problem." He started tapping on his keyboard, while looking at the monitor, with several different expressions on his face. He looked up at Soolchakan. "You said that this dimension…with the one star is called Serani Tan?"

Soolchakan nodded.

"Okay, just tell me the number."

"Forty-five," said Soolchakan flatly.

"That's amazing," sent Shalam. **"The translation is being done by their technology. Truly amazing**."

"How about the one…where you can observe us?"

"That's Fifty-three."

"What do you call…this one, the primary dimension?"

Soolchakan rolled his eyes. "One."

Gomez nodded while continuing the input to the computer. "Could you please…count for me?"

"How high?"

Gomez did not look up. "Just one through ten…for the moment."

Soolchakan sighed. "Tok, saw, pay, ser, tan, hoy, nak, kel, hig, tokani."

Gomez made an entry through the keyboard. "Again please."

Bonarain counted this time. This time, however, they came through as numbers that the crew of the ship could understand.

Gomez nodded in approval. "Are there…any other…ones that you visit…on a regular basis…that you might share with us?"

Soolchakan shrugged. "108 is another one where we can observe from. That one, though we can see you but not hear you. 68 is a very strange one, in that distances are irrelevant. Then…if we want to give someone a lesson…of some kind…where we are trying to stop you from fooling around with us…we take you to 92."

Milch huffed a little. "What's so special about this…92?"

Kiyalee wrinkled her nose in disgust. "It *stinks*!"

Schmitz, the forensic pathologist chuckled. "I've come across some pretty bad smells in my time…what's so bad about this…92?"

Kiyalee looked at Soolchakan.

He closed his eyes. **"Go ahead and give him a snort of that putrid air."**

Kiyalee got an evil grin on her face. She loudly sucked air into her lungs and vanished. Schmitz let out a surprised squawk and vanished. Several moments later, the two of them reappeared in the conference room. Kiyalee let the air out of her lungs and breathed a little heavily for a few moments.

Schmitz had a look of complete revulsion on his face. He ran over to a small door on the wall (a trash chute), opened it, put his face in the opening and vomited – much to the repulsion of every person in the room. He then walked over to the food processor and ordered a cup of mouthwash. He poured the mouthwash in his mouth and sloshed it around as he walked back to the garbage chute. He spat the mouthwash into the chute. He turned back to the people in the room still looking somewhat sick. "I will never complain about the smell of a…decomposing corpse again."

Doctor Lewis chuckled. "Come on, Bob, it couldn't be that bad."

Chyning sucked air into her lungs. She vanished. A moment later Lewis got a surprised look on his face and he vanished. Several moments later both Chyning and Lewis reappeared. Chyning had a big grin while Lewis looked a little stunned. He got up and did a staggering penguin walk over to the garbage chute. He opened the chute…and threw up as well. He spat a few more times into the chute.

Bonarain looked at the grinning Chyning. "**Was that really necessary**?"

"**Necessary doesn't matter**," sent Chyning with a grin. "**It was fun**."

Lewis sighed. "I have just experienced something…that I hope I never come across again. I have just…re-defined…the word…*stench*!" His entire body shuddered as he walked over to the food dispenser, and got himself a dose of mouthwash. "I don't really think that it was the smell that made me…lose my lunch. I think that there's some kind of…natural ipecac in the air…or some other…thing…that'll make you regurgitate…in gaseous form. One good whiff…and it's…heave ho! It's still…very shocking." His entire body shuddered again.

Soolchakan looked around the room with a big merry smile on his face. "Anybody else?"

"**I wanna send that high and mighty one in charge**," sent Kiyalee.

Milch held his hands up. "On, no, no, no, no, no. If two doctors, who deal with smelly cadavers all of the time, have that kind of reaction, I don't want to know."

Kiyalee shook her head. "**Too bad**."

"That one," said Emerson, "…the one you called '68' - you said that distance is irrelevant…what do you mean by that?"

Soolchakan disappeared and reappeared right next to Emerson. He grabbed Emerson's arm and both of them vanished.

Emerson was shocked at first because he was seeing a very unclear blur of colors. The blur only lasted for a few seconds. When his vision cleared, he was looking at... "No, that's... impossible," he said in a shaky voice.

Soolchakan was still standing next to Emerson, still holding the arm. "I looked for a structure...that appeared to be... unique. This one was one of several that are...rather unique. Do you recognize it?"

"Uh-huh," said Emerson weakly as he nodded. He looked at Soolchakan, stunned. The blur of colors went past his eyes again. When his vision cleared, he was once again in the conference room. He looked at Soolchakan, a little frightened. He swallowed hard. He went back to his post, still with that look on his face.

Milch stood up. "Ivan, what's wrong...where'd you go?"

Emerson gave Milch a weak smile. "Paris! France! I was standing on a rooftop. I was...looking at the...Eiffel Tower."

Milch now looked shocked. His gaze went to Soolchakan. "You were only gone...about ten seconds. Are you telling me that you went well over 3,750 light years...and back...in a matter of... seconds?"

Soolchakan looked smug. "As I said - distance is irrelevant...in that dimension." He mentally snickered. **"That'll give them something to think about**."

Milch sat back down. "Talk about *curved* space." He shook his head. "Uhm…are there any other dimensions…that you go to…frequently?"

"Not really," said Soolchakan. "Those are the most useful. Most of the others are too unfriendly or…of very little use…to us."

Emerson, still with a confused look on his face, spoke up. "Have you found anything…living…in that…stink?"

The four Owlam looked at each other with questioning and thoughtful expressions.

Soolchakan shook his head. "No, nothing that I can remember."

"The only thing that I remember seeing it moving…" said Bonarain, "…was a strand of some kind of…hanging hairy stuff…that was being blown in those nasty breezes."

Lewis smiled weakly. "Foul smelling breezes?"

Bonarain smiled. "Very foul smelling."

Milch let a small sound come out of his throat. "All right, let's get back to these…enemies."

Kiyalee scoffed. "Which ones?"

"The…uh…ones that you say were trying to say that they had the right to just come into your homes…and order you to line up for extermination."

Chyning waggled her head a little. "We did have a short,

friendly agreement with the Kalash and the Sodle…for a very short time. It was when we…were trying to figure out what to do about the Turgons."

Montalvo perked up. "Turgons?"

Chyning looked at the other Owlamites. They were all staring back at her so she continued her oration. "When that genetic bomb went off in the city of Turgon, it turned them into mindless, destructive, carnivorous, big nasty animals. They still stand up on two legs, but, they run like the wind. They have clawed hands, they have long snouts, with big sharp teeth and a very large appetite for anything living…that is meat. We saw them attack and kill one of the big plains predators. Only two of the Turgons were killed in the fight. The remaining Turgons ate the predator… and their own dead…and injured colleagues."

Emerson was shocked. "How could you cope with them?"

"We were still under the impression, at that time, that we should live and let live, while we discovered ourselves. The Turgons were not letting anything live." Chyning cleared her throat with a look of disgust on her face. "While the Sodle and the Kalash were trying to build a wall, to keep those monsters in, we used our dimension shifting capabilities to lead them way out west on that northern peninsula on the North Chilamte continent." She shook her head. "They were taking *far* too long to build that wall, so after we got the Turgons all out there on the far western end of the peninsula, we went back and finished the wall…*our* way."

Montalvo cleared his throat. "How were you able to keep away from them…even with that dimensional capability?"

Kiyalee huffed in disgust. **"What do we have to do to convince these *doovofts* that those dimensions leave us invulnerable**?"

Chyning giggled. "We'd let them see us, we'd run a little. When they started catching up to us, we'd shift to fifty-three. We'd then move a short distance away, come back to one and the chase would be on again. Occasionally, we'd accidentally come across some indigenous creature…and that animal would become a meal for the Turgons. After they finished…lunching…the chase was on again. We kept moving them west. When we got to the far western shores of the peninsula, we had the vast majority of them there…we went back to the wall and, again, we finished building the wall…*our* way…before all the Turgons got back that far east."

They had to continue on, telling the outworlders about how they built the vaults on the large moon and give them a lesson on how they *joined* two pieces of matter together. They also had to tell the visitors about the rules and regulations at the Turgon Wall. They also gave some more information regarding how the Teltermak were utilizing the internal organs of the Owlamites, supposedly, for potions and elixirs as well as some nasty experimentation. They continued telling the stories of getting rid of enemies by throwing them into other dimensions.

Montalvo was confused. "How long did it take to…get rid of an entire population of enemies? It just seems such a massive undertaking."

"We don't have to do it one at a time," said Bonarain with a smile. "We have the capability of moving…some rather large amounts of things."

Milch looked a little confused himself. "Like…what? Or should I say how much?"

All four Owlam closed their eyes and started concentrating. An alarm went off and red lights came on in every room of the ship.

Milch immediately got on his intercom. "Bridge, this is the Captain, report!"

Kasaki came back: "We…are suddenly not where we were before. The navigational computer is trying to ascertain where we are…but…it's very confusing."

Milch gritted his teeth. "How so?"

"We can only find one star…and it…I can't believe these readings."

Milch got up and headed for the bridge. He walked in and shouted: "Captain is on the bridge! What is going on?!" He looked up at big screen. There was a star on the screen that almost filled the entire thing. "Why are we focusing so closely on that star?"

Lieutenant Leonard Truax was the one currently on duty at the helm. "There's nothing else to focus on…anywhere! That star is the only thing we can find…other than a smattering of some space dust."

The four Owlamites walked onto the bridge.

"Welcome to dimension number 45," said Soolchakan

smugly. "Now you can see how we were able to move an entire population...without them being able to do anything about it."

Kiyalee snickered. "People...you are looking at *the* largest single object in all of the 239 known dimensions. The one and only star of dimension number forty-five."

Milch cleared his throat. "How...uh large is that thing?"

"Extremely hard to determine, Sir," said Truax. "There's so much radiation coming off of that thing...even at this distance it seems to be messing with our sensors."

Shalam looked around confused. **"What happened to our supply of spare spaceships? I can't see any of them...at all. Where are they?"**

Bonarain calmed him. **"Relax. We're on the opposite side of the star. All of our goodies are a long, long way from here."**

Aya of the Second had been following the Executive Officer, Kasaki. She was just as confused as Shalam. **"When have we ever been on this side of that star?"**

Soolchakan answered. **"We came here a long time ago. Long before any of you were born. We were wondering if there was anything on this side. We thought that maybe that star was blocking our line of sight for something else. It isn't. This is why we absolutely know that there is nothing in this dimension, naturally, other than one that big star."**

Milch looked confused. "How far away are we?"

Truax gave Milch a helpless look. "Again, I can't be exact because of the radiation coming from it...but that thing is at least...33 light years away...uh...maybe 34...or 32. I don't know, because, I can't get any non-fluctuating readings."

"What?!" Milch was flabbergasted. "34 light years... and the thing is filling the entire screen? What's the current magnification factor?"

Truax swallowed hard. "The current magnification is... one."

Milch stood there gawking, slack-jawed, at the screen. He slowly turned his gaze to Soolchakan. "You...pulled the...entire ship...into this dimension? How?"

Soolchakan smiled at Milch. "The bigger the object, the more concentration and effort it takes, however it can be done, since all four of us were working at the same time."

Milch stared helplessly. "Okay. You've shown us...how you got rid of those...Zalthas."

"*Zee*-Altha!" said Bonarain impatiently.

Milch smiled. "Thank you...Zee-Altha. Would you be so kind...as to take us back...to our regular dimension?"

The four Owlam all bowed their heads. Moments later the screen blurred with static and then cleared to show they were in orbit again.

"Standard orbit...around the...Owlam home planet of Hardooth...Sir," said Truax with a shaky voice.

Milch looked back at Soolchakan. "Thank you." He let out a big sigh. "Shall we...go back to the conference room?"

"Moving the ship, back and forth, took some effort," said Soolchakan. "We need to go...get a little rest. We'll come back later."

"All right," said Milch nodding his head. "We will anxiously await your return."

All four Owlam smiled and vanished.

Milch shook his head. "Egad!"

"Really," said Truax.

Milch looked to some of the other people on the bridge. "Science section...did you record how that was done...I mean moving from one dimension to the other?"

Lt. Salisbury shook her head. "Sir, we recorded that it did happen. The computer is still trying to...compute...*how* it happened. From what I'm seeing of the results...so far...I don't expect anything...positive or educational...any time in the near future."

Milch just hung his head and grunted.

Salisbury giggled. "One thing that we do know about them now...they do get weary...from some kind of strenuous, cerebral activity."

Milch just looked up and nodded.

All of the Owlamites were in Spy dimension on the ship.

Soolchakan was sitting there with a smile on his face. "I found out what we needed to know. They can use their equipment to determine they are in a different dimension, but they can't figure out how to go to those dimensions."

Bonarain was a little confused. "Why are you letting them know that we have a weakness?"

"This isn't anything about a weakness. I just wanted to find out if they can technologically find those other dimensions. They can't. That's good enough for me. That means that we still have a powerful weapon to use against them…if anything comes up that we need it." He looked at the three women. "Now…it's time for some kwatha."

All three women glanced back and forth at each other. They all shrugged and Jumped back to the gorge for their favorite meal.

The group was back in the conference room. They were all going over their notes again. A few looked at some of the notes taken by others. They talked quietly, sipping tea or coffee. Then the four Owlamites appeared in the conference room.

Soolchakan smiled. "We're back…for whatever questions you wish to ask at this time."

Chyning looked around a little disgusted. "**Oh… h'oolyach! We didn't startle them. They must be used to this kind of entrance.**"

Bonarain gave Chyning a sideways look. "**Don't start**

any sulking again. **They might just see you doing it and...give your true self away**."

Chyning wrinkled her nose and shook her head at Bonarain.

Doctor Lewis cleared his throat. "I have...a question about you...it's something that...is really puzzling me."

Soolchakan chuckled. "What?" He sniffed. "**We could probably read his mind and get the question, but I'll give him the courtesy of asking**."

"I...scanned you - all four of you - and each one of the other Owlamites - as each one came into the conference room. I...find that it's rather strange that the four of you...seated here... your DNA it appears as if it is..." he looked off to the side trying to think of the right word. "...corrupted. The DNA of all of the other Owlamites...it seems as if it is...somehow corrected - even to the point of them...all being so...perfectly healthy. I don't understand how...all of these other Owlamites could be related to you...if their DNA is so clean and yours is..."

Soolchakan raised his eyebrows. "Dirty?"

Kiyalee raised her eyebrows. "**He better watch what he says. He might have just stepped into...a place he can't get out of**."

Lewis grimaced. "I don't...mean to sound insulting...it's just that I don't...quite understand...how. All of the markers line up, which gives me ample proof that you and they are all of the Owlamite race. The problem is...how did their DNA get corrected so perfect and they're so healthy...and yet they came...from what appears to be something that was so…corrupted by those genetic bombs?"

The four Owlam looked back and forth at each other. All four bowed their heads and sat silently for a few moments. Mentally they were looking for someone who was in the later stages of her pregnancy while hatching a plot. Soolchakan looked up. A new Owlamite appeared in the room looking a little surprised and suspicious. The new one was female and was very late in her third trimester of pregnancy. She frowned as she looked at Soolchakan.

"Please introduce yourself to these people," said Soolchakan quietly.

She put her fists on her hips and huffed. She did not look at anyone in particular. She stared off into space. "I'm Jonokee of the Seventh," she said in a rather irritated tone. "What else do you want?"

The other Owlam women looked up at her.

"The ship's doctor is going to scan you and your baby," said Bonarain.

Jonokee looked at Bonarain in anger and shock. She vanished.

Soolchakan sat there with his teeth clenched. "*Jonokee, get back here!*" His voice sounded as if it were much louder, deeper and coming from a completely different person, in a cave.

She immediately reappeared looking a little frightened, with her fists covering her mouth. She stared at Soolchakan looking like a guilty child. **"You didn't have to get nasty**

about it. I'm just trying to protect my baby."

Soolchakan went back to his normal voice. "He isn't going to hurt you. He just wants to use his instruments to look at your child."

Jonokee stammered a little and placed her hands over her abdomen. "But…wh…what if…he…hurts…my baby? Wh… what…then?"

"If he does anything…stupid or harmful…you toss him into forty-five," said Soolchakan with a smile. He then glared at the doctor.

Kiyalee and Chyning got up, walked over and stood on each side of Jonokee with their hands on her shoulders.

Kiyalee sent a message to Jonokee. "**Don't worry child. We're here to protect you and your baby**."

Soolchakan smiled at Lewis. "You may start your scans." He looked at Bonarain. "**Start your little show for him**."

Bonarain simply smiled back.

Lewis looked rather nervous. "Yes," he said anxiously. "Just scans…uh…nothing more. I'm just looking at the fetus." He walked up to Jonokee and turned his medical scanner on. He held it near her abdomen as she glared back at him. "I'm seeing that the fetus…has a defective kidney…it's the left one…I…"

At that moment Kiyalee, Chyning and Jonokee all closed their eyes and bowed their heads a little. Their heads moved a little every few moments as they were communicating telepathically.

The expressions on their faces did not change as they continued their chore. Lewis, on the other hand, was gawking at his scanner in complete shock. He was so engrossed at what he was seeing on his scanner that some spittle came drooling out of his mouth. After several moments, the three women all opened their eyes and looked at the doctor. He gave his scanner another look, chuckled helplessly, cleared his throat, swallowed hard, shut his scanner off and walked back to his seat. Kiyalee and Chyning went back to their seats. Jonokee vanished.

Milch cleared his throat in a very loud manner. "What's going on? What happened?"

All four Owlamites looked at Doctor Lewis, smiling.

Lewis looked very rattled. "I...I...scanned...the fetus... and...and I found that...the left...uh...kidney was...very... defective...er...deformed...not right...or something like that. Now...I...could help and...and...and repair the...kidney... with my medical instruments. I...uh I, however watched as... those three...did something...and the kidney was completely... repaired..." He looked at the Owlamites with fear and awe in his gaping eyes. "HOW?!"

Kiyalee just started giggling. Chyning looked towards the ceiling with a big smile on her face.

"One of our...*acquired* talents," said Bonarain. "We found that we can repair our children while they're still in the womb. When I had my first pregnancy, with Shalam, I discovered this talent. I just thought about what was in my womb...and somehow...I don't really know how...I was able to see him...

and everything about him. His legs weren't developing correctly. They were badly deformed. I started thinking about his legs... how I wished they were...correct. Next thing I knew...his legs started...getting..." She looked up thoughtful for a moment. "...straightened out. His feet had been deformed as well...and I just thought the repairs on them...and it happened."

"This is intriguing," said Lewis looking at Bonarain with child's wonder in his eyes. "What...happens if the child...is born *with* the deformities?"

"We don't know," said Bonarain with a smile. "We've never allowed any child to be born *with* a deformity...or defective organ. We always make sure that they're healthy - and perfect - before they're born."

Lewis cleared his throat. "Uh...you said that you...were alone in that first pregnancy...uh...figuring out how to repair the fetus. I just observed that it took three...to repair the child of that one...just now...how were you able to do it alone?"

"**This *doovoft* needs to take a hint**," sent Chyning. "**He keeps on delving into the same area.**"

Bonarain pursed her lips trying to keep from giggling. "**He's a medical doctor who is seeing something that's beyond his mental grasp or technological capabilities. Let him ask his questions.**" She looked up and pondered a moment. "I accidentally figured it out...on my own. I did *not* leave the others wondering how to do it. The first time Kiyalee got pregnant - I showed her how to look the child over and repair anything that was wrong. When Chyning had her first pregnancy,

I did the same for her. Now, every new mother, we show her how to do it, during her first pregnancy. After that, she can do it on her own…if it needs to be done. Now that she knows what to do and how to do it." She smiled. "Of course, if any of them have any questions…I am still here to assist."

Lewis sat there, still open mouthed. "Incredible!" He looked down and shook his head. "You have a gift that…every mother…throughout the milky way…would love to be able to have - repair a child before birth…to make sure that the child is perfect…when born." He looked back up at Bonarain and shook his head still fearful and awed. "Incredible!"

The monitor in front of Milch beeped. He looked down at it. Gomez - who appeared to be pouting a little - had a question. Milch read it quickly. "In the observations, of your planet, we saw that there is, what appears to be, an animated plant. We're not sure whether it's a plant or animal…or just how to classify this…" He nearly choked on the word. "…anomaly. We were wondering if you know…what this plant, or creature, is and how to classify it."

Chyning chuckled. "That sounds like the Roistee."

Kiyalee looked at Chyning. "Yeah…I was trying to remember that. The Roistee! It is the Roistee."

Milch looked at them expectantly. When he got nothing more, he smiled and cleared his throat again. "Okay, you call this…phenomenon, you said Roistee. What we want to know…is it plant or animal…or what?"

"It just happens to be another Elf race," said Soolchakan. "They have rather dark green skin. They have, what appears to

be, leaves growing out of all parts of their bodies. They're…
somewhat mischievous…in that they try to hide all of the time…
in forests. They don't really hurt anyone or…seem to mean any
harm. They're…much like us…they just want to live and be left
alone. If someone intrudes on their territory they…play tricks on
them to make them go away…by scaring them into going away."

Again the monitor in front of Milch beeped. He looked
down and his eyes opened wide. He looked at Gomez with a
smile. He turned to Soolchakan with a bigger smile. "Would you
be so kind as to…give us a list of…all of the different Elf races…
and how to recognize them?"

Soolchakan looked a little perturbed for a moment. He
looked at his three wives. **"These people want to know
everything about all of the Elf races. Should we tell
them…all of it?"**

All three of them shrugged.

**"You're the one who decided to talk to these
people,"** sent Bonarain. **"I guess that telling them about
the other races isn't giving away anything strategic…or
secret."**

His eyes dulled and that strange voice came out of him
again: "Bikaropin, come to me!"

Once again, Bikaropin was on the ship. He looked a little
frightened. "Yes, Drey Sssorg, what is it?"

Soolchakan gave him a smile. "Our guests from another
world, would like to know about all of the different races on

Heart."

Bikaropin looked confused. "Uh…is that all? I mean you…used the *Voice*…Drey Sssorg…and usually…when you do that…I'm in trouble."

Soolchakan leaned back in his chair. "Really?" He frowned and contemplated the statement. "I didn't…" he looked back up at Bikaropin. "…think that…I did that." His eyebrows went up. "Hmph! Something for me to consider." He chuckled. "Anyway, our guests would like to know about all of the different Elf races."

Bikaropin looked a little fearful. "Do you…want a complete history of all of them…or…what?"

Milch's monitor beeped again. He looked down and read quickly. "No, any complete history can wait. All we were wondering, at this time, is just how many Elf races there are…and how to identify…the differences between them."

Bikaropin sighed in relief. "Oh, just something briefly… to identify. That's rather easy." He reached out at something with his right arm. **"Okay Inorim. Give me that scroll now. It should confuse the *h'oolyach* out of them."** His entire right arm disappeared momentarily.

Inorim was standing there with the scroll, chuckling. They had been listening in (mentally) to what was going on in the conference room. She snickered as she placed the scroll in his hand. **"Here you are husband. Is there anything else you want me to confuse them with?"**

"**Get a mug of that ninkanda brew ready for me,**" he replied. "**I'll let you know when I want it...thank you, my dear Inorim**." His hand then came back with a rather large scroll. He looked around. "Uh...do you mind...if I could have a place to sit down?"

Lt. Eli came up with another chair and placed it at the conference table for Bikaropin. Eli and Bikaropin exchanged smiles and Bikaropin sat down. Eli walked away looking rather mystified.

Bikaropin laid the scroll on the table and untied a string that was holding it shut. He started unrolling it. He looked around at all of the people at the table and smiled. "Are you ready?" He smiled and looked down at the scroll. "Let's see, we'll start with the Af-Ad. They're species has very dark brown skin and a very, very long nose. The adult is usually about 18 decimeters in height. They're a very common race and they're usually nice, however they can be pranksters." He looked around the table. "Is that enough of that one...or do you want more?"

Milch smiled. "Yes, just a brief physical description...that is used to identify that race...and commonality, along with a few things about attitude - just fine."

Bikaropin smiled back at him. He sniffed and looked back at the scroll. "Okay, next is the Af-Kawder. Their skin is..." He looked at Milch. "...I believe what you refer to as - caucasian..." he looked back at the scroll. "They're usually about 13 decimeters in height. Their noses are black...and flat. They're not as common as the Af-Ad, however, there are a lot of them. They like to live by their own set of rules. They don't like anyone telling them what to do.

After describing eighteen different Elf races he called Inorim again. **"Have you got the ninkanda brew ready**?"

Inorim chuckled again. **"Yes, dear husband. Pyree already brought it**."

He reached out with his right arm again and it disappeared again. When he brought it back, he had a mug. He took a long drink from the mug and then continued. "Number twenty…" He snickered a little. "…the Braquarsian. They are somewhat rare, they have medium brown skin, they stand about 18 decimeters, and they're another bunch that is *very* picky about following the rules…" He giggled. "…and they have these ridiculously long, floppy ears. If they didn't hear what you said, they reach up, hold one of their ears up and ask you to repeat what you said. If they attend some meeting, they usually tie some cloth around their head…in order to hold the ears up, so they can hear everything." He giggled again. "Looks ridiculous."

The crew of the ship had been watching his arm disappear and reappear. Several of them were rather disturbed, however, they did their best to cover their astonishment.

Bikaropin read on through the scroll. He would stop every now and then and take a swig from the mug. Twice while he was going along, he turned the mug to bottoms up. Inorim would then secretly refill the mug which added to the confusion and consternation of the crew. This only added to the enjoyment of all the Owlamites in the conference room. They were reading all kinds of interesting thoughts from the crew. So far, however, there was nothing that hinted anything about any attacking and conquering. These were just some very curious explorers…who were now rather awed and afraid of these Owlamites.

14

The ship had been orbiting 'Heart' for six days so far. Milch was in the sickbay, getting one of his scheduled regular checkups. Doctor Randolph was running the medical scanner over him. He noticed that she seemed just a little bit distracted. He cleared his throat, placed his hand under her chin and lifted her head. "Lois, is there something bothering you?"

She looked rather surprised. "Uh...no...uh...well *yes!*" She sighed. "I'm the mother of two children...and I never...saw anything like that...in my life."

Milch rolled his eyes. "Huboy! What new *thing* happened here at this strange planet of Heart...or should I really wonder about anything strange...in regards to these Owlamites?"

Shalam had been following Milch and Yamang of the Third had been following Randolph.

Shalam turned to Yamang. "Do you know what she's talking about?"

"She was the recipient of a special treat," said Yamang flatly. She snickered. "Listen and learn."

Randolph put the medical scanner down. She puffed her

cheeks out as she blew air out while thinking. "I'm the mother of two children. Both times I had the assistance of our modern technology and anesthetic capabilities and a few other little gadgets and gizmos that we use for medical reasons. Yesterday, however, I witnessed the birth of an Owlam baby. It was…so incredible! I never thought that…I would ever see anything…like that."

Milch snickered a little. "Are you telling me that there's another new surprise, in regards to our unusual hosts?"

She snickered back. "The capabilities that these people have…it's so unbelievable…what they did."

Milch was getting impatient. "Okay…WHAT!?"

She was slightly surprised by his abrupt irritation. "Uh… the woman…her water broke and she was in labor. They had her flat on the table. They were…doing that thing that they do…when they communicate telepathically. They were, probably, all three communicating."

Milch cocked his head to the side. "All three of whom?"

She closed her eyes and put a hand to her forehead. "The woman giving birth, of course, and two female attendants. The pregnant one was sweating and looking a little uncomfortable. They pulled her pants off. She lay flat…and the two attendants… their forearms disappeared. They moved their arms…I guess, into her womb. The pregnant one held her breath…and the two attendants lifted their arms. A moment later…their forearms reappeared and…and…they had a newborn…and the afterbirth… cradled in their hands. The mother's stomach flattened…just a little…after they pulled the baby out. When the mother gave birth…it was little over two minutes from the time the water broke, till the baby was out of the womb. They used that crazy dimension shifting to…get the baby out…without any pain for the mother. I would have loved to have had that…advantage…when my babies were born."

He was sitting there looking shocked. "They…reached through those dimensions…grabbed the baby…pulled it into another dimension…and then pulled the baby out…and brought it to this dimension…" He went through several different thoughts as he contemplated what he had heard. He looked back at Randolph. "From the look on your face, there seems to be another shoe… waiting to fall."

She chuckled nervously. "Is it that obvious?"

"You have a *certain* longing look in your eyes."

"Yes, Sir. I have a question…that I've been thinking about…for some time. I'd love to be able to find out something that's been bothering me about what they've said…and didn't say."

"Gimme a hint."

She gave a loud sigh. "They say that they're over 14,000 years old…but the oldest of their many, many children is…about 5,600." She shook her head. "Why didn't they…worry about any form of procreation…for over 8,000 years?"

Milch now felt the same confusion that was bothering Randolph. He shook his head. "That…is a…rather personal question…and a very, very interesting one…as well. I hadn't thought of that…" He opened his eyes wide in wonder. "…over an *8.000* year hiatus…from the bomb to the babies."

Randolph smiled expectantly. "Do you think that I could ask them?"

Milch sighed. "So far…they've been very open. They've answered all of the questions, candidly, that we've asked."

Shalam rolled his eyes. "These people wanna know everything about us."

Yamang scoffed. "I wonder just how much the first generation is going to give away."

Randolph scoffed. "Yeah, but most of that was to the anthropologists, the botanists, the geologists, the zoologists, the oceanographers…all of the sciences. This is…"

"…a part of anthropology," said Milch. "Do you want to be the one to put the question to them…or should we have Montalvo ask the question?"

She smiled. "It *is* my question. I'd like to be the one who does the asking."

"Okay," he chuckled. "We'll have you in on the next session…with the first generation." He crossed his arms and looked at her a little sternly. "Can you finish my exam now?"

She giggled as she picked up the medical scanner.

Yamang huffed. "Nosy *bimyocks*."

Another meeting in the conference room started. This time, Lieutenant Commander Lois Randolph was attending...to ask her question. All four Owlamites stared at Randolph with suspicion in their eyes, even though they had been advised of her question.

After the roll call was entered into the minutes of the meeting, Soolchakan looked at Milch with a bit of a smirk. "What questions do you want answered today?"

Before the anthropologist, Montalvo, could monopolize the conversation, Milch gave Randolph the floor. "One of our doctors has a question about your family. Specifically...well I'll let her ask."

Randolph smiled. "Thank you, Sir." She turned to Soolchakan. "I've been trying to think of some way to ask this question. I guess the best way is to just...blurt it out." She licked her lips. "You said that those nasty bombs went off...some...uh... how long ago was it?"

"Just over 14,600 years ago," said Soolchakan flatly.

"Yes...okay, 14,600 years...but, no children were born... until less than some 6000 years. Why did you wait so long...to procreate?"

The three Owlamite women looked around - at anything. Soolchakan looked at the women and grunted in disgust as he realized they did not want to give the answer to this question. "**Cowards**!" He took in a deep breath and let it out slowly. He turned back at Randolph with a sad look in his eyes. "We didn't really know that we *could procreate*...for a long time. Right after the bomb went off none of the women had any ovulation periods, none of the men could…perform the act." He looked down and sniffed. "It was…an accidental incident…" He gave Bonarain a sideways glance. "…that occurred…where we found out that we…were able to…procreate."

Bonarain sat there, staring at the ceiling, tight lipped as her face turned a little red. **"Do you really have to give them that information?"**

Soolchakan continued: "We have these strange looking reptilian scales on the back of our necks. For centuries we have excreted, what we call *Mushoshk*, from pores in the scales." He looked back at the women and they all were still staring at the ceiling. He cleared his throat and shook his head. He smiled at Randolph. "We didn't find out until the year 15 ATUT what it is. Again, as I said, it was somewhat of an accident." He gave Bonarain a bit of a disgusted stare. "Someone decided to go against, an unwritten law, where we cleaned this *mushoshk* off of our necks…in private. Bonarain decided to be nasty and she got a handful of her *mushoshk* and wiped it in my face. That was the first time that any Owlamite ever wiped their *mushoshk* on another Owlamite. For the first time in over 8000 years I got an erection." He gave Bonarain a nasty look. "I had a burning in my body and it was rather difficult to fight it. For some reason…I'm not sure why…I returned the favor, just to be facetious, I suppose, and wiped some of my *mushoshk* on her face." He looked at Bonarain. **"Why shouldn't I tell them?"**

Now Bonarain's embarrassment was in full bloom. Her face seemed to be glowing a bright red that rivaled the color of

Soolchakan's shirt.

Soolchakan smiled at Bonarain. "I know what I felt. Why don't you tell them what you felt?"

She gave him a dirty look. She wrinkled her nose at him. She looked at Randolph with a strained smile. "I had a..." She looked up. "...burning feeling...in my body...and especially my...female...private area." She looked back at Randolph. "I had an incredibly strong and irresistible desire...to have sex. It was still my understanding, after 9 millennium, that Owlam men were...incapable. I didn't know that he was having an equally strong drive for sex...until he dropped his pants." She blushed again and looked up at the ceiling. "When I saw that he was... in full bloom...my pants went down and we...did the deed." She snickered. "We went at it for...quite a while. When we were finished, we both collapsed...in complete exhaustion." She leaned back in the chair. She looked up as if contemplating. "We slept for quite a while, and...after we woke up...I did a mental...search of my body. I knew...I don't know how I knew...I knew that I had conceived." She looked at Randolph with a blank expression. "I knew that I had conceived even though that occurrence had not happened to any Owlamite woman since the bomb went off. I knew that for the first time since becoming an *Owlam* Elf, I was pregnant...and I knew that the baby was a boy." She sighed. "It was during my pregnancy that I found out...how we can... mentally, manipulatively repair the child...in order to get rid of any...defects...in the child." She looked at Soolchakan. "In the year 16 ATUT, the first ever Owlamite baby was born. My son Shalam...the first Owlamite Elf baby...ever."

Soolchakan turned to Randolph. "86 years later, she had a second son. His name is Monaha. It took a few more years to convince Kiyalee and Chyning…that procreation for them was possible as well. Bonarain gave them all of her…knowledge of how to correct any defects in the unborn child…in order to make sure that the child has a chance at a normal life."

Kiyalee gave Soolchakan a dirty look. "**Just how far are we going to go with our personal lives**?"

"**We've started it – we play it out and watch their reaction**," sent Soolchakan.

Kiyalee chuckled a little. "In the year 111 ATUT, I gave birth to a girl. Her name is Aya. She became Shalam's first wife."

Randolph looked horrified. "But…that…that's incestuous! You could come up with all kinds of…horrible mutations…and defects."

"Remember," said Chyning. "We can use our mental powers to repair any defect or mutation…while still in the womb. In the year 116 ATUT, I gave birth to my first child: Zina."

Soolchakan spoke up. "In the year 5575 ATUT, Xachool was born. He is the firstborn…of the 23rd generation." He looked at Randolph. "23 generations of Owlamites and we haven't had one single child born with any defects or mutations."

Doctor Lewis was looking rather confused. "Are you saying that the only time…that any of you…have, or can have sex…is when you wipe your…what did you call it - mucus - on each other's face?"

Soolchakan gave Lewis a condescending look. "*Mushoshk!*"

Lewis cleared his throat. "Thank you…for the correction," he said with a guilty look on his face.

"The answer is - yes," said Soolchakan. "None of us…of any generation, have ever been able to have sex, or are interested in sex, or conceive…unless we…share our *mushoshk*."

Chyning grunted in a disgusted manner. "That was one of the things that we were hunted for. Some of those monsters that… hunted us down and killed some of us…they got our *mushoshk* from our glands, for the purposes of making, and selling, a powerful aphrodisiac."

Gomez sat there laughing. "Are you telling me that this… stuff…that comes *only* from an Owlam…it affects other races…as an aphrodisiac?"

All four Owlamites glared at Gomez.

"Excuse me," said Upton the zoologist. "It does seem a little strange that a substance, that's peculiar to Owlamites, would affect other species in the same way that if affects you."

Soolchakan and Bonarain looked at each other with an evil grin on both their faces.

"**They don't believe us**," sent Soolchakan irately.

"**The only way that they're gonna believe us is if we dose them**," responded Bonarain bitterly.

Both disappeared. Kiyalee and Chyning both giggled.

Soolchakan reappeared next to Upton and wiped some mucilaginous excretion on her forehead. Bonarain appeared next to Gomez and wiped a similar substance on his face. Soolchakan and Bonarain disappeared again - they both reappeared in their seats…wiping something off of their hands with cloths.

"**Have fun, you two *bimyocks***," commented Soolchakan mentally.

Gomez and Upton were both panting heavily with strange looks on their faces. They both tore their pants off and headed for each other. Without any care for what was around them, they immediately began having mad passionate sex, right there on the floor, with no concern for whatever or whoever else was in the room.

Milch looked at the four Owlamites in horror. "How long…uh…are they going to…keep doing that?"

Soolchakan sat there with a smug smile. "Until they pass out, or the *mushoshk* wears off."

Milch tried to avert his eyes from the activity. "Which do you think will happen first?"

Soolchakan just shrugged with a smirk on his face. "I've never used it on an Earthling before. Who knows?"

Milch shook his head with his eyes shut. "Let's reconvene somewhere else. Right now, let's give those two…some privacy." He looked at the four Owlam. "Please join us…in recreation room…4."

The four Owlamites disappeared.

Before everyone could get up Milch snarled at Randolph. "Okay, Lois, this was your idea. You stay here and watch them."

Randolph looked mortified. "For…what?"

"To make sure that they don't kill each other…sexually."

"I'll stay," said Doctor Lewis.

Milch looked at him angrily. "I told her to stay."

"I'll stay…as well," said Lewis.

Milch grunted in disgust. "Who's going to represent the medical staff in the meeting in the rec room?"

"We can send Dodge," said Lewis.

"Dodge is an RN. Dodge can be there," said Milch. "I want a doctor."

"All right," said Lewis. "The only other doctor, on board, is our pathologist - Schmitz…and he's part of this group anyway."

Milch sighed. "Fine!"

Schmitz gave the nervous laugh. "Uh…whose going to represent the main science section…now that Gomez…is… occupied?"

Milch closed his eyes in disgust. "Someone call Riley. He's the second in the science section after Gomez."

Yeoman Aua looked around. "Uh…who should we get… to represent the zoology section?"

Milch opened his mouth. He looked over at the *pair*.

He looked back at Aua. "Tough! We won't ask any zoological questions until…later." He looked back at the pair. "*Much later.*" He thought for a moment. "Either that or we keep it to the ornithologist…what's-her-name?"

"Lieutenant. Maxine Veach," said Aua.

"Fine, call her, let's go," said Milch.

After four hours of questions and answers in recreation room 4, Milch was getting rather concerned. "Look, I know that they probably deserved this…sexual shake up…as a lesson… but…no human being can go this long…without some detrimental problems resulting from it. Is there anything that we can do…to stop their…*insatiable* desire?"

Soolchakan chuckled. "Have a woman clean his face off and have a man clean her face off. That way, whoever is doing the cleaning, won't be affected…themselves."

Milch called to Lewis on the intercom. "Did you hear that?"

"Absolutely," said Lewis. "We're on it…right now!"

"Let me know what happens," said Milch.

"Yes, Sir," came the response.

"**I wonder why they're so concerned**," sent Chyning. "**Are they really that fragile**?"

"**Possibly…probably**," sent Bonarain.

After several fretful moments Milch was hailed on the intercom.

"Go," said Milch.

Lewis came back. "They've both collapsed in complete and total exhaustion. We examined them and their respiration and blood pressure have gone back to normal...but they're both in a state of complete physical collapse."

Milch looked at Soolchakan, a little perturbed. "Take them to their quarters. No point in trying to wake them up...maybe for several days."

All four Owlamites giggled.

"We're getting them to their quarters now, Sir," said Lewis.

"Thank you," said Milch. He looked back at Soolchakan. "Okay, let's get back to those very *large* blue birds in that country you call...Lower Oosam."

Three of the Owlamites looked at Kiyalee. She smiled and gave them, what she knew, about the birds.

Two days later, Gomez tried to attend the conferences. After his head slammed down, with a very loud bang, on the conference table - from falling asleep in his seat, he decided to give up and go back to bed...for a while longer. He got up from his chair - and fell flat on his face. One of the security personnel gave him assistance getting back to his quarters.

After a total of four days of rest - for both Gomez and Upton - both came feebly staggering into the conference room.

Milch looked at both of them. "Gomez, do you think that you can stay awake…this time?"

"Yes, Sir," said Gomez. "I'm doing fine now. Maybe not up to 100%, but, I'm at least at…80%."

Milch grunted approval. He turned. "Upton, how're you feeling?"

She gave him a tired smile. "I can make it, Sir." She went to her place and gave out a squawk of surprise as she sat down. She gingerly adjusted her position, sitting on just one hip, in the chair and looked up at Milch. "I can make it, Sir."

Bonarain snickered. "Uh…Doctor Lewis…why don't you examine her?"

Lewis looked confused. "For what?"

Bonarain rubbed the lower part of her abdomen. "What do you think?" She gave him a haughty smile. "**I'm pretty sure that these Earthlings are affected the same way we are**."

Lewis grunted, got up, went to Upton and turned on his medical scanner. He scanned from the top down. When he got to the lower part of her torso his eyebrows went up. He cleared his throat. "Congratulations, Joyce…you're pregnant."

She glared at him. "That's impossible! It ain't my time of the month!" She looked thoughtful for a moment. "Not for…at least another five days."

Lewis leaned closer to her. "There *is* a zygote, a fertilized ovum...in your uterus. You *are* pregnant."

Upton's jaw went slack. She turned and looked at the Owlamites.

Bonarain had a friendly smile on her face. "Male Owlam *mushoshk* will make a female...*any* female of any species... ovulate."

Upton went limp in her chair and shook her head.

Lewis cleared his throat. "You can make any important decisions later. For now, let it be known, that you *know* that you are definitely pregnant.

Upton looked at Soolchakan showed her teeth and snarled.

"She's not very grateful, is she," sent Soolchakan? **"They wanted to know how it works and we showed them. For some reason, they don't like it**."

Chyning huffed. **"How rude**!" She had to fight to keep from giggling.

After one of their conference meetings, Doctor Lewis again wanted a little private conversation with Milch.

Milch decided that it should be done in his office, next to the bridge. "Okay, Doctor, what's on your mind?"

Lewis sat down after getting a cup of coffee from the food dispenser. "I've been...forbidden by the Owlamites...to do any more scans. Okay, for the sake of diplomacy and harmony and all of that good stuff, I stopped. The only thing that I could go on, for a closer look, was the scans that had already been accomplished." He sipped his coffee. "What I found…is…I know you won't like it, but I found another mystery…in regards to our hosts."

Milch groaned and put his hands over his face. He took in a deep breath. His hands dropped to his sides. "Okay, give it to me."

Lewis chuckled nervously. "These people have an extra organ that I…just haven't been able to figure it out. They have a liver that functions very much the same way that ours does. They, however, have…what appears to be an extra liver, just below the normal one. Everything that I see about it, shows that it is definitely another liver…but it does not act the same way. Our liver helps to filter the body of toxins and it creates over six billion different chemicals that our bodies need, daily. This extra liver of the Owlam…it only creates…one enzyme…I think. It does absolutely nothing else that I can find. Their systems are, daily, flooded with this enzyme. I have tried to analyze it…but… the only way that I could do a comprehensive analysis…is…an autopsy. I don't think that…any of them are willing to die for our…curiosity."

"What about a biopsy? Do you think that they'd go for that?"

"I'd have to dig…too deep. I'd have to go around, or through a couple of other organs…and I don't know…if I'd have the right place. I don't know how much it might hurt them."

"So…this one has to remain a mystery."

"I'm afraid so, Sir. I wish I could find out more, but with this I can't. We have established a good relationship with them and I certainly don't have any desire to do any damage to that. The results could be very…" He turned his head looking rather frustrated and confused.

"Yes, they could be…very….!"

Odan of the Third had been following Lewis. He shook his head. **"These Earthlings are still maintaining that they want a peaceful relationship with us. They say that we have an extra liver in our body, but they don't want to pry in our bodies…and maybe in our minds as well. This is another example of how they…they're just here to learn and not conquer."**

Soolchakan ate a lump of kwatha while contemplating. **"Thank you for that Odan. So far these people have been consistent. They make friendly meetings with others…*any* others."**

After two years of questions and answers and research, the visiting ship departed. They had gained a wealth of information about the system and all of the inhabitants of the planet Heart. They were very grateful when they were told that they would be welcomed back – if they wanted to come back. Just remember to be friendly…*or else.*

The ones assigned to watch the people on the spaceship

waited until the ship departed the star system entirely. They had waited for any kind of secret message about coming back and conquering. Nothing like that happened.

Soolchakan was sitting in the dining area in the gorge apartment that had been home, for so long, eating some sliced fruit from a plate that Bonarain had prepared. The three women came in and decided to join him in the repast.

"I'm happy that we finally found someone we can get along with," said Soolchakan. "After all those millennium, having to battle and destroy all of those…invaders…this was very pleasing."

Bonarain nodded. "I guess that there's hope for the future. If there's someone out there who can get numerous planets to join forces for peace and protection…I like it. It gives me hope for the future of for all of us."

Kiyalee looked somewhat worried. "They might ask us to join in on some fight…if they do find some other arrogant conqueror out there."

"We'll have to think real hard about joining any of their fights," said Chyning.

Soolchakan scoffed at Chyning. "You won't have to think hard. You'll be out there trying to get to all the good stuff first."

Chyning grinned and wiggled her eyebrows as she chewed on some fruit.

Bonarain smiled. "Yes, we're looking at a much brighter future…I hope."

Soolchakan shrugged. "I'm not worried." He looked around at the women. "Bonarain, with you on one side educating everybody with your teaching talents and Kiyalee giving her all, regarding mechanics and technology...how can we lose?"

Chyning now looked affronted. "You like Bonarain because she teaches, you like Kiyalee because she keeps all of those trucks...and other stuff working...WHAT AM I?"

Soolchakan looked at her with a dull eyed stare. "A monumental pain in the butt."

Chyning was giving Soolchakan a very nasty glare with her nose out of joint, while Bonarain and Kiyalee were holding their stomachs and laughing hysterically...while doing everything they could to *not* spit a mouthful of food across the room.

www.ingramcontent.com/pod-product-compliance
Lightning Source LLC
Chambersburg PA
CBHW072053020726
47501CB00003B/568